Acting the Part

# Acting THE Part

## Z. R. ELLOR

HARPER TEEN
An Imprint of HarperCollinsPublishers

HarperTeen is an imprint of HarperCollins Publishers.

Acting the Part
Copyright © 2022 by Zabé Ellor

Library of Congress Control Number: 2022938054
ISBN 978-0-06-315788-0

Typography by Chris Kwon
22 23 24 25 26   PC/LSCH   10 9 8 7 6 5 4 3 2 1
❖
First Edition

To Alexandra Overy,
an amazing author and friend

Acting the Part

# One

After hours of hair and makeup, I finally look like I've crawled out of hell.

Greta Thurmway, who sits in the makeup chair to my left, bites off a yawn as technicians glue rhinestone ornaments to her wig and paint her makeup to stand up under harsh studio lights. But I play the space warrior Morgantha Moonblade, and I need to look professionally messed up.

My long black wig is curled and tangled—but not too tangled—every lock expertly positioned to cast dramatic shadows on my otherwise round face. The stylists and the director of photography argued all morning over which shades of eye shadow Morgantha could feasibly access on the swamp planet where her Season Five character arc begins. Someone suggested painting a bruise on my chin to cover a cluster of zits. Someone else pointed out I'd look like a victim in a domestic violence PSA.

As they work out my look, I thumb through fanfics on my

phone, tilting my head as the makeup technicians ask. I trust they'll do their jobs, and I'll do mine. Besides, I've already had my creative input in the hit sci-fi drama *Galaxy Spark*. My beloved ship #Morganetta will become canon in Season Five.

Morgantha, who treats men as (a) mentor figures, (b) brothers-at-arms, and (c) murder victims, comes off as such an obvious lesbian. When Greta's character, Princess Alietta, was introduced in Season Four, fans latched on to the idea our fictional counterparts would get together—especially after I came out as queer in a video I posted on Quicshot. Viewers flooded my mentions with heart eyes, crossed fingers, and rainbow-flag emojis, begging me to make #Morganetta canon. I read countless fanfics about sheltered, shy Princess Alietta falling for the loud, boisterous Morgantha. Then I screwed up my courage and asked the showrunners to let Morgantha and Alietta fall in love. It took some off-set battling of my own, but Peter and Wes finally agreed.

But once Morgantha and Alietta start dating on-screen, people will ask me and Greta how we feel about representing a queer couple. I'd rather give mouth-to-mouth to a cactus than have a serious conversation with that prickly perfectionist, but I need to learn how she feels about LGBTQ+ issues before the new season premieres, if only to stop her from saying something awful to the press. Nothing will ruin the fandom's joy like discovering the actor behind their beloved Princess Alietta is a homophobe.

"Do we have to do full makeup?" Chris Arden, my

stepbrother, says from the chair to my right. A stylist is meticulously texturing the stubble painted down his cheeks. "We're just shooting promo photos."

"Millions of people will see these," Greta says. "Do you want the world to think of you as the guy with half a beard? This is premium cable, not a Syfy original with a five-dollar budget."

"Chris is very image-conscious," I joke, trying to melt the awkward tension Greta injected. She's always talking about her image. I bet she runs every photo she takes past her publicist before posting it. "Remember that time he tried to bring socks with sandals into style?"

"It was my first time in New York in fall," Chris says. "I only brought one pair of shoes and my girlfriend had a migraine. Someone had to run to the drugstore, and I didn't want my toes to get frostbite and drop off on the way."

"But think how impressed she was by your heroic sacrifice," I point out. "Is she coming to the first-reads party tomorrow?"

"Probably." He angles his coffee mug to drink without smudging his lips. "Did we figure out the food? Dad texted he made cupcakes."

"I ordered from that shrimp barbecue place. I don't want to volunteer the cast as test subjects for Will's baking."

"Got your wig," says a makeup technician, offering Chris a model head covered in foot-long silky black curls.

He snorts. "You've made me wear those for five seasons, and they always look terrible. Until this crew hires some Black stylists, Bryken Moonblade is bald." He shaved his head this morning—and used my sink to do it, even though our house has five bathrooms.

The tech coughs nervously and holds up a piece of paper. "Mr. Arden, we have a style sheet."

I snatch the style sheet and a pen and write *Bald* next to Chris's name. "Put him in a helmet."

The techs dig through their big bin of prop hats. All the official *Galaxy Spark* armor is stored on location back in Northern Ireland, but they do find a passable substitute: a spray-painted bowl with molded plastic panels on the sides and a thick leather chin strap, left over from Season Three's promo shoot.

Chris mimes pouring his open bag of Doritos inside, laughs, and puts it on his head. I snatch the Doritos bag off his knee while he's busy. Chris and I fumble for the chips until the contents spill across the floor in a tide of orange powder.

"Stop," Greta whispers. She hasn't moved her chair so much as an inch all this time. If a tech's hand slips while they're gluing on Princess Alietta's wig, her hair will be pasted to her eyelid. I guess she's been watching us in her mirror. "You're making a mess, and you'll get us all in trouble."

"I know how to behave on set," I say. "I was filming diaper commercials when I was five months old."

"It's just that most people grow up and stop throwing food off their high chair."

"I'm mature." I'm not just a child actor who got her first jobs because her mom owns a production company. I'm giving queer fans the on-screen representation they crave, not just a kiss in the background but a love story between stars. I'm showing straight viewers that Morgantha and Alietta's romance should be celebrated, not just accepted. My contributions matter.

I change the subject. "Greta, are you coming to the first-reads party?" A tech hisses as his hand jiggles, smearing my mascara. "I know it's a long drive to my house."

"I'll be there," Greta says. "Still the shiny mansion that looks like an ice cube, right? I want to make sure I don't miss my turn because a literal house blinded me."

"I'll pay you a hundred bucks to tell my mom how much you hate it."

"I make it a rule not to disagree with Kate Ashton. Unlike a certain actor who got last year's party ended early when she argued with her mom about not allowing bubble bath in the hot tub."

I flush. Of course she brings up that specific humiliation.

If I didn't need to ferret out how she really feels about our on-screen romance, I might not even have invited her to the party. I don't need her high-and-mighty attitude around when the LA-based cast gathers to read the Season Six scripts. Learning where Peter and Wes are steering my story will be stressful enough without Greta criticizing me for breathing wrong.

My phone dings as an email lands in my inbox. The subject line: CONFIDENTIAL CONFIDENTIAL CONFIDEN-TIAL. A password-protected attachment—the Season Six scripts. Chris touches his waistband, where he's tucked his phone. Greta's phone beeps atop her makeup table. She bites her lip, leaving trails through the layers of painted gloss. Staring at her phone like it's a rattlesnake.

"Don't mess up your makeup, Miss Perfect," I say. No response. Can't I even needle her back? "Don't peek at the script until the party. It's—"

"En garde!" Chris shouts, poking at me with his plastic stellar sword. I draw Morgantha's blade—or at least the replica prop I'm wearing for the photo shoot—from my belt and whack it against his. He drops into a fencing stance. We both got master lessons when we were cast on the show, and even though I usually lose two of three bouts, I always relish a chance to test myself.

Greta sighs. "I mourn the day Wes and Peter decided to put swords in their space show. Why are our twenty-ninth-century warriors running around with fourteenth-century weapons?"

"It can shoot plasma beams," I remind her, showing off the amethyst power crystals in the hilt. They match the purple tunic I wear, stitched with the crest of Morgantha's adopted family, House Moonblade. My silver leggings are as shiny as if they really came from another world. "It's super-high-tech nanosteel."

"It's because the showrunners don't trust viewers to watch more than twenty minutes without hooligans bursting into fight choreography."

"You're just jealous because Princess Alietta doesn't get any cool battle scenes." I dig through the prop bin, grab what seems to be a quarterstaff with an umbrella hot-glued to the end, and offer it to her. "Join us! Lighten up."

"I'll lighten up when I'm not on the clock. Enjoy getting fired."

*Is this wrong?* Uncertainty fizzes in the pit of my stomach like warm soda. Maybe Greta really knows something I don't. "Maybe you'll get fired for being boring," I say. The retort feels as clumsy and awkward as I am, but hurt flashes deep in her big brown eyes. With something sharper beneath it, like the shark from *Jaws* circling under a boat. Fear.

I don't know what to say.

"All done." The wig supervisor gives Greta's head a final tap. "You three can head in now. They're all ready for you."

Chris's sword whacks across my shoulder. I laugh and curse, chasing him down the hall from the makeup room to the photo studio. My sword pokes into his back, his leg.

"You're dead!" I shout. "You're dead again!"

"Then why am I still running?" He flashes me the famous Arden grin over his shoulder, and I chase him down the hall, Morgantha's long black boots squishing with every step.

Head over heels, we tumble out into the studio. The doors bang against the walls as we knock them open. Photographers and lighting techs stare at us. A costumer winces at the sight of Chris's helmet, now knocked sideways.

"Miss Ashton. Mr. Arden." The creative director clears her throat. "Where's Miss Thurmway?"

Greta. I look back over my shoulder. She didn't follow us. My heart sinks. How can I ask something as personal as *How are you on gay shit?* when I can't even seem to get us into the same physical, mental, or emotional zip code?

We get started without her. Chris and I pose on purple-painted papier-mâché rocks, a green screen hanging behind us where another world will be pasted in later. We draw our swords, flex our bare-arm biceps, crack up laughing. That gets the camera clicking, and the photographer suggests I swoon in Chris's arms.

"How about he swoons in mine?" I say, and Chris obliges. I stagger to hold him up, but we grab some good photos anyway, and I'm sure the obsessive fans who want Morgantha and Bryken to wind up a couple (*ew*, and also *ick*) will go nuts for them. In the actual canon of the show, Morgantha and Bryken haven't even talked since midway through Season Four, when he was captured by Queen Aylah's space marines. I'm hoping we'll reunite in Season Six. I can't wait to shoot with my brother again.

"Bench-press him, Lily!" Peter shouts, laughing from the sidelines. The younger of the two *Galaxy Spark* showrunners eyes us over the lid of his massive travel coffee cup. His hair and beard are a mussed-up mess, and he's wearing one of his fifty interchangeable wrinkled black tees, which probably reeks from his motorcycle drive here. If someone asks about his appearance, Peter brushes them off by saying he's on a big script deadline. Kate sent him some fancy shampoo as a Christmas present, but I don't think he took the hint.

With Greta still absent, the photos grow sillier. Chris tries to clamber up onto my shoulders, piggy-back style. I crouch forward and try to accommodate, but he's almost a foot taller than me. I can't get the leverage to swing him into place. Peter sets down his clipboard, rushes over, and kneels down behind us, supporting Chris with his back.

"I can see you," the photographer complains. "Could you stick your face down behind that boulder?"

"Can I be in some of the shots?" Peter says. "I'm part of the story, too."

"Photograph Peter!" I say. "It'll be hilarious." If Wes, the older showrunner, was on-site, I'm sure he'd shut us down. He doesn't approve of Peter and me being friendly, of how Peter taught me to drive his motorcycle and took me and Chris fishing when we shot in Vancouver. But I've heard stories of terrible bosses in the industry—just ask anyone what Hitchcock put his stars through. It's nice working for someone who wants to be likeable. "Just call him, like, the new super-secret villain we're introducing in Season Five. The Hideous Scraggle-Bearded Swamp Smuggler."

Peter winks at me as he tugs his scraggly beard. "I'd have to write one hell of a death scene for myself." Peter and Wes love writing twists and turns to keep the fans buzzing. They're especially famed for their creative death scenes. Just last season, a pop star with a cameo appearance was blown up after Queen Aylah flung him out an air lock, and Sir Henry Pellsworth, distinguished British Shakespeare veteran, saw his character die of infection after Morgantha stabbed him in the groin

9

(sure, they should have antibiotics in space, but I cracked up watching a man famed for his King Lear roll around in front of a green screen shouting, "My jewels!" as fake blood capsules spurt through his hands). Season Five will contain the biggest shock death yet—Alban Moonblade, Bryken's father and Morgantha's adopted dad, leader of the resistance against Queen Aylah, will nobly sacrifice his life attempting to rescue Bryken from the evil queen.

I'm expecting Morgantha's Season Six story line to include fabulous, devastating twists. But the thought she might die makes me sweat through my plastic tunic. Morgantha has so much story left to tell. She's destined to find the mystic spark at the galaxy's core and defeat Queen Aylah for good. *Galaxy Spark* should give her and Alietta the most shocking ending of all time—a happy-ever-after. Anything else would devastate the thousands of queer fans who made #Morganetta trend globally even before Morgantha and Alietta ever met on-screen.

"Seriously, where's Greta?" Peter asks. "I want some shots of her with Lily. Need to promote how we've written her into a subplot viewers will like."

Princess Alietta debuted in Season Four. Greta, who grew up in a suburb outside Pittsburgh, aced an open-call audition, and made it on the show. "I couldn't imagine a better fit for the part," Peter told me at the time. "Some people are just born to be stars." But the reviews of Princess Alietta's story line—she's the last member of the mysterious House Dustborn, a traveling diplomat who promotes interplanetary peace—were mixed, to say the least.

"People like Princess Alietta," I say. "It's just they're all girls, and the male fans complain loud enough to drown out their voices."

"You're right," he says. "Sorry. God, it's stupid—I've been watching all these YouTube videos about why Alietta's story makes me a bad writer."

"Dude, don't. Just because someone's got a camera and an internet connection doesn't mean they know what they're talking about."

"I'm here." Greta quietly stumbles into the room. She's in full Alietta mode, tight purple silk dress, LED locket flashing the crest of House Dustborn, blond wig glittering with gems. Normally, in character, she carries herself with a regal bearing that draws every eye. Now she's chewed through her lipstick, and she's hiding her bunched fists in the folds of her gown.

Something's wrong.

Greta spreads out her fractal-patterned skirts and perches on a fake rock. She crosses her ankles with an easy, ladylike grace I've never been able to master. Her cool brown eyes are deep and full of secrets as she stares into the camera. Acting on instinct, I step up and stand tall behind her.

"I like that direction, Lily," the creative director says. "Put your hand on her shoulder. Like you're protecting her."

I swallow. Greta's dress is bare-shouldered. Her skin is cool to the touch. I give her shoulder a squeeze, trying to convey everything too awkward to say out loud—*I really hope you don't hate me because I'm a girl, doing this*—and give the camera a death stare. *Morgantha won't let anyone hurt her girlfriend.*

That's the nice thing about acting. I can slip into someone else's skin, wrap myself in a cool, badass identity straight out of a script. Things between Greta and me have always been strained as hell—the first time we met, on set, I said, "Hi, I'm Lily Ashton," and she pivoted and fled for her trailer. But under the lights, with the cameras snapping, I can pretend I'm standing behind the love of my life, even though I don't know what that feels like. I've never had a real girlfriend.

Finally, the creative director nods us finished. Greta shrugs me off and brushes at her shoulder where I touched her. Like it itches. God, it would explain so much if she was actually allergic to me.

"Want me to get us some sandwiches?" I jerk my thumb at the catering table. "We could go eat on the balcony. And talk."

"I don't eat gluten."

*I can't even eat right*, I think as I stomp to the table in my squeaky pleather boots.

Just as I reach the mountain of carbs and sweets, a pre-teen girl tugs on my pant leg. Her T-shirt reads *Sunset Meal Supply*—one of the caterer's kids. "Are you Lily Ashton?" she says. When I nod, she says, "You're my hero."

Did I look that young in middle school? Nuh-uh. No way. "Your parents let you watch the show? It's got adult content."

"I know their streaming passwords. I watch everything

you're in because you're gay, like me." She says that without hesitating. Completely unafraid. Like I'm a magic talisman. "Can I have your autograph? Please?"

A grin breaks across my face. I'm used to people asking, but I'll take any opportunity to make a queer kid's day. Life can be so hard for us, especially when you don't have rich, supportive parents like I do. An autograph is the least I can give them— and soon, I'll give them even more. That kiss scene in Episode Three. Canon #Morganetta.

I scribble my name on one of the menus, and she hugs it with an excited blush.

"Want mine?" Chris asks, coming up at my side. His plate is loaded with ham sandwiches. I snatch one and stuff it into my cheek. "I know. I'm just the boring buff guy who carries Morgantha's sword."

"Hey," I say as the starry-eyed girl hands him the menu, "I carried *your* sword for, like, a whole episode after you got poisoned by that scorpion on the desert moon. Not my fault that thing's a foot taller than me."

"Do you want my autograph?" Peter says as Chris signs. "I'm the showrunner."

"You're the boss?" asks the girl.

"Not in a boring suit-and-tie way!" Peter spins his keys around his fingers. "I'm the one who taught Lily how to drive a motorcycle."

"Okay. Bye." The girl clutches her menu to her chest and skips away. Peter frowns. The look on his face tells me he's taking that rejection seriously. For a grown man, he acts like such a kid sometimes—but considering how Chris and I spilled Doritos all over the makeup room, who am I to judge?

"Can I borrow your bottle opener?" I say, fiddling with my cream soda. Peter tosses me the key ring. The souvenir Key Largo bottle opener, parrot faded, is so worn it barely hooks under the lid. Peter's disappeared by the time the bottle fizzes open, so I tuck the keys in my waistband and go looking for him.

He isn't talking with the director or back in the makeup studio. He must have gone outside to smoke. My tightly stitched tunic rubs tight against my chest and stomach as I tramp down the fire stairs. Hot air washes over me as I step out into the Burbank afternoon. The desert stretches out before me, dry and biting, the broad sun in the blue sky painting everything in primary colors.

*What's she doing here?*

Greta's leaning against a battered old pickup, chewing on her fingernails, staring at the road. Her shadow stretches long and black, washing over the road to the slumped white strip mall on the other side, tall and lonely like a palm tree ringed by asphalt. I'd think she snuck out to vape if I didn't know how obnoxious she thought vaping was.

Oh, god. Maybe she snuck out here to avoid me. Maybe she hates #Morganetta so deeply she'd rather tunnel to the center of the earth than speak to me.

Careful as I approach her, I weave my fingers together

behind my back and keep space between our shadows. "Hey," I mutter. "What's up?"

"I skipped ahead in the script." Her whole body trembles silently. Her head is tipped back so the tears rolling out can't smudge her makeup.

I rub my chin, confused. Does her favorite character not get enough screen time? Did she have a personal fan theory proven false? "Please tell me they didn't write us a sex scene." I don't turn eighteen until principal photography is over, in late April, but Greta's birthday is in November, so they could tell her to do it with a body double and green-screen in my face. It's part of acting professionally, yeah, but I'd like to have sex in real life before I have to fake it covered in mocap dots.

Her head does a tiny, tightly wound shake. Her eyes don't even flick my way. I'm not sure of the right thing to say to reach across the distance between us. Probably not "Are you weirded out by the idea of people making you film topless, or weirded out by pretending other girls turn you on?"

"No. I—" She chokes off and passes me her phone.

EXT: A field outside the burning village.

ALIETTA stumbles out of the smoke, disguised in a stolen army uniform. We have a moment of relief: she survived the terrible raid. BRYKEN enters, covered in the blood of the civilians he failed

to save. We're so excited to finally see
these two characters meet at last, it
takes a beat to realize he thinks ALIETTA
is the enemy.

                    BRYKEN
          You did this. You and your
          monster queen, Aylah of
          House Sinheart.

                    ALIETTA
          It isn't like that. I'm not
          on their side. I belong
          to House Dustborn. Aylah
          held me captive. I've been
          running from them, too--

BRYKEN cuts her off by slapping her across
the mouth. Stunned by the blow, ALIETTA
sprawls back in the dirt.

                    BRYKEN
          Shut up. What do you know
          of being Aylah's captive?
          You were a princess on
          Neublon-6. Aylah locked
          me up on her prison ship.

```
Killed  my  father  right
before my eyes. She wanted
to teach me to fear her.
I'll teach House Sinheart
to fear me.
```

BRYKEN draws his stellar blade and stabs
ALIETTA through the heart. She dies.

"Holy shit," I whisper, lowering the screen. My voice comes out as a high whine, like it isn't even mine to control. "This is sick." I feel nauseous. Grossed out by how selfish I've been, spending this whole day thinking about how awkward and annoyed I feel around her. Because Alietta and Morgantha matter to the whole world. At least, the queer-lady fraction of it. At least, they will. Soon.

And Peter and Wes will break all their hearts when Alietta gets brutally murdered on-screen next year.

# Two

Bury your gays. They buried their gays.

For years and years on television, having a character come out as gay meant they'd die within a season. Not just back in some ancient heyday of homophobia—last year, the bi main character of *Ancient Are the Ways* and the trans lady prisoner on *Breakaway* both got stabbed to death in the exact same way (piece of glass in the throat, fake blood everywhere). It's the sort of awful you get when writers say they want more diversity on-screen but don't bother to craft story lines for their gay characters beyond "I'm here, I'm queer, I'm coughing up blood."

When I was twelve, Kate sat me down to watch her all-time favorite TV show: *Buffy the Vampire Slayer*. It was cheesy and predictable in places, but we both loved the badass female characters. Kate said Buffy made her feel seen and taken seriously as a young woman. But then one of the recurring lesbian characters was murdered and her girlfriend went insane, and I felt depressed for days. Even before I knew I was gay, I knew how it felt to have my heart made a punch line in a cruel joke.

"This has got to be a prank," I say. "Peter and Wes—they wouldn't do this to Alietta. They wouldn't have Bryken do it. Not after all that bad PR we got in Season Two, in that scene where it looked like Trade Magnate Hal sexually assaulted Aylah—"

"You don't get it." She shakes her head. "Ever since my first episode aired, the show's male fans have rooted for Peter and Wes to kill me off. Because my character's super feminine, and that bores them, or some bullshit. You're fucking Morgantha. They sell T-shirts with your face on them. Everyone loves you."

I'm confused for a second. Is she talking about me or the character I play?

"I know it looks bad, but I think we can fix this," I say. "It's just a first draft. Peter and Wes make changes to their scripts all the time." How often have I arrived on set to see Peter running up with a stack of scrawled papers in his fist, overwriting the lines I've spent all day rehearsing? "I'll explain why it's wrong to kill off one of the only gay characters on the show and how they'll squander the good PR from Morgantha and Alietta getting together." #Morganetta is supposed to blow up the internet, yes—but for a good reason. Not because we're burning down the internet to protest a narrative catastrophe.

She wipes her nose with the sleeve of her dress. Her platinum-blond wig is coming off sideways, rhinestones

19

hanging by threads of glue. I'm making things worse. If she was anyone else, if she wasn't so upset, I'd let it go and walk away. But I need her. After everything I've invested in #Morganetta, it still takes two actors to bring it to life.

"We can leak the scripts online!" I continue. Sure, we're both under NDAs, but it's only a thirty-thousand-dollar penalty per infraction. And the public outrage it'd generate, especially after Episode Three with the kiss airs—they'd have to keep Alietta alive. "The moment it goes viral, the internet will hold them accountable. They'll be so grateful we've stopped them from making a bad decision that we won't get in trouble at all."

"I'm going to lose my job," she croaks out.

The zip and beehive hum of my angry thoughts swirls to a stop.

That's what's bothering Greta. Of course. Not the loss of the on-screen representation. The loss of her job.

And I didn't even stop to think what that means to her.

"I'm sorry," I say, and my voice sounds smaller now. "This must be scary and upsetting, and it absolutely sucks you found out this way. Would a hug make you feel better?"

Behind her tear-streaked makeup, her eyes get big and seething. Like she's afraid my awkwardness will rub off on her. Like she's mad at me for thinking there's anything I can do to help.

Like she doesn't want another girl to touch her.

"Honestly," she says, "can we please just . . . go?"

*We.* That's what catches my attention. *We.* Greta's never been a *we* with anyone. She doesn't talk about dates she's been on or friends back home or even much about her family. Every conversation we've had is about work, even while practicing stage kissing during the Season Five filming. This is my chance to figure her out. To do her a favor. To get her on my side re: #Morganetta.

And when I see someone that sad, I just want to make them smile.

Before I can overthink it, I grab the helmets off the back of Peter's motorcycle and offer one to Greta. "Put it on. Let's get out of here."

"Right now?" Her eyes widen. "We're still in costume!"

"The helmet will keep your wig safe," I say, strapping the other one down over my own as I straddle the driver's seat. It's not like these are our real costumes, stored carefully back on location. Just cheap facsimiles made for the photo shoot, which they'll recycle after.

"Peter will be so upset. It's his bike!"

"It's fine," I say, hopping into the driver's seat. My heart is pumping faster now, head spinning with frantic energy. Peter has given me a few motorcycle lessons on deserted back roads between shoots and in parking lots before makeup call. I'm pretty used to controlling it. I've never taken it out on the highway, but I've driven there in one of Kate's cars, so how hard could it be? "He gave me the keys. He likes me."

"Well." She bites her lip. "I mean, he does always treat you like his kid brother. You could burn down a set and get away with it."

She straps on the helmet, hikes up her petticoats in one arm, and slides the other arm around me as she swings into the seat. I glance back to double-check her visor is down, and notice through the glass how long her lashes are. Like butterflies perching on a velvet-brown flower.

My stomach drops like I've gone over the crest of a roller coaster.

*Greta Thurmway has the most important eyelashes in the world,* thinks some absolutely idiotic part of my brain. I've never been this close to a girl when I wasn't filming. Every part of her body lines up with part of mine.

What a useless thing to notice. I don't even like her as a friend.

"Hold on." I try to make my voice low and firm as I key the ignition. The engine growls between my thighs.

I twist the throttle. The bike jumps beneath me like a rearing stallion (like that pinto bastard who threw me filming the TV movie *Ghost Pony*). Greta squeezes me like a toothpaste tube.

And we're off. An arrow from a bow, a bullet from a gun, streaking across the pavement before I can blink. All I think is *Oh shit, we're dead* and *I'm going to kill Greta* and *Don't flip the bike don't flip the bike don't flip—*

I spin us out onto the road in a spray of gravel. My stomach lurches. Greta screams and yells curse words I didn't know she knew.

Five fast heartbeats later, we're speeding down the asphalt into the haze and vivid blue hovering over LA.

"I've got this!" I shout, to reassure her, and mutter, "Shit, I've *got* this." Then I laugh so hard the sounds feel solid in my mouth. The engine's roar seems to crawl inside my lungs, animating me. A pickup truck speeds past the opposite direction—the driver honks and shouts at us like an asshole—and Greta flips him the bird and lets her violet petticoats stream out in the wind.

"It's like we're in an action movie!" she gasps near my ear, warm breath and a tiny, intimate shared pocket of sound. Cars and dust and desert whip by us, a river of motion and fuel. The skintight tunic and leggings trap a simmering layer of sweat next to my skin. As the bike punches its way south, mountains rise all around to dwarf us, the sun beaming down like a magnifying glass. Something wild and speed loving rises up inside me and escapes as a cry of joy.

The long, snaking coil of the Golden State Freeway twists through the hills like an electric cord—and snarls when we hit traffic. Packed in tight with the heat and rumble of stopped cars, I pull up the bike behind an exhaust-belching delivery truck and rest my foot on the ground.

"Lily," Greta mutters. "Just behind us."

A middle-aged white woman hangs out her car window, jaw agape, phone up and filming.

"Hey!" I shout, lowering my voice to sound tough. "Put that down." She doesn't budge, and my skin starts to crawl. She's looking at us like the free latte you get when you hit ten thousand points on your reward app.

"Holy shit!" Two boys lean out the back seat of an SUV on our left flank, both phones up. "It's those chicks from TV!"

My teeth click into a snarl. I shoot them a deadly glare. If we weren't frozen dead in the middle of traffic, I'd hop off the bike and kick both their asses. I didn't spend seven years in stage combat training without picking up a little of the real thing.

Greta, as usual, has her mind on practical concerns. "They could be streaming this live," she groans. "Oh, fuck. We're so fucked."

Everything that fled my mind when I read Peter's script—years of Kate's careful training and my costars' warnings about paparazzi encounters gone bad—now rises to the center of my thoughts. How many viewers could their stream attract? How viral could this go? What will Kate do to me if she finds out?

Will I also get Greta in trouble?

"Hold on tight." I set my jaw, kick off, and gun the throttle.

We fly between the stalled trucks and cars, up the white of the lane marker. Sunlight glares in my eyes, and I lower my brow to keep my focus up ahead. Greta's petticoats flutter perilously close to car doors and windows; a scrap of fabric rips off on the window of a too-close Land Rover. But we slide through the mess and down the exit ramp, racing off into the sunbaked quiet of Griffith Park.

I park the bike at a trailhead and help Greta get down. A seam splits on my tunic, opening it from my armpit to my bra strap. Black asphalt dust litters her embroidered hem. Tourists point and snap photos. An old lady shoots us a vicious stink eye and shouts, "In my day, we treated costumes with respect!" I fumble so nervously sticking the key in the helmet lockbox that my hand slips and leaves a gash in the red paint.

"Where are we going?" Greta asks as I lead her onto the least-crowded trail I see. "Are we hiking to the observatory?"

I shrug. "The observatory is usually pretty crowded this time of day, but we could go there. I wanted to show you this place Kate took me as a kid." At least, I think it was Kate who took me there. It might have been a nanny.

"Lead the way. I've never been here."

"Really? You've been living here for two years."

"I have work!" She hikes up her long skirts in one hand, stepping over loose rocks and roots on the path. "It's not like I can run around doing whatever I'd like."

"I've got the exact same job," I point out, "and I do."

"You're *you*." She sighs. Like there's something big and obvious between us I've cluelessly missed.

But she sounds happier. She's rolling her eyes at me, not crying or shouting. At this point, I'll take all the eye rolls I can get if it means we're bonding.

The crowds thin out as we hike higher, until we're alone in the world and the cameras stop snapping. A stitch twinges in my side. I never realized walking in a park demanded actual physical skill. Growing up on a steady diet of film and television taught me miserably tromping up a trail is how the average white person bonds with their family.

I'm not from an average family. But Greta practically grew up in a Hallmark film. I read as much in her interviews after her casting. She's got two parents still married to each other, three older brothers, a dog. They made pancakes on Christmas and hunted eggs on Easter and even once went to see the groundhog on Groundhog's Day. With her freckled cheekbones and small-town charm, she feels factory-made to sit at the center of a story. A girl plucked from her normal life to shine among the stars.

Which makes her the polar opposite of me. I'm not stupid. I'm a decent actor, but I got this role because my mom runs a production company. Greta's better than me by any measuring stick, and both of us know it. She embodies *actress* and *glamor* in a way I never will, and it's hard for me not to be a little jealous. Her correcting me and Chris on set just salts the wound. Because I already feel like an imposter, a fake. I don't need Greta to rub in everything I do wrong.

I squeeze my fists and push myself to keep up as we hike, even as the sun beats down on my too-tight, torn tunic. The costume crew must have made it off my old measurements, since I've grown—out, not up—since Season Five wrapped. Kate says the boobs will be an asset when I move into playing more adult roles, and it helps to be short so smaller male actors won't mind working with me. But far as I'm concerned, puberty's a lottery where everyone loses.

Since I'm wearing a sports bra underneath my costume, part of me wants to tear the gross, sweaty thing and ditch it in the scrub bushes, but littering is illegal and, besides, some weirdo would find it and sell it online.

"Up there!" I say, pointing toward an overlook rise. Greta charges ahead. It's a clear day, and her eyes light up as she peers out at the horizon, her dusty costume slippers touching the trail's very edge.

"Lily, come check this out!"

I come up beside her. The city rolls and rattles across the valley and hills, like the long swoop of a superhero's cape flourished against the sea. The knots of interchanges, concrete wrapped around palm trees and scrub brush, send cars racing off into a thousand lives that aren't mine. The wind whips at my wig, drying the sweat to salty trails on my throat. It's every bit as gorgeous a view as I remember. My eyes sting and I'm getting a blister from one oversized boot and my heart has never felt so full. "Look! You can see all the way to the ocean!"

"I can even smell dead fish on the wind." She gives me a sidelong glance. Her eyebrow wiggles, and suddenly it's ten times more important than even her eyelashes. "Oh, wait. That's you."

I whack her on the shoulder, which is as high on tall, reedy Greta as I can reach. She cackles, which should be a point in favor of her secretly being a movie villain, but suddenly I feel like I'm standing here with the real Greta. Not the person I know from press junkets or on set. My grand-theft-motorcycle partner in crime with red hair, freckles, and the most important eyebrows in the world.

"Cut that out!" she laughs, manicured fingernails scrabbling for my wrists before I can get in a second blow. I lean in, struggling for leverage, and slam my nose into her shoulder. "Shit!" She grabs my cheek, twisting my face upward. "Did I break it?"

"No?" I stumble, nostrils clogging with snot. Her palm is still pressed to my skin, warm and soft. *She must use really good moisturizer*, I think as my heart churns like helicopter blades, and then—

Greta leans down and kisses me.

Her lips press tight against mine, and I imagine a film score swelling, sweeping me up like a wave. Her fingers tangle in my hair. Her breath rolls down my lip. It feels like everything. Like the sun rising, or a curse breaking. Like the whole mountain is spinning around us as the camera sweeps out and cuts to credits.

Sweat traces glittering lines down her cheek as she pulls away. All I can hear past her heavy breathing is the pounding of a flock of woodpeckers on a dead tree, tapping faster than even my racing heart.

"That was . . . whoa." I can't speak. It's like I'm high but I also want to start skipping. To throw my arms around her and do it again, because *why not?* I came here to figure out who the real Greta is, and if she's a girl who wants to kiss me, all my problems are solved and life is better than wonderful.

She winces. Bites her lip. "That was . . . I mean. Yeah. That certainly . . . happened. What's there to say?"

*What's there to say?* It was a kiss. On the lips, with some tongue behind it. That's important. Even more important, it was *us* kissing. Not our characters. Her kissing me and me kissing her back. It was Greta and Lily and it matters. It matters to me.

I don't think I realized how much it matters to me until now. When it sounds like it doesn't matter to her.

I fumble for words. "Well, when Episode Three airs, there'll be questions. Online and in interviews. About us and our identities. Everyone knows I'm gay, but you're mysterious and shit. Why'd you kiss me?" My voice spikes on the word *kiss*. Weak. Incredulous. I'm slowly dying of how uncool I feel and sound. Hoping she'll push me into the brush so I can roll downhill and mercifully snap my own neck under the weight of this failure.

"Honestly," Greta says, very quickly, "I wanted to know what it would be like. Kissing someone for real."

"And?" My voice is a squeak.

"It was . . ." She looks down at her hands. And then she shrugs.

A shrug. That's what kissing me is like. Like a one-star Yelp review with no comment.

Fuck. I was such an idiot. It didn't mean anything at all to her. And it shouldn't mean anything at all to me. It hurts, yeah. But that's just because I want to be good at kissing in general. I don't want to be good at kissing Greta, of all people. Especially if she doesn't think I'm worth her time.

"I'm sorry," Greta finishes, and I shake my head. Even though it takes everything I've got to keep from panicking and running; I can't ditch her in part of the city she doesn't know well. My cheeks burn with embarrassment and the start of a wicked sunburn.

"It's cool," I say. "You don't have to apologize." She doesn't have to like me. I'll survive. Whatever. Maybe I'll find a girl who wants to talk with me more than once in a blue moon. One who isn't an anime poster on my wall. "We should head back down. Out of the heat."

Very calmly, I lead us back down the trail. Neither of us speaks. Which is good, because I don't know what to say.

When we get back to the parking lot, two LAPD officers wait by Peter's bike. And my gut says they're not asking for autographs.

# Three

"I've seen a lot worse, ma'am," the officer says as Kate furiously answers the door. "Once stopped a pop star from punching her dealer for selling okapi turds as a club drug. Sometimes kids go for a joyride without a license. No one got hurt. Pay the fine and her record is sealed at eighteen."

"It's all over the internet," Kate says, in the same voice a TV mom might complain about a mess on the floor. "This isn't going away so quickly."

The look she shoots me means *I* might be going away. Like, to a locked box in the middle of the Arctic Circle. Feverishly, I envy Greta. The cops dropped her at the apartment she nominally shares with her mom, whenever she can make it to town to visit her. Since she's eighteen, and I told them I'd lied to Greta about having a motorcycle license, they let her off with a warning.

I'd rather be before a judge in a courtroom than under Kate's harsh gray eyes.

"You're not slapping my star with grand theft auto charges, right?" Peter steps out from Kate's shadow, his typical grubby black T-shirt more wrinkled than ever. A worried note lurks beneath his joking tone. "I gave Lily permission to use my bike. I only called the cops because she and Greta took off without telling me. I thought some deranged *Galaxy Spark* fan had kidnapped them."

"Hey!" I say. "I could totally take on a deranged fan. I'm short, not weak."

"We were all worried about you two," Peter said. "Seriously, kid. I try to keep things fun and jokey on set, but what you did—that's serious."

Kate glares daggers at the officer. "I appreciate the prompt customer service. Wish you'd been as polite at that Pride block party I threw in '04. I can still smell the mace when the wind blows off the valley. Have a nice day."

He grunts, shoves a stack of papers at Kate, then turns and jogs off down the driveway. Like an extra in an action movie escaping the blast radius of a bomb.

I wish I could be that lucky.

"Well, Lily," Kate says. "Now we can talk. And I can decide if I'm shipping your stuff off to Alcatraz."

She makes *talk* sound like a punch in the gut. Even Peter hears it. "Come on, Kate. I'm not pressing charges. We can let this all go."

"You should leave," Kate says. Point-blank and heavy. "You wanted to make sure Lily was alive. She's alive."

"I'm trying to help."

"You've helped." Kate jabs a finger down the driveway. Peter holds his hands up—like he's signaling her not to shoot—and her frown only widens. Down the driveway he goes, with a last sheepish wave back at me. I return it and don't blame him for ditching.

"Did you have to kick him out like that?" I say when he's gone.

"Do you want me to discipline you in *front* of your boss?"

*Oh.* Yeah. I guess I don't want that. But ever since the officer led me to the door, all I've heard from Kate is how mad she is. All I ever hear from Kate is the next step in her plan for me and how well or how poorly I'm living up to it.

"He's not just my boss," I say. "He's a friend. At least Peter cares if I'm safe. You didn't even ask where we went."

"When I was your age, I hitchhiked through a thousand miles of desert. I trust you to be competent. But you're almost an adult. You should understand your choices have consequences." She sighs, runs a hand back through her hair. "Peter isn't responsible for raising you right. He's responsible for *Galaxy Spark*, which means, to an extent, keeping you happy. My job is to be your parent. Come on."

*Her job.* Kate's had plenty of those. When she was sixteen, she ran away from home to tote coffee around movie sets—assistant to the assistants of the stars. She broke a director's hand when he groped her on a set, got sued, and ran off to Singapore to develop her career at an international film distributor. The company boomed. Every studio in Hollywood offered her fortunes to return; she turned them down and started her own production company. She had me and was back in the office the week after giving birth, me in a carrier. When she met Chris's dad, Will, a pro wrestler turned movie star, she got him to propose a few weeks after their first date. Kate gets things done, so efficiently all her naysayers get trapped in her dust.

And I'm the next project on her to-do list.

Kate waves me forward. I follow her back into the kitchen, through our all-white box of a hallway and the porcelain dome of the atrium. Polished and spotlessly clean. Even the trash cans sparkle. Unlike me, in my shredded, dusty spandex, looking less like a space hero and more like I tumbled out of a dumpster behind a drag show.

"I swear to god," Kate says as we enter the kitchen, where Will's baking, "to whatever deity may be listening, to whatever higher power governs teenage idiocy, to Thalia the muse of public relations—"

"Muse of comedy," Will corrects. My stepdad inspects his rising bread with a practiced eye, broad shoulders hunched over the stovetop. Six jars of sourdough starter rest on the counter. Chris and I love his new hobby—fresh hot bread, plus the chance to make countless yeast jokes.

"Raising teenagers makes me feel like the gods are playing tricks on me." Kate pops an aspirin and gives me a hard look. "Do you know what you did?"

I squirm. Kate's glare is known to make grown men quake

in their Italian leather shoes. "Gave Greta a lift?"

"Stole your boss's bike. Committed multiple traffic violations. And you got photographed, through all this, wearing costumes that inextricably link this dumbass stunt to your careers!" Kate laughs. It's the sound the Joker makes before burning down a building. "What were you thinking?"

"Come on. You did the same stuff when you were my age." My cheeks burn. The sheer unfairness of it all simmers in my chest. "You packed an overnight bag and hitchhiked from Phoenix to LA, slept behind a soundstage, broke into a supermodel's set trailer to shower for a job interview—"

"I don't want you to be me," Kate answers. "I want you to have everything I didn't. Starting with a clean juvenile record."

"You're a good mom," Will says, stepping between us to massage her shoulders. "Lily's a good kid. She wanted to cheer up Greta. It's a big shock, the first time a friend gets fired."

"She's not my friend," I mutter, ducking around them to pull an energy drink from the stainless-steel fridge. Mmm. Purple flavor. "And how'd you know about that?"

"Peter couldn't wait to blab about the 'awesome plot twist' he came up with high on Adderall at three a.m." Kate rolls her eyes. "The press will ask questions, and we need a cover story. You picked a hell of a time to stop griping about how she's an annoying perfectionist, kid. We can't tell everyone 'I'm sorry, but Lily was upset Greta's getting fired.'"

"Why not?" I say, dropping my pull tab in the recycling. "What Wes and Peter are planning is wrong. It'll hurt the show's queer viewers. Going public will get enough other people angry to stop them, and I can afford the fine for one infraction—take it out of my *Galaxy Spark* money. I want to do the right thing."

"God help me, I somehow gave birth to a kid with more heart than sense." Kate pinches the bridge of her nose. "I know you feel hurt. But you better find another way to deal with this, because once you break an NDA, fine or no fine, no one's going to trust you not to do it a second time. It'll ruin your career. Say goodbye to Ann Elise."

Ugh. The Ann Elise books. The new film franchise Kate plans to produce. Based off a bestselling series of novels about a shy college student hired by a handsome billionaire to revitalize his dying fashion magazine (turns out he's mistaken her for another, much older and more experienced editor with a similar name). When I'd pointed out a billionaire should background-check his employees (and maybe not *date* them), Kate had shut me down with "One hundred million copies sold worldwide—one hundred million. After this role, the whole world will know who you are."

I'm not sure how I'll go from badass monster slayer to blushing bookish virgin turned accidental fashion editor, but I'm an actor. I'm good at pretending to be someone I'm not.

"Did you figure out when we're filming that, *Kate*?" This earns me another glare, half power this time. Kate doesn't like that I use her first name, but I grew up dragged along to her meetings and events. I heard more people call her Kate than I knew kids who called their parents "Mom." So *Kate* can deal.

"I have a writer attached and the budget approved. We can start once you finish filming the next season of *Galaxy Spark.*"

I exhale and try not to look relieved. I've got some time before I need to take on this new, extremely heterosexual role. Kate's sent me a million articles about why Ann Elise is a feminist icon—she stands up for her goals, she grows strong female friendships instead of backstabbing other women for career advancement—and I understand. I should be excited to play this part. In a way, Ann Elise might be more groundbreaking than Morgantha.

But she just doesn't click with me. And that deep-down feeling of *mismatch* is so embarrassing I can't voice it out loud.

"How does Lara Brown feel?" Will says. "That you haven't started shooting yet?"

"Lara," Kate says diplomatically, "can kiss my ass. If she wants the hero of *Galaxy Spark* to bring Ann Elise to life, she'll wait until Lily has time for her. Not the other way around."

Lara Brown. A midwestern housewife with big hair and bigger ambitions, who hit it big when her self-published romance novels blew up into an international sensation. She's the Kate of Ohio, which would be great if it didn't mean two Kates trying to crush me between them.

"You're sure Lara's okay with me being gay?" I ask, sliding onto one of the leather-padded barstools at the kitchen island. Will had the set custom-made for him, so my legs swing in empty air. "She knows, right?"

"Yeah," Kate says. "I wouldn't make you work with a homo-phobe. It'd be an absolute nightmare."

I wince. *Thanks for having my back.* I'm glad she took care of it, but I hate how it feels. Like we're coworkers, not family.

I have plenty of coworkers. I have only one mom.

"However," Kate continues, "she's already sent me several angry emails about working with a motorcycle thief."

"To be fair," Will says, "if I knew absolutely nothing about someone other than they were gay and a motorcycle thief, it would be the second part that concerned me."

Kate's phone buzzes. She presses her fist against her mouth, like she's trying to trap a frustrated scream inside. "It's Lara's agent. Shit. Lily, go to your room. I need to make some adults-only strategy calls."

"Am I being grounded?" I ask, shrinking down in my chair.

"You're being sent away. The real punishment comes later. Be glad I'm not going to cancel the first-reads party and ruin all your professional relationships."

I grab an apple from the bowl on the island's center, tap it to make sure it's not wax, and bite down. My phone buzzes—a text from Chris, asking if there's anything he should pick up on his way home. I should be glad my party's not canceled. Heck, I should be glad that being maybe-grounded is my big-gest problem.

But I don't feel grateful right now. I feel pissed off.

Kate hasn't even bothered asking why I'm really so upset.

I jump off the stool and duck off to my room. It's on the

top floor of the west wing, with an ocean view behind my half-closed blackout curtains and clothes scattered across the floor. Everyone in my family calls it my "cave," which is, honestly, accurate. Kate's offered and threatened to hire an interior designer to redo it in any style I like—a major concession, since the rest of the house is her ultra-modern baby—but I've resisted even that. My room is my sanctuary, papered in posters from anime I liked two years ago, centered around the high-backed gaming chair Will calls my throne.

I drop the apple core in the trash and fiddle with my phone. Open a newly updated fanfic—a #Morganetta coffee shop AU over a hundred thousand words long—and read about Morgantha and Alietta studying for their SATs. Everyone in the comments section is gushing over how clumsy Morgantha (for some reason, she's always clumsy in the fics) knocks her latte onto Alietta's test prep books. *Jeez those things cost eighty dollars!!!* says the most upvoted comment. All I can think is *Huh, eighty dollars is a lot for some people* and *Am I supposed to take the SATs?* I guess I should be grateful that's what runs through my head, and I am. I just hate feeling there's a wall between me and the rest of the world. Between me and people I'd want to be friends with, if I could ever be only another fan.

It's not like I get to be a normal teenager. Go to an in-person high school. Attend dances. Decorate a locker. I only even know about these things from TV. But when I interact with the #Morganetta fandom, behind the safe anonymity of a made-up username and avatar, no one knows or cares I haven't done that stuff. They're all looking for a safe space, too. To imagine. To dream.

Maybe it's a little egotistical of me, to read about my character's imagined romantic life—it was super awkward that time a fan ambushed me with topless #Morganetta art at Comic-Con—but the love the fandom invests in the ship shines in each word. It makes me feel like I'm part of something. Like all the work I'm doing on *Galaxy Spark* is making people's lives better. And I can smooth over every last fear and worry I carry because I know I'm doing something right. I'm putting other people first.

My alarm goes off. I set down my phone. Fifteen minutes until the raid starts.

I shower quickly, drop my ruined costume in the trash, unpin my wig from my plain brown ponytail, and pull on shorts with my favorite cozy sweatshirt before returning to my throne. The massive high-tech desktop I bought last summer whirls quietly to life. The familiar breath of the fan washes over my bare legs as I jam on the headset and log in to *Swordquest Online*.

You'd think I'd get enough nerd time in my day job. That, after hours in the makeup chair, sweating under focused lights, I'd be through with playing pretend. But the massive online world of *Swordquest* is a haven for me. In this brightly colored fantasy adventure, I'm not Morgantha, with all the weight that carries. I'm Frey of the Wildlands, huntsman and archer extraordinaire, my avatar a hairy, wild, leather-strapped human dude in his mid-thirties way too buff just to carry a bow.

I'm no one. I'm normal. I mean, I'm a heroic veteran of three magical wars, but so is everyone else.

"Am I late?" I ask, charging through the portal into *Swordquest*'s newest twenty-person raid. The rest of my guild waits just inside the entrance, passing out potions and healing gems as the boss, a demonic pirate king, waits patiently down the corridor for us to kill him.

"You're right on time, Frey," says Hawk, guild leader of the Warhawks and our main tank. "Thanks for showing up exactly when we're fighting the one guy you need loot from."

"Some people have jobs," says a high, unfamiliar voice. A priest, whose display name is Aida—must be a new member of the guild. "I'm sure he was just late at work."

See, here's the thing about Frey: everyone assumes he's a guy. When I made my character two years ago, I didn't realize that most girls—and lots of guys—prefer playing female characters. I just fooled around with the available models and he was the one I wanted to represent me. And since I didn't want anyone recognizing my voice from TV, I bought modding software, the kind that drops your voice a full octave. When I speak, they hear Frey.

It started out as a joke, or at least, something I'd joke about, privately, in my head, to make it make sense why I loved him so much. *Look how quirky I am! Playing as this enormous dude!* Like I'm such a good actor, I can pretend to be a guy and no one will notice.

Frey doesn't feel like a joke anymore. He feels like part of me. "You don't know Frey," Hawk says, a warm edge to his teasing. "He's always got some crazy excuse for being late to raid."

"Like the time he tried to convince us his mom took him to a party at the Japanese embassy and they didn't have Wi-Fi," adds Clay, our mage.

I roll my eyes. I'd been telling the truth, but I guess normal teenagers don't often find themselves in that scenario. "Sorry, team. I had a long day at work. Plus, my mom yelled at me." It sounds so simple and easy when I put it like that. Like the weight of two media franchises isn't resting on my shoulders.

"Aww," Aida says. "Thought I was going to get a cool story." She pulls a magic hat from her inventory and throws it at me. My avatar morphs into a tiny white rabbit. I laugh, fling it back, and suddenly the whole guild is a foot-high pack of fluff.

"I like this new healer," I say, and Aida's character curtsies on-screen. "Give me back the hat. I want to try something."

She passes it to me. I turn and toss it at the boss. He shrinks into tiny rabbit form—and bellows, charging straight at us.

I've accidentally started combat.

Quickly, I click off my rabbit form and fire Mirror Arrow at Clay. The elven mage, who happens to be standing farthest from the group, lights up like a sparkler. The roaring rabbit chomps him once, and Clay falls to the floor. Then, because I redirected the boss's attention at one, now-dead target, he turns and runs back down the hall to await us from his starting position.

"I'm so, so sorry," Aida says, resurrecting Clay. "I shouldn't have been messing around like that. I nearly got the whole raid killed."

She sounds nervous. Even more jittery than I'd expect from someone trying out for a spot on our team. "Hey, don't worry about it. I wipe us out every other week."

"He loves wasting our time," Clay says. "Aida, last week he convinced us we'd unlock a secret boss if twenty people jumped on this switch in the same millisecond. We wasted twenty minutes syncing our jumps."

I bite my lip and force down a giggle. "At least I didn't 'forget' to summon my fire elemental for eight pulls in a row."

"And you didn't get booted out?" Aida says. "You guys are way nicer than the assholes in my last guild."

"I have a high dumbass tolerance," Hawk says, grumpy and grudgingly affectionate. "Right. Let's do this for real."

Seamlessly, my mind slips into the flow of play. Arrows fly from my gold-trimmed bow in perfect combos, fingers flying over my keys from muscle memory. The boss summons lethal patches of lightning and fierce winds to buffet the raid. I glide around obstacles, thumb rolling up and down my mouse.

"Stack!" Hawk shouts, and we group together in the hallway's heart. I grappling-hook–swing into the pack as our healers fling up a massive shimmering shield. In the next heartbeat, the hall collapses on our heads.

Aida swears and mashes her keyboard so hard I hear it click over comms. My health bar winks up into yellow, and I weave through a maze of crashing waves as I sink bolt after bolt into the boss. *Come on.* If this wasn't a game, where my arrows vanish after hitting home, he'd look like a pincushion instead of a grumpy giant sailor. "Die," I grunt as the boss flings Hawk against the room. "Die, die, die!" Our tanks are dead. He's coming for me now. I back away, still firing in the pattern I could twitch through in my sleep. His health is at two percent—one—zero—

"Finish him!" Aida screams.

The giant's fist crushes me. I punch my desk and curse. Frey lies in a fetal position on the raid floor.

We've died with less than ten hit points remaining. One arrow away from victory.

We've made it to this stage three times and haven't beaten him yet.

"I'm sorry," Aida says. "If I hadn't stepped in that lightning puddle—"

"Just don't do it next time," Hawk says, and charges back into battle. "All part of learning the fight."

For the next three hours, we throw ourselves at the boss. The luck's bad, or maybe we need stronger stats to kill it. Some players grumble to themselves about how frustrating this all is, but I don't mind. Everything's been frustrating today. It's better to be frustrated *with* people, as part of a team.

"I'm off for the evening, boys," I say finally. "Need my sleep, since I'm hosting a big party tomorrow."

"How many people counts as a party for a nerd like you,

Frey?" Hawk laughs, sarcastic and teasing. I don't mind. It's different when guys tease other guys, especially their friends, a layer of fondness running under it all. "When I was your age, we'd call it a party when we had four people together in a basement for D&D."

"When were you my age?" I say back. "Like, five minutes ago?"

As I speak, my elbow jams the cable connecting my headset and PC. Sound blips as the connection deactivates and restarts. My voice reverbs for a heartbeat—my real voice, high-pitched and *wrong*.

Clay laughs. "I knew it! You're filtering your voice deeper. You're like, twelve, in real life."

"No," I blurt, even though they've all heard me. I can't exactly deny my own voice.

"It's okay to be twelve, Frey," says Hawk, and even though he's just joshing, it hurts. Like he's accidently poked me in a weak spot.

Filtering my voice lower just makes me more comfortable than filtering high. Tuning my voice up makes me sound awful, horrifying to hear—so wrong, the sound made my palms sweat. And playing as a guy is easier than playing as a girl. Some of the assholes I met before joining the Warhawks would harass anyone with a high voice out of the game.

But these guys are cool. They're happy to have Aida with us. They wouldn't care if they knew their ranger was a girl.

Only I'd care.

"Aida, you did good after those first few pulls," Hawk says. "The raid slot is yours, if you want it."

"Yes!" she gasps, like she's shocked to hear it. But she did well. Her quick thinking and spellwork kept us standing through two pulls when multiple lightning bolts struck the raid at once.

"Can't wait to play with you next week," I say, deliberately pushing my voice lower. Just in case. Static cracks through the voice channel.

"Compensating for something?" Clay says. I wince.

"Be nice to Frey," Aida says. "People have all sorts of reasons for using vocal mods."

A smile cuts across my face. I don't mind the teasing and trash talk, but for some reason, these jokes feel like they go too far. Aida's not just a great healer. I think she'll be a great friend.

"Yeah," says Clay. "He's totally a serial killer playing from max-security prison. Or a wanted terrorist."

"Don't make me send my criminal minions after you," I laugh, glad now the conversation's shifted off my mods. I portal out of the raid, repair my busted armor, turn in a few quests, sell some ore I've mined. Five minutes later, a private message from Aida pops up in the corner of my screen.

*I had fun raiding with you tonight! Want to do some questing this weekend?*

*Sure!* I type back. *I'll DM you when I'm free.*

*Sorry those guys were ribbing on you for using mods. They strike me as good people, but they probably don't understand how many people game to be themselves in a way they can't IRL.*

*Yeah. There's just some things I'm not comfortable sharing with them.* Like the fact I star in America's biggest cable sci-fi drama. Or how my voice sounds in real life. *I don't want them thinking I'm some girl who plays a guy character for weird reasons. That's not me.* It is, but it isn't. There's nothing wrong about me playing as Frey. It just feels right. *It's just a queer thing, I guess.*

*That makes sense. My old guild was made up of all queer people. I'm an ace panromantic cis girl. It's nice knowing I'm not the only queer person in the Warhawks.*

I fight the urge to smile. At least I've made this mess of a day happy for someone. *Why'd you leave your old guild, if you don't mind me asking? I love hanging out in queer spaces online.* That's why #Morganetta fandom matters so much to me, after all.

A pause. Three dots pop up in her corner of the chat box. *On good days, I tell myself we just grew apart. But sometimes I feel like it's all my fault. That I was a bad healer, or a bad friend.*

*I don't think you're a bad friend. You seem really nice. Unless YOU'RE the one who's secretly a serial killer.*

*Lol. It's nice to meet you, too, Frey. And if you ever want to talk about being trans, I'm here for you.*

That hits me harder than Captain Storm's meaty fist. Reflexively, my fingers key the strokes to wipe out my chat log. My heart hammers, pounding fast against my ribs. I close the game client and shut down my computer, hyperventilating. Like a spy who's intercepted a secret message he's got to destroy.

*Whoa.* This feels . . . intense. A rush like speeding down the

47

highway on a motorcycle. What the hell is going on? Aida's wrong. I can see how she'd make that assumption—but *no*. I'm hiding my identity because I'm Lily fucking Ashton and this game is the only place I can escape that.

I should have just told Aida I'm cis. I shouldn't have logged off like I was guilty.

I shouldn't *feel* guilty.

Especially not because part of me suddenly wishes she could be right.

That I could be Frey. Because, some days, it feels like he's the most real part of me.

# Four

The next afternoon, the cast gathers in the poolside living room, where the wall folds open onto the sharp-edged black marble deck. Beyond the fence and hedges, the yellow and green of the city below fades into the blue haze of the Pacific. We sit on Kate's fashionable black-and-white minimalist stools (big plastic cubes she paid a lot of money for) eating mini bacon-and-shrimp skewers and sipping fresh-squeezed-orange juice-and-Sprite imitation mimosas (for me, Chris, and Greta; the adults get the real stuff). I tried to sneak in a beer under my sweatshirt, but Kate is watching me closely for once, and Will's liquor cabinet is in his private gym. All those posters of him in a Speedo with muscle grease slathered on his arms twists something strange and confusing inside me.

*If you want to talk about being . . .*

I can't finish that sentence, not even inside my own head. It fizzes into static, like an old TV set humming in the back of my head that I don't know how to turn off.

Thankfully, Chris cannonballs into the pool, spraying up cool water and breaking through my swirling thoughts.

"How're you doing, kid?" Ruby sits down on the stool beside me, which is absolutely dwarfed by her bulk. She's another wrestler turned actor, and she plays Captain Thorta, Queen Aylah's evil right-hand henchwoman. Thorta's supposed to be getting a redemption arc; she gave a big speech in Season Five about wanting to be a better person and helped Bryken escape Aylah's prison ship. We're all hoping Thorta will join the good guys in Season Six. But my hopes sink further every time I remember Alietta's terrible death scene.

"I'm fine," I say, tossing back my glass of orange juice. My eyes accidentally meet Greta's as it goes down, and I turn away so fast some slides down the wrong pipe, leaving me coughing. The stupid kiss hangs between us like a flashing red traffic signal. Like the headlights of a motorcycle I never should have touched. If I had a time machine—okay, first I'd kill Hitler, then I'd save Lexa on *The 100*, then I'd erase yesterday afternoon from history.

"Your mom isn't being too hard on you about the motorcycle thing, right?"

My stomach sinks further. I only saw Kate once today—glaring at me from across the living room as she argued with someone on a video call—but that upcoming punishment hangs over my head like a guillotine blade. I'd hoped the first-reads party would be an escape, even knowing that one terrible spoiler. But between Aida's DM and the upcoming

Kate-pocalypse, I feel like I'm crawling out of my skin with anxiety.

"If she kicks me out, will you adopt me and teach me to wrestle?" I say. Joking. Mostly.

Ruby ruffles my hair. "Any day, kid. What about you, Greta?" She looks across the table. "You look sort of green."

Greta shakes her head. Even her picture-perfect eyeshadow can't hide the tired rings under her eyes. She looks like she didn't sleep at all last night.

"C'mon," Ruby says. "Is it boy trouble? Do you need me to kick someone's ass for you?"

The cast looks out for each other. They're like my extended family—better, since Kate's family in Texas has barely spoken to her since she ditched them for LA. No one tells the press that Callie had skin cancer treated during Season Two filming or that Sir Henry would shake and tremble when he didn't get his meds. We keep each other's secrets. We help each other balance our public and private lives.

I should feel like I can be myself around them. The Lily Ashton who exists beyond the press, wigs, and pressure. But even around the cast, I still feel like no one sees me as I am. That the real me hasn't yet shown up at the party.

*If you ever want to talk about being trans . . .*

I shiver as Aida's words echo down my spine. It's like I'm back in Griffith Park, but it's midnight and the mountains are shrouded in fog. I'm stumbling up a peak with only a flashlight of internet knowledge to show me the way. I follow some trans and nonbinary people on social media, but their genders and lives are so diverse, with nothing specific to guide me to my truth. I know there's some "girly" stuff I don't enjoy, like wearing skirts and dresses, but maybe I'm just butch.

Being Lily Ashton is hard enough without needing to learn how to be someone else.

"I brought 2009 Moët," says Callie Liu, waving a green bottle. She plays Queen Aylah, the leader of House Sinheart, who rose from obscurity to take over half the galaxy, and she always carries herself like she's standing on the command bridge of her own personal spaceship. "Trust Kate to show me up with 2006 Clos Lanson." In real life, she's a globe-trotting supermodel famous for dumping a Swedish prince after he told her she'd have to get baptized to marry him.

"Hey, we can always use more champagne. We have to toast the Season Six casualties," Chris says, his swim trunks still dripping. His girlfriend, Shyanne, sits down beside him, expertly balancing a tray of finger sandwiches and vegan bacon on her knee. She's an actress, too—a comedian. With her hilarious delivery and knack for bringing characters to life, I know it's only a matter of time before she makes it big.

Shyanne raises her champagne flute. "To the best and the deadest of you all!"

"I better make it to the final episode," says Callie. "Then I want Morgantha to kill me. Not sure how. Knife through the belly, burned to death, poison—something dramatic."

"As if Morgantha has ever killed anyone in a way that doesn't involve a stellar sword or a gun," I laugh, and try to make myself feel it. To ignore the feeling my own personal earthquake has tilted the ground beneath me.

Chris hums his best impression of the theme song, and we're off. Shyanne reads for the bit parts, swapping between different accents for each. I turn to my first scene, where Alietta and Morgantha discuss their future as a couple.

"Nothing would make me happier than ruling the galaxy as your wife." Greta smiles at me, wide and earnest. Light dances off her long, perfect copper eyelashes. If it was any other girl, my heart would fizz like champagne bubbles. But chatting with Aida reminded me just how naturally I connect to so many other queer people. I have plenty of other, better options.

"We can't," I say, chewing a mouthful of vegan bacon around my line.

"Swallow before you talk," Callie says. "You just spat fake meat on your shoe."

"Sorry!" I dip my foot in the pool. That cleans off the red bits, but soaks my sock. My cast mates give me concerned looks. "Sorry. I'm, uh, distracted." I clear my throat. Channel Morgantha's cool passion for strategy. "Alietta. You're the last princess of House Dustborn. If you don't marry and produce an heir, the secrets of Nebulon-6 will die with you."

"Let the planet crumble," Greta says. Fire burns in her eyes. Every word she speaks is bright and clear as a lit match. "You're a true hero, Morgantha. You can win the hearts of every solar system for light-years. Just like you've won mine."

She says it so ringing and real, selling every beat of the line. *Damn, she's good.* Even knowing what's coming, Greta radiates Alietta's optimistic hope. This scene will make Alietta's death hit even harder. Peter and Wes want this to hurt.

I pull on my best game face and read through Morgantha and Alietta's war-planning scene. They're going to travel to the mysterious Nebulon-6 and seek an army from Alietta's mother's family. Their allies applaud and cheer (Shyanne switches to a heavy New York accent for this) and Morgantha—

"A warrior must be cold as well as ruthless," I read. "This fight is bigger than just House Moonblade. The freedom of the galaxy is at stake, and Bryken is only one man. Leave him to rot in Aylah's prison ship. We'll free him when the war's won."

"Pretty cold, sis," Chris says, laughing uneasily. "Ditching me right after our dad died, to run off with your new girlfriend? That's a dark turn."

"She *is* a motorcycle thief now," Callie adds. "That's pretty dark."

In the show canon, Morgantha and Bryken grew up together after Bryken's dad adopted her into House Moonblade. Even though they compete against each other for attention and status, they love each other deeply. Their father died in Season Five—it feels out of character she'd abandon Bryken now. Like he's disposable.

The pit inside me deepens. Even my upcoming mega-grounding, or whatever terrible punishment Kate devises, doesn't unsettle me like this.

Shyanne clears her throat and says in a cockney accent, "If I had any balls, they'd be crawling back up inside me right now." When everyone gives her a look, she points at her script. "That's Lieutenant Selven's line. You know. Because he's a mutant, and they, uh, castrate those so they can't mess up the gene pool?" She continues. "All the little hairs would be prickling and I'd have to— Gross, gross, he's got a whole speech like this, gross."

"Oh my god," Callie says. "We get it, Selven doesn't have balls. Does it have to be such a big thing?"

"Be fair to Peter and Wes," Greta says, laughing for the first time all evening. "They're men. To them, nothing in life matters besides their junk."

Normally, I'd laugh along. But this comment itches. Rubs me the wrong way, in ways I know she never meant it to. Makes me feel like I've got something missing.

*What's wrong with me?*

Our characters meet with the prime minister of Nebulon-6, who's yet to be cast—I think they're finding someone really famous to do a cameo. He tells Alietta he'll never ally with her because she's failing her duty to perpetuate the lineage of House Dustborn. "I'm sensing a running theme," I mutter darkly after he sends spies to kidnap Alietta and clone her. Too many story lines that reduce characters down to their gender— no, not even, to their . . . parts. Am I the only one who catches that? Am I being too sensitive?

Thankfully, Thorta appears out of nowhere and saves us

from the assassins. Ruby pumps her broad wrestler's fist—
"Redemption arc!"—but then her character is injected with a
strange drug. As the next episode opens, Thorta develops strange
rages and deep green streaks growing through her muscles.

"I can feel it changing me," she says to Alietta as our ship
docks on a busy space station. "Making me see things that
aren't there. Making me want to hurt people. Please, Alietta,
help me. Put me out of my misery."

"What?" Callie says, eyes wide above her mimosa glass. "Are
you asking Greta to kill you?"

Ruby squints at her page. "I get out my dagger and place it
over my heart. Wow. That's very . . . wow."

"I can't," Greta whispers her line. There's a single tear bead-
ing in her left eye, summoned like magic. "I'm not a killer. I
won't be like Aylah."

"Morgantha is a killer, too," Ruby says sadly. "You think
you're better than her? Better than all of us, with your pretty
dresses and— Wait, it says here that Thorta is angry. Why am
I angry?"

"And why don't you just ask Morgantha to do it?" I butt in.
Peter and Wes are trying to be dramatic, super dark. It just
comes off as . . . unmotivated. Like they're just yanking on the
characters' puppet strings, instead of telling a story.

Alietta refuses to kill Thorta, so Thorta runs off, transforms
into a hulking mutant, and smashes up the space station. She
and Morgantha battle. Alietta and Morgantha flee to a planet
under attack by Aylah's troops. Three improbable plot twists

later, Bryken kills Alietta. The room goes quiet. My faux mimosa is sour on my tongue.

"This is the worst," Greta murmurs. "Is this supposed to be dramatic irony? Does Alietta deserve this because she spared Thorta's life?"

"If it is, the script doesn't say so." Chris shakes his head. "Reggie told me when he left last season it'd all be downhill from here."

Reggie didn't tell me that. He may play Morgantha's adoptive dad, but in real life, he's way more interested in launching his cologne line than socializing with kids. I didn't realize he and Chris were friendly. But looking at Season Six, it's pretty damn clear he's right.

"One more," Callie says. "Let's read one more episode and see if that cheers us up. Greta's contracted two more seasons. Maybe they bring her back to life with fancy space tech. And if that doesn't work, we can head downtown and get shit-faced."

I take a deep breath, trying to find some inspiration to act out Morgantha's sorrow. When I played a starving orphan in three different Lifetime original movies, I imagined our dog who died when I was six. For the Season One scene where Morgantha discovers the murdered bodies of her biological parents, I dredged up all my personal feelings about not having a dad.

But the one spark I can find to mourn Alietta as Morgantha is the crushing failure I feel that I can't secure a happy ending for the fans. They're losing a chance to be seen. The chance to matter, on a big, important stage. And that doesn't exactly make me want to read lines. It makes me want to take Kate's car, hit the road, and leave this whole industry in the dust behind me.

It's getting up past eleven at night. Chris fiddles with his phone, exhausted and listless. Greta sneaks herself a pour of champagne, long fingers shaking; Ruby comes over and gives her a hug. "It's okay, sweetie. It's not the *worst* script I've ever read."

I shake my head—*how does that make anything better?*—and open the script for the next episode.

It starts with Morgantha beating the crap out of some random henchmen on a tiny planet, calling them murderers, demanding they renounce Queen Aylah or . . . wow, Peter and Wes have some pretty graphic imaginations. Then she runs off on a quest seeking a mysterious invention said to be able to bring the dead back to life.

"Am I still on the space station?" Ruby asks, sounding a little left out. "Did they forget about me?"

We start skimming. Captain Thorta never reappears. Morgantha slaughters soldier after soldier—because, apparently, she can only process her grief through anger. Bryken has a threesome with sex workers to—

"Process his grief about Alietta?" I squint at the page. "But *he* killed her! Why does he get to grieve about it?"

"These scenes don't even connect with each other," Greta sighs into her champagne. "It's like they ran out of time and jotted down the first things they could find."

"I know why it's so disjointed," Callie says, dropping her script. "It's because Wes's father is sick. He's rushing, and Peter's working alone."

"Most shows have way more writers," Ruby says. "But Wes really wanted this one to be under his control, and now he's short-staffed thanks to his family issues."

"It's not just staffing issues," Chris says, taking a deep breath. Shyanne squeezes his hand. "Bad enough he's killing off Alietta, but having the only Black character left on the show do it? That's never been Bryken. He's an honorable dude. He can kick ass, sure, but he'd never murder an unarmed girl."

"It's a really racist plot point," Callie says. "Like, mega huge. Remember that dumb belly-dancing scene they made me do in Season Three? Peter and Wes didn't listen when I told them to cut that."

*They've talked before?* I swallow. *And Peter and Wes didn't listen?* Peter has always treated me like family. He gave me this job. He taught me to fish and do a kickflip on a skateboard. I had a front-row seat at his wedding.

But them being nice to me has jack shit to do with whether they wrote racist tropes into their TV show. I can't let my privilege excuse me from helping my friends—especially since it sounds like I've been keeping my eyes shut too long.

"You talked to them about it?" Chris says.

Callie nods. "They said they'd think it over, and then I never heard from them again."

"But that . . ." Chris's mouth moves without sound as he searches for the right word. "Shit, I'm sorry. That sucks."

"I'm sorry, Callie," I say. I'm sorry for all of us. So much has gone into *Galaxy Spark*. Years of our lives. Hundreds of hours of labor by our production crew, everyone around me. I reached out with my own heart to push Wes and Peter to craft the love story behind #Morganetta.

And now it all feels icky and strange. Like it was never ours at all.

A wind cuts across the hilltop. Will walks up from the kitchen to drop off some handmade cupcakes. I breathe a sigh of relief Kate isn't with him. "Doing okay?" he says when he sees us all sagging on the couches and hard plastic stools.

"Hey, Dad," Chris says. "Season Six isn't what we expected."

Will gives him an understanding nod. "That's too bad. Hopefully you'll get to shoot cool scenes at least."

"Anything can be 'cool,'" Callie says. "Queen Aylah could start her own fashion line. That'd be a *cool* twist. Cool doesn't matter. What matters is how a show makes people feel, and right now, this makes us feel like crap. Do we want to do something about this?"

"We might get in trouble," Greta says. "I know we care about these characters, and especially about the fans of the show"—she looks at me as she says this—"but they're our bosses. We could face real retaliation if we speak up."

"I'm down to talk with Wes and Peter," Chris says, "but not if I'm the only one. How are y'all feeling?"

Ruby muses. "Maybe if we catch them in a good mood . . ."

Maybe, she says. That's not good enough. "There's no maybe about this," I say. There's something so cruel about ruining the stories of all your marginalized characters. Representation invites all viewers to imagine themselves in the world of the story. Killing off those characters cruelly feels like inviting someone inside your house only to slap them in the face. I pushed for this plotline. How it turns out is my responsibility. "I'll talk to them about killing off Alietta. I can let everyone know how they react. Would that help?"

"Worth a try," Callie says. Chris nods. I clench my jaw, already planning in my head how this conversation will go.

I'll save this story. #Morganetta's fans deserve a real hero. And the other cast members deserve the best friend I can be.

# Five

I wake up and make the mistake of checking my phone.

The blurry photos of me and Greta, in costume, on a motor-cycle, have been memed across the internet. My mentions are full of middle-aged women declaring I'm no longer a good role model for their daughters and other queer people upset over how I let them down. One viral tweet says *LOL I love Morgantha but Lily Ashton can get fucked. #Morganetta*. Even the *LA Times* has a piece headlined *Lily Ashton's Wild Ride Draws New Attention to Teen Driving Safety*.

I bury my head in a pillow and fight the urge to throw up. *Fuck*. All these people, especially the queer fans of the show, are counting on me to be something for them. And with one big, thoughtless mistake, I let them down. I didn't mean to hurt anyone. I just wanted to cheer up Greta.

I guess that's what happens when you do something nice for your nemesis. The universe snaps back into order, like a tugged rubber band, and you get stung.

As I'm about to go looking for more #Morganetta fanfic, my phone buzzes. A reminder I've got a meeting with Kate Ashton in fifteen minutes. Location: dining room. She's even attached an agenda.

I throw on PJ pants and an oversized hoodie with the entwined swords-and-spaceships logo of *Galaxy Spark*—a gift from Peter and Wes at the end of shooting last year—and clomp downstairs. Greta's already waiting at the long, polished black steel table. She slept over after the party went late, and she's already changed into the fresh clothes she responsibly remembered to bring. She's even wearing lip gloss. I get that she's perfect. I just don't like remembering how awkwardly I fit into my own life.

Greta sips her orange juice and gives me an awkward wave. I fight the urge to pull up my hood and vanish beneath it. "Your mom sent me a meeting invitation on my phone," she says. "Like we were at an office or something?"

I look around at my world, with its white walls and tiles and carefully framed swirls of abstract art. Stark, icy, and clean. I'm the only mess here. "Yeah. I mean, we sort of are? She sent me one, too. It's a Kate thing."

"That's . . . a lot," Greta says. There's a shiver in her voice. I guess no matter how perfect she is, it takes a while to reach Kate-level polish.

I never will. I know why Kate's called this meeting: to punish me for stealing Peter's motorcycle. But why did she invite Greta? Does she want an audience for when she feeds me to the sharks?

"Girls!" Kate says, entering the room. Behind her stands Johann, Greta's manager, slouching a little in a sweatshirt and jeans. I'd say he's not up to working on weekends if I didn't know he always looks like that. "We need to talk. Lara Brown's still sending me upset messages. Pictures from your little joyride are all over the internet. Including both of you making a very rude gesture at passing cars."

I want to yell. Kate's a fiend in traffic. But that won't get me anywhere. Me being like Kate isn't good enough for her. I have to be better.

"How could you do this, Greta?" Johann says. "I've spent years planning your career. How am I supposed to book an actress who breaks traffic laws?"

I glance at Greta, arching my eyebrows in a can-you-believe-him? Johann is the laziest excuse for a manager I've ever met. There's a million things he should do for her that he doesn't. But Greta looks away when I try to catch her eye. She grabs her juice glass like it's the only plank to float on after the *Titanic* sinks.

"I messed up," I say, pushing ahead. Greta's disdain for me doesn't matter right now. I need to accept my punishment and get through this. "I take full responsibility."

"No," Greta says. "I got on that bike, too. It's also my fault."

I turn to Kate. "There's got to be something we can do to make it better, right? Give people something else to talk about?"

"Well." Kate rubs her temples. "That's what we need to

happen. But generating positive publicity is hard. People prefer spreading negative stories. We need to craft a story people want to share. Here's the best idea I've come up with. We can take a page from the old Hollywood playbook and tell the press Lily and Greta are dating. Studios used to set their stars up in fake relationships so no one would know they're gay. Now we can do the same so no one knows they're dingbats."

"I love it when the girls kiss," Johann says unhelpfully. "So progressive."

"Absolutely not," Greta says. "No one would ever believe it. Lily Ashton and *me*?" She says it like we're fundamentally incompatible, a laugh track and a slasher movie. Like I'm the last person on earth she'd let anywhere near her blush-pink-glossed lips and too-tight ponytail.

I scowl. Now she's, like, actively poking at my flaws to push me away. When *I* need to push people away, I just vanish into a role and bury my real self out of sight.

"What about me?" I say. "I'm queer, not desperate. I don't want all the single girls in LA thinking I'm stupid enough to fall for the first person who bats her eyelashes my way."

"Just for a few months," Kate says. "Once we start filming Ann Elise, it'll be like this never happened. You're the ones who messed up, kids. You want to take responsibility and make this right? This is what responsibility looks like."

"It's a great opportunity, Greta," Johann says. "It'll help you get another role after Season Six. Think of how much more attention you'll get if the world thinks you're bisexual!"

"Attention from creeps," Greta says. "Openly bi people face so much gatekeeping. I don't want strangers putting my entire personal life under a microscope to judge if my identity is valid."

She's right. When people say they're bisexual, too often the internet responds by asking them to provide gender-categorized receipts of their sex life. I remember our kiss in Griffith Park. Her hands soft on my cheeks, her chest pressed so close to mine I felt her adrenaline-shot heart racing. Warm and *purposeful*.

I still don't understand why she did it. Maybe she wanted to figure something out. To confirm to herself she could never want to date a girl. It hurts a little, to feel useless and used. But whatever that kiss meant, I'm glad it's only ours. No one deserves to be publicly judged by the list of everyone they've made out with.

"What if I find an actual girlfriend?" I say. "Someone who wants to date me for me, not just for a PR stunt?"

"Oh, honey." Kate slowly shakes her head. "I'm sure that'll happen one day. But you barely interact with girls your age outside of Greta. It's not like that's going to happen anytime soon."

*You're not living a normal life, Lily. You don't go out and meet people like normal teen queers.* It rankles, but Kate's right. The last girl I talked to was in a video game. Why should I even worry about my dating life when I'm already facing the terrible, looming threat of losing #Morganetta for good?

*#Morganetta.* My pulse kicks up a notch, and I haven't even

snagged my morning latte yet.

"Everyone loves Morgantha and Alietta," I mumble, mulling it over. "They're not even a couple on-screen yet, and the whole internet wants them to be together. Greta, if you're interested, I could send you some great fanfic recommendations."

"You read fan fiction about yourself. Like, do you even have room for a girlfriend beside that ego of yours?" Greta shakes her head. "Just because strangers ship our characters doesn't mean we should pretend to be a couple. We're our own people."

*Really?* I haven't felt quite separate from Morgantha in years. But that doesn't matter right now. "Us dating isn't just good PR for us—it's good for the show. Once Peter and Wes see how many people watch to see us together, it'll give them a good reason to keep Alietta—to keep you—in the cast."

Greta stares at me like her shoe leather came to life and started talking. "You're seriously considering this. Why would you do that for me?"

It's not only for her. #Morganetta isn't just about me or her or our characters—it's about thousands of people in the fan community. A passionate, wonderful community that always surprises me with its creativity and depth.

And I need to keep #Morganetta going for myself. Playing a girl who loves girls gives an easy answer to the question Aida raised last night: *I'm a lesbian, I'm a queer girl, this is who I am and what I care about.* A sentence, instead of the storm of unfinished words inside me, that neatly sums up my identity.

"I just want to tell a good story," I say. And as Greta rolls her eyes and grudgingly mutters "Okay," I can't help thinking what I really meant was *I want to tell the right one.*

Greta and I pose holding hands by the pool. I smile at her, she smiles back, and we upload the video to Quicshot with heart captions. That'll be enough of a teaser until we make our "relationship" public at the Season Five premiere.

So, it looks like this is really happening. One more role I need to balance in the juggling act of my life.

Greta takes off as soon as the photos are posted. I stomp up to my bedroom, tighten my blackout curtains against screen glare, pull on my headset, and log in to *Swordquest Online.*

"What are you up to this afternoon?" I ask Hawk.

"Killing thorn elementals to build the Shield of Creeping Brambles," he says. I've only seen a few tanks carrying the powerful armament around. It's a very cool-looking shield with animated thorn vines dancing around the edges. "And technically, it's tomorrow morning here in Okinawa."

"I thought you lived on the West Coast. Weren't we in the same time zone last week?"

"I was on leave visiting my family in Portland." There's a pause as he sips a drink. "Now it's back out on duty. I use a VPN to access North American servers on base."

"Oh." Another thing I didn't know. It's strange, hearing someone's voice in your ear for months, working beside them to take down the biggest challenges *Swordquest Online* can offer, but never seeing a whole facet of their lives. "I didn't know you were a soldier."

"I'm a Marine, kid. Don't call us soldiers." He laughs. "Let me guess. You never met one of us in real life."

"Sorry," I say, ears prickling red. "Um. No? I come from a pretty artsy family."

"That figures. You rich?"

"Yeah."

"Lucky you." There's bitterness in it, but not pointed at me. "I joined up because I didn't have the money for college. Convinced my best friend to sign up with me, too, and got a six-hundred-dollar bonus. His truck rolled over a left-behind mine in Afghanistan, wrecked his hearing and balance for life."

"I'm so sorry," I say.

"It is what it is." He sighs. "Use the chances you've got. Be sure to make your rich family send you to college."

College. It's *an* option, I guess. But playing the lead in the Ann Elise franchise is the hundred-million-dollar option. Still. I could go to literally any college in the country. I have opportunities other people my age would risk everything for.

It makes me wonder what I'm doing with my life. Why I haven't even thought about options for my future. *Kate does that all for me. My acting roles, my classes, now even who I date.* People joke about laid-back Californians, but have I laid back out of my own life?

When I picture the future Kate's laid out for me, it feels bright and brittle as her beloved plastic cube chairs. Like it's not really part of me, but it's the direction I'm pointed in and I'll roll downhill like a stone until I hit it. That's what it means to be Kate Ashton's daughter.

That's what I love about *Swordquest Online*. When I'm here, I'm just me. Whoever that is. And maybe when I figure out who *me* is, I can figure out what I want to do next.

"Hey, guys." Aida comes into our channel. Her yawn sends static clipping across the comms.

"What's up?" I say. "You sound beat. Doing okay?"

"Parent stuff. Work stuff. I just need to get away from it all."

"So, can't you just move away?" I say. "If it's that bad, and you have a job?"

"I mean, maybe," Aida says. "I *am* eighteen. I just graduated online high school, and they're acting like I'm still eight years old. I got in trouble, and now I just want to run away rather than look at my mom's face."

"Come out to LA," I suggest. Knowing she's close to my age makes me feel better. Sometimes, I'm convinced all the cool people my age are out at parties and concerts, hooking up and having awesome adventures. It's nice to know I'm not the only one spending all their time on video games. "I'll show you around town, we'll go to Disneyland, and if your real-life drama follows us, we'll hike out to Death Valley and strand it in a canyon. We'll have to avoid my mom, though. Because she's also scary as hell when she's disappointed."

She laughs. "I practically live out there for work, anyway. I meant run away into *Swordquest*. Not be me for a while."

"Relatable," I say, inviting her and Hawk into a group. *I practically live out there.* I wonder what sort of work she does. If our feet have scuffed down the same sidewalks. If we've ever brushed elbows in a crowd. Finding an online friend who lives close to you is like picking two stars at random from the night and learning they orbit each other. "But I think 'you' is a perfectly nice person to be. Even if your awful old guild didn't appreciate your awesomeness."

"Hey, if it wasn't for them, I wouldn't have met you guys. They got me into the game so we could stay in touch when I wasn't in town."

"They were your friends in real life?" I wince. "I'm so sorry. Like, I know I said sorry before, but that's a whole new level of messed up."

"It's fine. Okay, it's not fine. My therapist says I need to be better about expressing my feelings."

"I went to a therapist in middle school," I say. "She said I needed to develop a filter."

"How's that coming?" Hawk quips. The deep, sarcastic tone is like a pin in a balloon. Hawk's my friend, but for a moment, I wish he wasn't here. I want my conversation with Aida to stay just us, private and curled up in the safety of my headset.

We pick up a mage and a druid, then teleport to the Broken Avalanche dungeon, where snow demons lurk to plot their attack on mortal realms. Right away, it's obvious the other players aren't worth shit. The druid only uses his area-of-effect attacks, even when we face a single enemy, and the mage keeps strolling into groups of frost trolls, dying before Hawk can taunt their attention his way.

Accepting that this will take the better part of an hour, I fire an Illusion Arrow at Aida and turn her into the mirror image of one of the giant frost beasts, a massive fuzzy hulk. She laughs, filling up half the corridor as she casts healing spells. *I can't see past u turn it off!!* types the mage, fatally blundering into their fifth pack of trolls. Hawk pretends to cremate them with a magic torch while Aida sighs and brings them back to life.

*I'm sorry if what I said the other night was weird and too personal,* Aida says in a DM. *About . . . you know. Queer stuff.*

*No problem,* I type back. And it really is no problem. I love talking about queer stuff.

As long as those conversations don't crawl into my head and echo forever like new Lizzo songs.

"Do you like LA?" I ask her. "I've lived here my whole life. I don't know anything different."

"I didn't at first! It's like walking into a blast oven, and everyone thinks they're living in some enchanted fairyland where the real world can't touch them. Especially this one girl I work with—she's, like, super important and that makes her completely oblivious to other people's problems."

"I know what you mean," I say, thinking of Greta. Blowing away audiences and charming the showrunners with just a few words in her open audition. Her flawlessness radiates out of her until she's practically floating on a cloud. Kissing me like it was nothing because I'm sure she kisses people every week.

"It's hard to deal with people who are always happy when you're not," Aida says.

"You're not happy?"

"I mean, I try to be. I'm in a good mood when I'm gaming or watching movies. It just doesn't always work. LA is fine when you get used to it. And I like how I can always find people to talk about movies with."

"Yeah," I say. Tons of people move to live and work in this city because they love film. They really, really care, even when they're making no money and get no reward but the occasional flash of their name in the credits.

Do I have that same passion? Film has always been part of my life. Something that comes naturally, effortlessly, like flexing a limb. But do I love it? Will and Kate, even Chris, can talk about acting techniques and film history for hours. I'm not magnetized like that. The closest I come to that level of passion is hanging out in the #Morganetta fandom, but even there, I'm just a spectator.

I float by. I'm fine. Fine has to be good enough. Right?

"Anyone watch the show *Galaxy Spark*?" Aida asks.

I bite my lip and say nothing.

"That's the sci-fi show with the hot evil space queen?" Hawk says. "Never seen it. My friends really like it."

"It's just okay," Aida says. "But I heard rumors Princess Alietta and Morgantha are going to get together this season. Frey, you might like to get into it."

"That'd be cool, I guess," Hawk says as I bite down a laugh.

Then a monster picks him up and flings him to the ground, and we're too busy getting his hit points up and dodging flying spikes to talk.

Everything that seems so big and heavy, so life-wrenching and important to me, means literally nothing to Hawk. Which comes as a relief. I don't want to be the kind of famous where my own sense of self-importance eats up my brain. *Everyone's world doesn't hinge on who I date. On whether I star in Ann Elise or whether Morgantha's character arc in Season Six sucks balls.*

But Aida cares about Morgantha and Alietta. Someone's world hinges on the stories I tell, both about Morgantha on TV and about me and Greta on social media. Just knowing she'll be watching brings home why I'm doing all this. I don't need everyone to like me or care about the show. It's not about me at all. Thousands of queer girls like her need to see that representation on TV.

"Don't worry," I say. "Lily Ashton—that's the actor who plays Morgantha, right? She's queer. I'm sure she'll do her best to make it canon."

Aida laughs. "I mean, it's not like they can say no to Kate Ashton's kid. I'm not the biggest fan of hers, but I know she tries her best."

Those words clunk down into the confused, messy swamp of me. *I try my best.* I do, hopefully. But the way she said *Kate Ashton's kid* . . . like doing my best only works because of who my mom is. Like so much of my power comes from her and I don't really matter at all. Because I do everything my mom wants. Because my biggest, only deviation from her plan is that I play video games.

But those emotions can keep festering inside me. My feelings about my life, about Kate and her plans—none of that matters to anyone but me. #Morganetta matters to a whole community. I have to protect it, and that means focusing on getting Peter and Wes to fix the script. That means holding my breath and pretending to date Greta, even if it hurts. It means pushing aside the mountain-weight feeling Aida pulled to the surface the other night.

*If you ever want to talk about being trans . . .*

It's not like I'm lying about who I am and how I feel. I'm playing a part, with a purpose. I'm doing my job for my community.

It's *like* lying, but no one gets hurt. Except me. And I can take it.

# Six

Thursday afternoon, when we arrive at the Grenadine Theater to celebrate the Season Five premiere, you can't see a trace of queer on me. I'm stuffed in a tight green dress, frilled and fitted with a wide bust. My shoulder-length hair is curled in a bun high on my head. Heavy makeup covers my zits, and my blush and eyeliner are bright and camera-ready.

"Showtime," Kate says. She took a separate car to the theater, wanting all eyes on me and Greta entering together—but video-called me the moment she got inside. "You look great, honey. How's Greta?"

I turn my phone around. Greta sits across from me, scowling. She'd probably slouch into a heap if that wouldn't risk popping the stitches holding her into her designer dress.

"Smile, dear," Kate tells her. "Try to look happy. You're young and in love. Not that I remember what that feels like! When I was your age, having a relationship, let alone one with another girl, would have absolutely ruined what little

I'd scraped together of a career. But it's supposed to be a nice feeling."

My eyebrows arch. I twist back my phone so Kate can see my expression. "Would you have dated another girl? If it was an option?"

"Huh. Never thought about it." She pops in a stick of nicotine gum. "You should be proud of yourself tonight, kiddo. This show you've created is going to mean a lot. People are rooting for you."

Rooting for Morgantha and Alietta, at least. Rooting for the story me and Greta are weaving, where we flirt with each other and post cryptic hints.

"That video of us sharing smoothies got three hundred thousand favorites," I tell Greta as Kate hangs up. "And only a handful of comments calling us delinquents. So at least we're getting the motorcycle story out of people's minds."

"A clip of my brother's dog jumping on me got two *million*," she says. "Great how our magical gay love story is less like-worthy than a golden retriever."

My heart sinks lower. This absolutely sucks. It sucks because she doesn't like me that way. It sucks because I felt a flicker of connection with her back in Griffith Park, a hope I couldn't even label, and now the tidal pull of Kate's planning and my need to save #Morganetta has wiped everything else away. It sucks because I want to fix everything and don't know how.

"You don't have to do this," I say, very quietly. "There's plenty of things we can try to change the headlines and fix the script. I don't want you to pretend to be something you're not, if dating a girl makes you uncomfortable."

"What?" She cocks her head. Three shiny reddish strands fall from her high chignon and stick on her cheek. "I'm not uncomfortable with dating a girl. I meant . . . people only follow me for dumb cute pics and information about the show. They don't care about my personal life. They don't see me as a person."

"I mean, yeah?" I'm confused now. "That's what social media is *for*. Controlling your brand. I'd think the most professional teen actor in Hollywood would understand that. You just need to have a life outside it."

She says something I can't hear.

"What?"

"I said, it's hard to have my own personal life. And it's scary. Because I'm also queer."

*Oh.* My cheeks redden under my makeup. *Way to go, genius.* She's been trying to tell me something important, and I've been teasing her. "I'm sorry for all the joking around," I say. "I thought—I don't know what I thought. You never talk about it in interviews." I've heard more interviews with her than we've had real, genuine conversations.

There's a lot of LGBTQ+ people on the planet I can't stand, especially in Hollywood. But I don't like feeling that I've missed out on seeing some big part of her. I've assumed so much about her that I might as well have made up my own Greta in my head.

"Because I'm strategic. I don't want to reveal anything about myself that might hurt my acting career."

My stomach's doing something weird and crawly beneath the corset I'm stitched into. My head spins as I mentally sort through every interaction we've ever had. Remembering how she didn't even seem excited when Peter and Wes agreed to make #Morganetta canon. I thought she was just straight. Does she not like the ship? Does the representation not matter to her? "Being queer doesn't mean you can't be an actor."

"Maybe not if you're Kate Ashton's daughter. The rest of us have to make hard choices." She sighs. "This is why I said no one will believe we're actually dating. Your life is mansions and movie stars, motorcycle joyrides, and Morgantha. I'm just some random girl from the real world. Who's going to believe you chose me?"

*She seriously thinks no one would choose to date her?* Greta's gorgeous, tall and copper-haired, brown eyes framed by firefly lashes, and hands annoyingly soft when she's touched me. Who wouldn't want to date her? Sure, it would mean putting up with her prickly professionalism and the aura of perfection that makes me feel I'll never quite live up, but from the outside looking in, I'd be the lucky one. If we could stand each other. If she didn't hate me so much.

"You know," I start, because this has been bugging me for days, "I don't read #Morganetta fanfic because I'm egotistical. I do it because it helps me to see that I'm giving something back to the queer community. Like all the work I put into this show matters to more than just me."

"Of course it matters. Thousands and thousands of people watch the show, Lily. They could just, I don't know, watch *Jeopardy!* reruns? Why in the world would you think the show doesn't matter to people?"

"I mean . . ." I squirm under her piercing brown glare. "Sometimes I feel like I don't matter. Or like I'm not really a person at all."

"Huh?" She looks at me like I've grown a second head. Which, all things considered, would be a perfect *Galaxy Spark* plot twist.

But before I can say more—before I know what I *want* to say—the limo rolls to a stop. An usher opens the door. We step out into a forest of flashbulbs and cheers. My eyes sting, so I tilt them up and focus on the impossibly high puff tops of the palm trees rising like reedy basketball players around the theater's Grecian-pillared entry doors.

"Smile and wave," Greta says, plastering on her warmest stage grin. Up ahead, a familiar tall, skinny man with messy hair talks animatedly to a reporter. *Peter.*

Forget smile and wave. I'm here to talk to him.

I drop her arm and slide off through the crowd. One of the handlers grabs for my elbow with a murmured "Miss Ashton!" but I twist free and press to Peter's side.

He's surrounded by photographers and reporters, a ring two ranks deep, but they part for me. Camera flashes streak my vision, but I came prepared. I've already locked his position in my mind and it's easy for me to slide my arm around his waist.

"Here's our star!" He mimes giving me a noogie, though he knows better than to mess with my six-hundred-dollar pressed curls. "Morgantha! The scourge of three solar systems! The girl who eats all the green Skittles from the pack!"

I stick out my tongue and wink. Of course that's what Peter thinks when he sees me. The kid who used to break into his office and rob his candy jar. But I don't mind that he likes me. I can use this to speak up for the cast, for my friends. We'll see how he reacts to our feedback about Alietta's death and use that to strategize about fixing everything else. I channel Morgantha's courage when I stretch up to his ear and whisper, "We need to talk. At the party. After. It's serious."

He stiffens. But he whispers back, "You can always talk to me," and I take that to heart. Peter would never write a season this problematic out of cruelty. He just doesn't know better. It's all simple mistakes that the right advice can fix. I can't fix the weird, numb lostness inside me. But I can fix this show.

Maybe that will be enough.

The reporters want to know what I'm wearing, and I'm happy to tell them who did my dress, hair, and makeup. I pivot and spin, showing off the green silk sheath. I don't normally like dresses, but this one isn't so bad. I enjoy giving the designers and stylists credit for their work, and reciting their names reassures me. Only a girl would know this much about her own clothes, right?

I'm exactly what they want, I tell myself, grinning and

posing. Spotlights illuminate the silk begonia on my left shoulder. *Lily Ashton. Morgantha Moonblade.* Playing the part they all came to see.

There's a thousand great actors in this town, but there's only one me. Someone who's been acting so long, I can't tell when I'm not doing it.

"What happened?" Greta says as I slip out of Peter's orbit and back into hers. Casually, she threads her skinny arm through mine. The inside of her wrist brushes my elbow and electricity dances down my spine. She's got a tattoo there, a simple outline of a heart. I wonder when she got it. "Please don't tell me you called Peter out on his crappy writing in front of everyone here."

"Not yet," I say. My pulse races. Even the inside of her wrist reminds me of that moment we kissed in Griffith Park. The spark of that moment, before she turned away. "I'll do it later. When we've got time and space to talk." The premiere party at Wes's mansion will be the perfect opportunity. Everyone will be gathered in one space, and it always goes late into the night.

"And, Lily," she says, light but firm, like the feather brushes on my arm are reinforced with steel, "you're not going to drag my name into it, right? You won't tell him I'm complaining?"

"Of course not." I'm already forced to spend time talking about her in public. Pretending to date her. Why would I bother bringing her up when I don't absolutely have to?

But I spoke too loud. Too snappy. A hairy-armed photographer turns our way. "Trouble in paradise, ladies?"

"Everything's great," Greta says, sweet and brittle as a jaw-breaker, and tugs me onward.

"I don't know how much dating experience you have," I mutter. "But I'm supposed to be your girlfriend. Not your tractor trailer."

"Technically, I'm your life jacket. Since this is the best thing your mom can think of to keep her Ann Elise movie from sinking. So, you better cling tight."

"We need each other," I say, but it comes out weak. "I mean, the more PR we bring to the show, the more reasons Peter and Wes have to keep you around."

"It doesn't work both ways. You're too short to strap around my shoulders."

"Hey!" I squeak. "Am not."

"You're five two." She rolls her eyes. "At least I'm being honest with you. You're the only one I *can* be honest with, if I'm going to spend the next few months pretending to be interested in someone I'm not."

"We're," I argue. Something hard and jagged jabs into my chest. It's not like I chose to be short. "We pretend stuff we don't feel every day."

Her perfectly plucked eyebrows arch. "So that motorcycle ride—that was you playing a part? Which one? My tour guide? My friend?"

I bite my lip. A film of lip gloss builds up on my teeth. Because the truth is that ride was the most honest thing I've done in years. Blurring through traffic with her felt even more real than playing *Swordquest Online* with my guild. But it got me in apocalyptic trouble, and it got me here, and nothing in my life has changed. Only an embarrassing mess of feelings rushed through me for a moment before Greta stomped them flat.

"That ride meant something," I start, and that's all I get off as the reporters surround us.

"Greta, Lily, hi," says a skinny man with an *LA Times* press badge. "Good to see you. Want to comment on why you two were pictured on an unlicensed motorcycle joyride last week?"

"Rumors say you two have never been close on set," says a woman reporting for E! Online. "Why are you suddenly involved in high-speed chases?"

Showtime. I take Greta's hand and lean into the mic. *Sell it. Pretend you're in love. Just like you do on the show.* It's hard to summon Morgantha when I'm wearing a taffeta petticoat, but I pull enough of the space warrior into my red-carpet self and give a fearless grin. "Actually, the two of us have something to share. We're together now."

"So, you've become friends?" *LA Times* speaks across his phone mic, recording us. "Excellent, excellent."

"Greta," says an old guy burdened under a tangle of shoulder-mounted cameras. "How do your hometown friends feel about you replacing them with a famous actress?"

"Lily and I aren't just friends," Greta says, voice tight. Like she's trying to keep the air inside her from escaping. "We're together. Get it?"

"You're . . . best friends?"

"Oh my god," she mutters, and smashes her lips to mine.

Flashbulbs fly. My brain short-circuits. I let her dip me backward, her hand on my lower back, like we're Catra and Adora at the goddamn Princess Prom. *Oh my god, oh my god, I'm kissing Greta Thurmway.* It's like lightning. An injection of adrenaline straight into my veins. *I don't even like her*—but my jackknifing heart doesn't know that. Her copper eyelashes, fluttering above me. The smell of her, rose perfume and spotlights. For all my melting body cares, we're on a beach honeymoon drinking rum from coconuts.

But the milliseconds tick by, and the kiss draws out, like she's giving the cameras plenty of time to capture all our angles. My back aches. Her lips are dry and sticky under layers of gloss.

But it's not that she's bad at kissing. It's pretty skillful kissing, all things considered.

It takes skill to kiss someone and convince them that kiss means nothing at all.

Episode One, Season Five plays beautifully across the big screen, the costumes detailed down to the last button, the interlaced branches of the Belfast forest woven tight together overhead, flashes of an orange alien sky poking through. Our cinematographers and VFX artists know just how to blend the otherworldly and concrete, and the music swells and rises dramatically with every emotional line, with every beat. To the casual viewer, there's nothing like it on TV.

But, sunk into my super-plush love seat of a theater chair, I can't help noticing how holes thread through the story. Scene after scene passes with no connection to the one before, or to anything that happened in previous seasons. Queen Aylah's motivations shift from scene to scene. Seeing my own sneering, enraged face on-screen as Morgantha—the character I love, who before Frey, was the character closest to my heart—only drives home how Morgantha always reacts to struggles with violence. If she was a real person, she'd have a court order to attend anger-management classes.

It's not bad to write angry women, I don't think. But it's weird how Peter and Wes only see a strong female character as one willing to murder at the drop of a hat. That her strength is being even more violent than the men around her.

Credits roll across the screen. Everyone claps. Wes and Peter take a bow. We stand up and filter out past the producers and journalists; Chris and Shyanne, in matching yellow tuxedo and gown, pose for fashion photographers. Someone sticks a mic in my face and says, "Lily, does your relationship with Greta mean anything for Alietta and Morgantha in Season Five?"

Kate slides between me and the journalist. "No spoilers," she says, and herds me to the limo. "Let's get you out of here. Good job tonight, kid."

We hold the cast party at Wes's big, fancy house up in the Hollywood Hills, a Mediterranean-style mansion built in the late 1920s and shimmering with fairy lights across the high stucco walls. Every time I walk up the white stone pathway, I feel like I'm slipping into a fairy tale, and I hold my breath as I arrive. Hip-hop pounds through the downstairs speakers.

Champagne flutes sparkle in white-gloved hands. The night feels ripe with magic. I know I can make Wes and Peter listen to me.

Wes greets his guests in his three-story atrium, standing proudly before his fountain, a marble lady pouring out her basin behind him. I haven't spoken much with the senior showrunner since his dad got sick. He's lost weight in a bad way, his tux pulling loose on his frame. When he claps me on the back and pulls me into a hug, I notice he's using concealer to wash dark circles out from under his eyes.

"Are you as excited as I am to get back on the set?" Wes asks me. It comes out as a tired grumble. He's in his fifties, but he usually has the energy of a little kid. I've never heard him sound so defeated and old. "It'll be a great challenge for you, playing a grieving Morgantha. Real heavy stuff. Bet this is the year you get nominated for your first Emmy."

Oh my god. My heart drops like Thelma & Louise off a cliff. I almost plunge in—*Wes, let's talk about burying your gays, fridging women*—but the other guests are packed tight behind me, and I want to talk about this with Peter first.

*Peter will be different.* I break away from the hug, letting the hordes of other people stream in to talk to Wes. He's young. He's liberal. He's even got a *Resist* sticker on his motorcycle. He'll have to listen to me.

I wade through the crowd. Ruby steps on my hem, nearly sending me sprawling into a server, and murmurs apologies. Callie whispers she's acquired three bags of very good quality weed—"It's lavender-infused. Don't tell anyone or you'll start a land rush." I mutter, "Later," and push my way to the grand piano in the center of the glass-chandeliered living room, where Peter is filling his plate from a server's tray.

*Breathe.* My heart thrums beneath the heavy green taffeta. I can do this. Navigate this conversation. For the cast. For the fans. This is so much bigger than myself.

"Lily!" Peter grabs a second champagne flute from the server and offers it to me. I take it, and say, "Thank you," as she walks away. "Congrats!"

That's not what I expected to hear. "For what?"

"About you and Greta! C'mon, kid, I've been watching you film together for years now. You think I didn't notice your big crush on her?"

I roll my eyes. "I know you're busy, man, but take some time off to get glasses."

"No way, kid. I may be a decrepit old husk of thirty-two, but I know puppy love when I see it. Even the lesbian version. I'm happy you're happy. And it's great PR for the show."

I know. Kate's already having an intern plan social media promo surrounding our relationship, scheduled to post right before Episode Three. The big kiss episode. Suddenly, the world feels too tight around me. I'll explode if I don't ask him. If I don't do something.

"You're happy about us being together in real life," I say. "But don't you know how important it is to have a gay couple on the show? An actual couple, with a romantic arc and every-thing, not just something you hint at by having two hot people of the same gender stare longingly at each other."

"Of course," he says. "That's why you wanted Morgantha and Alietta to get together in the first place. And you showed me all those tweets and fanart when we wrote Season Five. I always wanted *Galaxy Spark* to have a diverse cast—that's why I cast Chris, and Reggie Ainsley." Peter waves toward the bar, where Reggie, a middle-aged Black man in a gold-trimmed tuxedo, shows a group of girls a card trick. He played Alban Moonblade, Bryken's dad and Morgantha's trusted mentor—until he got offered his own superhero franchise, hence his death scene in Episode Five. "It's important for all fans to feel represented on-screen."

He sounds just as enthusiastic about #Morganetta as he did the first time I brought it up. Which is why I'm so confused. Has he not thought about this besides just . . . putting a few marginalized people on-screen? *Being seen takes more than I see one person like me on the screen.* "But, Peter, how will they feel when they see Bryken kill Alietta in Season Six? How will Black kids feel when they see Chris's character turned into a murderer? How will queer girls feel when the first fictional relationship they identify with ends in violence?"

He winces. "I spent months writing these episodes. Had to crunch everything in since Wes took off to deal with his dad's cancer. Kind of sucks to hear you talk like that one scene is the whole season."

*The whole season isn't all that great either.* Still, that isn't the matter at hand. "That scene is all I can think about. All I can remember." I don't want to get vulnerable. I want Peter to see me as the cool, chill person who loves riding motorcycles and messing around. But he needs to understand. "It was physically painful for me to read. You may not feel those feelings like I do, but if you're my friend, you'll trust me when I say it hurts."

"Jeez," Peter says. His cheeks redden. I hope that means he's listening. "Huh. I guess I never saw it that way."

Our intense conversation must have caught some attention. Wes slides into our group, a little off balance from drinking. "What's going on here, kids?"

*Kids.* Suddenly, that strikes me as off. Peter isn't a kid—he's thirty-two, and he and his wife had a baby last year. Kate's Motorcycle Incident reaction was all about how I need to learn to be a responsible adult, think about how my actions reflect on me, influence my career and my opportunities. But Peter's been an adult for, like, ages. He should be responsible by now.

"We were just talking about the new season," Peter says. "Lily here has some, er, editorial notes."

"Oh, really?" Wes turns to me. "Pitch me your vision."

*Shit.* I pause. It's not like I have an idea for how I want the season to go, aside from a #Morganetta happily-ever-after. I just know what shouldn't be on-screen. Haltingly, I explain myself again.

"When I started writing for TV in the nineties," Wes says, "when my dad was a producer on *Windy City Danger*—yeah, I'm a nepotism baby, no comment needed—I got my feedback from the senior writers and the production team. They were the experts in how to keep viewers tuning in each week. Nowadays, everyone with an internet connection needs to tell you they could do your job better. I'm working on a reboot of this eighties movie—can't say which—"

"Wes, if you butcher *Back to the Future*, you're dead to me," Peter cuts in.

"—and the whole team's bringing me these random internet memes about why the original is crap and needs an update. We had a conference call last week about whether the female lead should wear heels in an action scene. If we want to show viewers she's an empowered woman, we need to pause mid-apocalypse to show her pulling on some Nikes. Problem is, that says nothing about the character or her power. It just says 'please don't shit-talk us on the internet.'"

"Why shouldn't the internet get its say?" I ask. "People can make their own choices about what to watch. You can't make people watch something that goes against their values."

"Sure, but it's easy to make yourself sound high and mighty. When I was a kid in the eighties, my mom hated every woman in an action movie. Either she was useless and weak, lewd and bossy, or too butch and a bad role model. Turns out, Dad cheated on her with an actress once. She was scared every woman in Hollywood was a threat to her marriage. People project their own feelings onto art in ways that have nothing to do with writing. You're scared of homophobia—that's reasonable—and you're reading it into scenes that have nothing to do with that."

"Nothing to do with homophobia?" My voice is rising. I hate how thin and feeble it sounds. "You wrote a gay woman bleeding out for no reason."

"Not for no reason. To tell a good story, you need to raise the stakes with time. Morgantha's faced plenty of dangers, sure, but she's never faced a danger to her heart. She's always had Bryken to lean on and a bunch of admirers cheering her forward. The way I see it, this scene is what'll push her to stand on her own and make her own choices. When Peter sent me his outline, I was in the hospital, watching my dad get chemotherapy. Before I signed off on his direction, I thought profoundly about how loss and struggle help us grow. We're not doing this for cheap shocks. To me, it's the only way to push Morgantha forward."

*There has to be another way.* Wes's words swirl around my head. What would I have written if I had the pen? I think it through. My blood is up and steaming; I want to pull out some answer that'll blow his mind. But honest to god, I'm blank. I'm not a writer—but I know bad writing when I see it. I'm not a chef, but I know when my meat is overcooked.

I just need to give them a reason to care. A reason to want to change the scripts, to do better. I need to find a way to fight. If Morgantha can take on a whole galaxy of enemies to defend House Moonblade, then I can stand up for the real-life queer people who need me most.

# Seven

Still dumbfounded, I pick through the tray of no-sugar chocolates and tofu lemon tarts left out on the dessert table, trying to find something genuinely sweet. At last, I find a bag of Halloween candy tucked behind the linen-draped serving table and shove a Snickers down my throat.

"Sweetheart?" Kate's voice grabs my attention. I straighten up as my mom drags over a short white woman wearing a hot pink suit and layers of jewelry. "This is Lara Brown. The author of the Ann Elise books."

My jaw drops. I didn't know she planned to spring this on me.

"Lily's starstruck!" Kate says. "Look at her! She's such a fan of yours. She's never met a real writer."

*Considering Peter and Wes, maybe I haven't.* I fix on a smile. Like Kate always says, good manners come free. "I love Ann Elise. She's wonderful!" I haven't actually read any of the books, which adds another twist of guilt to the mess inside me, but I did read the Wikipedia summaries of the first four, and I *do* know how to improvise.

"What's your favorite book, honey? I'll sign it for you." Lara opens her purse—a pink leather bag big enough to fit a golden retriever or very patient child—and shows me a stack of fifty paperbacks. She's got to have arms of steel, lugging those around. Why is she a writer when she could make a fortune as an elite bodyguard?

"*Ann Elise Strikes Back*?" I say, reading the spines and picking the one that sounds most interesting. Like *Star Wars*.

"My, you have interesting taste. Most people hate how I made Ann Elise break up with Michael in that book. They never liked how she dated Wyatt for two weeks. It *was* a daring choice, but how else was I to make Patricia's plot to ruin her life because Ann Elise exposed the unethical practices of her fashion show really have teeth?"

It feels like *Star Wars* now. Or *Galaxy Spark*. A vast, labyrinthine fandom. A pit to which there is no bottom. Guilt prickles in the bottom of my stomach. The girls and women who love Ann Elise deserve someone equally passionate in that role.

"I'm so happy to hear you're dating Miss Thurmway," Lara says, signing the book in a flourish of script on her knee. The giant diamonds in her earlobes flash in the chandelier light. "Young love! So romantic and wonderful. I mean, I only ever was in love with my Breyndon. But I suppose it's just as lovely when it's two girls involved."

"We're . . . very happy," I stammer, pulling on a tight smile.

I'd be even happier if the earth would open up and swallow me whole.

"Tell me." Her voice drops low. Conspiratorial. "You don't . . . you don't do that awful scissoring thing? I read about it online. Researching you."

Kate makes a choking sound. For once, I can't read her signal. Drag Lara to hell? Or smile, play along, and save the hundred-million-dollar deal?

I can buy one hell of a gaming computer with a hundred million dollars. "No, ma'am. Never. Pretty sure that's not a real thing."

"Good. It doesn't sound sanitary."

Kate clears her throat. "Lara, I'd like to introduce you to a few more of the producers who'll be working to bring Ann Elise to life. Be good, Lily."

"Yes, Mom," I say. As soon as she's led the author away, I scan the room for Greta. She needs to be warned that Lara's typed "what are lesbians" into Boomer Google. Her flash of red-blond hair catches my eye over by a tower of mini salads on toothpicks.

It's only when I reach her side I realize she's not alone. She's joined by a tall woman with her same red-blond hair and a scowl.

"You must be Lily," says Greta's mom. She speaks my name like she's about to vote me off a reality show. By her side, Greta cringes. "My baby won't stop talking about you. She said you introduced her to Los Angeles."

I try to smile, since I know Kate's watching. Something about this lady rubs me the wrong way. "I might have sat her down and explained we don't have a real subway." I'd have done more if she hadn't spent all of Season Four filming avoiding me in her trailer.

*Go*, Greta mouths at me. The fall of her smile makes me wilt inside. She's doing her best to melt into the potted cactus behind her, and she looks like she couldn't be more uncomfortable if it stabbed her. It's a complete one-eighty from her body language in the limo—not the whole "Greta doesn't want me around" bit, but the bit where she looks uncomfortable speaking her mind.

What's changed? Is her mom making her feel bad? Kate and I may not always agree, but I know she's on my side.

Greta's mom continues. "Well, I'm sure you'll miss my daughter when she comes back to the real world next year." The arc in her lip. Like she's holding it still so she can hold herself above me. "Now that Greta's obligation to *Galaxy Spark* is ending, she's coming home and going to college."

I stare at Greta. "You're giving up? You're not even bothering to look for another role?"

"It's time she started building herself a real future," her mom says. "You can't shoot for the stars forever. You'll only get burned."

Greta stares at her shoes. Her fingers flutter, perfectly manicured half-moons now bitten to stubs. So upset she's even letting bits and pieces of perfection go. "It's okay, Lily. Just . . . go away."

I don't feel like going anywhere. Wes and Peter can treat me like I don't understand good storytelling, and maybe I don't; maybe I'm a clueless idiot who's only in this room because my mom is important. But I know what pain looks like, and Greta looks like she's slowly collapsing under the weight of her own spine. She doesn't want to stop acting. She just needs someone on her side. "Greta's a great actor," I snap. "She can still build her career. And she deserves to make that choice for herself."

"Excuse me?" gasps Greta's mom. Harsh as sandpaper. "That's none of your business."

*"Lily,"* Greta whispers, more urgently. "Seriously."

I back up, still staring at them, confused. How does Greta deal with her mom? Speaking to her for thirty seconds made me want to scream. Small wonder Greta doesn't talk a lot about her life. If I lived with someone that negative about my dreams, I wouldn't bring them up in conversation either.

As I duck away into the maze of guests, my phone buzzes. I untangle it from my tiny clutch and read a short text from Greta.

*Thanks for standing up for me.*

*Fuck.* My throat swells, snotty and painful. I've been so convinced her closed-off-ness means she hates me, that I never even considered she might have problems too painful to share. Problems I don't know how to solve. Even if I save her role on *Galaxy Spark.*

I don't know what to do.

I'm only seventeen and the whole world knows it, but they also know I'm rich and famous and the bartenders Wes hired don't card his star. Two vodka shots sicker, I slink over to the back of Ruby's red Ferrari convertible and borrow her pipe. She gives me a sad look—she also hates crowds. "You're a Virgo, right?"

I shake my head. "Taurus."

"Oh, poor baby." She pats the top of my head. "This is not your night."

Greta steps out a side door and looks our way. Tears glitter on her cheeks. Ruby reaches out to extend her the pipe. Greta takes one look at her and me, shakes her head, and marches down the driveway. An Uber is already waiting for her. She climbs in, without even waiting for her mom. My stomach sinks further back into the swirling mess of a crossfade.

"You two fighting?" Ruby asks.

"We're fake. PR stunt. Kate's idea."

"Does your heart know it's fake?"

"That doesn't matter." What I want doesn't matter. What happens between us in real life isn't anywhere as important as the love story we can show people on-screen.

After another hit, I wander back inside. The lower level of Wes's house has been transformed into a massive *Galaxy Spark*–themed arcade, full of props, games, and activities, and all the younger guests have drifted downstairs. My nerves and rush of anger from confronting Greta's mom have stilled, but I'm not as chill as I'd like to be. I want to find Chris and dare him to drunk-climb the boulders behind Wes's house with me. That might help.

I don't find Chris, but I do find Shyanne drinking a pink martini while sitting inside the life-sized replica of Alban Moonblade's iconic spaceship bridge, complete with blinking LED screens. "I saw you talking to Lara Brown!" she squeals when she sees me, rising to her feet and nearly toppling onto the plastic dashboard as she grabs the book from my hands. "Oh my god. Did she sign that for you?"

"Um. I'm guessing you like the books?"

"They're my heart and soul. I hid them under my bed in high school because my dad thought they were trash. I made fake covers that looked like *The Scarlet Letter* so I could sneak-read them in school. Lara wants you for the movie, right? I'm so happy for you!"

"What's your favorite part of the books?" I say. Maybe if I can figure out why she loves them, I can find my way in. I can make myself love playing Ann Elise like I love Morgantha.

"It's the feelings. They're so . . . sharp, so relatable. Ann Elise captures what it's like looking for your place in the world, trying to surround yourself with people who care about you, who you can trust. People say it's just about dating and fashion, but it's more than that, really. It's about finding the courage to be who you want to be. Whenever I'm worried about my career, I pick them up and remind myself my dreams matter."

Courage. I could use that. I need that. In her own way, Ann Elise is a hero just like Morgantha. I should be excited to play her. I can do this. I want to understand why other girls love that story. I want to understand what I want. What my heart and gut are trying to tell me. But I don't. I've never listened to any of that. I've listened to Kate.

"Lara's got copies of her books in her purse," I say. *Instead of the fifty-nine kittens she could squeeze in instead.* "I bet if you asked, she'd sign one for you. She's back over there."

"God, I want to, but I'm way too drunk. I'd never live it down if she saw me such a mess!" A group of selfie-snapping guests have queued at the entrance to the replica bridge. They're shooting us weird looks. Are we too loud? Shyanne squeezes my wrist. "Let's get out of here before we both accidentally humiliate ourselves!"

She pulls me off to the poolside photo-booth pavilion, where guests laugh like kids as they have cat whiskers and fake wounds painted on by the makeup artists Wes hired. Dimly, I realize Shyanne is also protecting me, dragging my intoxicated ass out of an area where people might see what a mess I am. I kind of love her for that.

"Look at me!" Callie roars, flexing the fingernails a manicurist tech just applied. Long acrylics, sharp black. The middle nail of each hand has a dragon painted down its heart. Along with her gold and crimson gown, she's wearing a Batman mask, her eyes painted dark. "I am the *night*. I *am* the night. Who do I need to dangle off a building to be the first Asian Batman?"

"You mean the first Asian Batwoman?" Shyanne suggests.

"No, fuck that. Batwoman never gets her own movie. I'll just strap on a Bat-dick and drop my voice." She lowers her tone. Ruby laughs. I freeze like I've just stuck my finger in an electric socket, like a curtain has dropped and left me naked in public.

"Put on a costume." Shyanne pulls a fake beard, brown and bushy, from the box behind the booth. The knot inside me twists.

"I don't want—" but she swoops in and slaps it over my face. One of the makeup artists grabs my chin, slathering on costume glue. A few brushes with a blending pen, shaping shadows over and around my cheeks. My skin blazes. I'm going to look like one of the extras from *Lord of the Rings*, but I'm too intoxicated to say no, so I pull on a smile and roll with it.

"Callie!" I hook an arm around her shoulders and grin. Trying to match her energy, her vibe, in the way I feel is expected of me. "Shyanne! Let's shoot our fashion roll!"

We squeeze into the booth together. Callie presses her cheek next to mine, Shyanne sprawls out on my lap, and we vamp it up for the cameras, all puckered lips and seat-sprawled screaming and both our middle fingers lifted high. Callie's yelling something in my ear, and I can tell she's glad to be here, with me, and I feel a hot flash of embarrassment I don't occupy this space nearly as well. Shame and drunk squealing mix into one high frequency in my head.

I pick up the photo roll and—

*Oh my god.*

It strikes me like lightning, like a slap of cold water from a crashing wave. Like walking through a stranger's door and finding yourself at home. Like that moment in *The Lion King* where Mufasa appears in the clouds to tell Simba to remember who he is.

*I look a little like Frey*, I think. Maybe that's why the alarm bells in my head flash in soul-deep recognition. But that's not it. I look like me. More than that—for the first time ever, it's like there is a me, me draped in a suit jacket and a stage beard, drunk and high and captured on cheap photo paper in my fist.

It's like I'm holding a piece of my own soul.

"Can I see?" Callie says.

"Sorry," I say, and slide the photos in my bag. She gives me a weird look, but I'm not worried what she thinks about me right now. *Me.* I'm the person in those photos with a heavy brow and beard. I'm that. I'm Frey. I've never been more certain. I don't have a magic bow and ax and I've never been to a fantasy kingdom, but he is me in a way I never realized—

Aida. I need to talk to Aida.

I don't even remember calling Kate's driver to take me home. Everything is a blur until I pound up the stairs into my bedroom, fling off my sweat-soaked dress, and drop down in my gaming chair.

"I use voice mods because I'm trans," I blurt into the comms. "I don't want you to hear my voice and think I'm a girl. I need one space in my life where I can just be myself."

Silence. I wait. Barely half the guild is online, and I don't even know who would care about such an announcement on my part.

Then Hawk says, "I'm glad you feel comfortable telling us,

man—I mean, is it okay I call you that?"

"Yes." The words bubble out of my throat, fast and needy. "Please, god, yes."

"I'm so happy for you," Aida says. She sounds exhausted— it's past 3:00 a.m. on the West Coast now—but I can feel the joy behind her words. "And I'm proud you felt comfortable telling us." A ding alerts me to new mail. I check the nearest postbox to find Aida's sent me a heart-shaped box of virtual chocolates and a letter full of heart emoji.

*It was all you,* I type to her in chat. Tears clog my throat. I can't even say it out loud. *Thank you for giving me the push. For giving me a reason to think about this stuff.*

*I'm always here if you want to talk. But you're the brave one. It takes a lot of courage to be yourself.*

Courage. I never felt like I had any. Not Morgantha-level courage. I certainly didn't feel brave when talking to Peter and Wes at the party.

But I guess it's easier to be brave online than it is in real life.

# Eight

*Do I need to tell someone?*

The question rattles around my head the next few days as Season Five premieres across the rest of the world and the staged photos of me and Greta go viral. Mostly, I hang out in my room, slogging through my online classes (Kate insists I need a high school degree, and it's easier to study than fight her about it) and raiding with my fellow Warhawks.

At last, we kill the pirate king boss and move on to the next boss encounter. Three dragons, in succession, drag us through obstacles corresponding to elemental signs while we beat the crap out of them. We quickly master weaving through swirling winds conjured by the air dragon and running the gauntlet of crashing waves down the water dragon's back. But there's a murderous segment on the third and final dragon, the earth dragon, where he pulls us through a collapsing tunnel and our healers just can't quite figure out the perfect sequence of spells to keep us alive.

"It's my fault," Aida says, frustrated, after our fifteenth death. "Even using both Divine Blessing and Chosen of the Faith can't keep everyone standing."

Hawk pulls her numbers. "You're not getting enough spell-power from your Ring of Titanic Might. You need to grind Fate Essence to get it up."

I volunteer to go with her. We spend the next three days running through the world of *Swordquest Online*, killing monsters to fuel her ring with their power. I tell Kate my stomach is bothering me, that I've got period cramps, that I need to finish an essay for my tutors. It gets me out of a brunch with Lara Brown and a photo op with Wes at an art gallery opening. It also means more time with one of the few people I can stand, doing everything I can to avoid thinking about the looming nearness of Season Six filming.

But the day before Episode Two drops, Kate shows up at my door with a new dress and heels.

"You have a date," she says so grimly that I almost expect her to add *with death*. "Try not to argue with Greta like you did with Wes and Peter at the party."

I gulp. "You heard?"

"Look, you and I both know you shouldn't be arguing with your bosses." She laughs. "But personally, I can't stand Peter either. I'm glad you realize you deserve better scripts, and I'll get those for you."

*The Ann Elise movies*, I can hear without saying. "Okay?" I mutter. It's not the reaction I probably should have, but nothing with Kate and me is normal.

"You're allowed to be passionate, Lily. Just be smart, too. Remember, there's a lot of ways to get what you want. Think about the long game and the career you want to have." She taps her phone in her pocket like it holds the answers to the mysteries of the universe.

Kate's not mad I argued with Peter. I should be relieved.

But one look at the dress, and I'm distracted. All I can think about is that it's a costume for a shoot, a wardrobe for a commercial selling girlhood.

I don't think Kate knows what I want. Only what she wants for me. She doesn't like Peter and Wes, and she won't raise a finger to defend them. But that doesn't mean she'll defend me. I'm not even sure she's listened the ten billion times I've told her how important #Morganetta is. Not just as a role, a beat in my career. She doesn't care how much it matters to me.

And that leaves me just as jittery as pulling on this dress she bought for the girl I'm not.

The car takes me to a French brunch restaurant in La Brea, where Greta and I have been positioned by a big plate-glass window, ensuring plenty of photos will be snapped and uploaded to the internet to assure the world that this is real. The red-checked curtains and walls stacked with fresh bread will make an excellent backdrop, I'm guessing, but I don't know how photogenic we'll be. Greta fiddles with her phone while I chow down on brioche. I get the feeling she's just counting the seconds until she's allowed to let go.

"What do we . . . do?" Greta whispers.

"What do you mean? We pretend we like each other." I fix on a smile and brush a loose lock of hair back behind her ear. My fingertips tingle where they brush her freckle-dusted cheek. The this-is-fake memo clearly hasn't reached all parts of my body. "Whatever normal people do on dates."

"I've never been on a date. How would I know?"

"You've never been on a date?" I stare at her. I mean, it's not like I've got any dating experience. Kate watches me like a hawk, and even if I escaped her, the whole world will notice me. I figured out I was gay because of my preteen anime obsession, not because there was a real person I liked. "You're, like, normal. All-American small-town girl. And you're gorgeous—I mean, like, objectively gorgeous. I mean, you're a model and an actress and—"

"I never wanted to go on a date." She folds her arms over her chest. Like a clamshell closing. "Okay?"

It doesn't feel okay. It feels like I've pressed something sensitive without meaning to. I scramble to change the subject and find my salvation when the server brings out my shrimp cocktail.

"Guess how many shrimp I can fit in my mouth?" I poke Greta's leg with my heel and squeeze another shrimp into my cheek. "Go on. Guess."

"Are you twelve? Don't waste food."

"I'm not wasting it." The next shrimp goes under my tongue, making it hard to talk and also giving me a good excuse not to.

"I'm going to eat them all anyway. I'm just eating creatively."

"I don't understand how you can be seventeen years old and still think this is funny."

*I* don't understand how she looks my age when she's obviously eighty, but I don't say that because there's too many shrimp in my mouth.

I top out at twenty-three.

"Can we just talk?" Greta asks as I swallow and wash the shrimp down with orange juice. Thank god I didn't pick up on the conditioning that gives so many girls in Hollywood a problem with food. Maybe that should have been my first clue I wasn't a girl at all. "Like adults? Since we're stuck here in this fishbowl from hell?" A bus has pulled up outside. Tourists lean from the windows snapping candids.

"Talk about what?" I roll my eyes. "The show? The shitty script? *Star Wars*? I get it. You're a mature professional legal adult. I'm sure you think you should be babysitting me instead of pretending to date me. But this fake-dating thing will go way easier if you don't freeze me out."

"You think I freeze you out?"

"Duh. The first day we met. I was so excited to have another kid my age on set. The moment I introduced myself, you fled like I had the plague."

The tips of her ears turn pink, clashing with her yellow-tinted eyeshadow. My lips quirk up. "Okay. Yeah, that was awkward. I didn't mean to hurt your feelings. You were the first famous person I'd ever met. I got scared."

*Scared? I wasn't even five feet tall.* But I can't even remember the first famous person I met. Kate once asked an Oscar-winning actor to hold baby me while she dug some important papers from her briefcase, and I threw up on his shoulder. "What about when Chris and I were gonna steal our horses from the set and race to the ocean? You ratted us out to Wes, and he called Kate on us. We got grounded for two weeks when we came home. Then you said you'd done it for our own good."

"You could have broken your legs. Or gotten the horses killed. Not every problem can be solved with Kate's money."

I shrug. "I mean, I bet she could pay someone to invent a horse wheelchair?"

"I can't believe you." Greta rolls her eyes. "Your head's full of more dreams and fluff than a Ghibli film."

Before I can ask if that's a good or bad thing, a shadow falls over our table.

"Excuse me?" says a server, a girl maybe a few years older than us whose French chef's cap can't quite conceal her dyed purple hair. We both jump. Greta pulls on a smile faster than a sports car accelerating. "I never do this, but I want to say how much it means to me, seeing the two of you together—both on and off the show. My girlfriend broke up with me last spring and #Morganetta helps me still believe in love!"

Warmth flickers in my stomach, a sort of awkward flush. I nod, buying time to figure out what to say, wishing she hadn't mentioned that bit about her girlfriend. Sometimes people think they know me better than they do because I'm on TV. I also need to figure out how to manage Greta's reaction so she won't say something hurtful—

"Anyone with hair cool as yours is bound to find happiness." Greta squeezes her wrist. "Believe me. You'll be okay."

The server squeals out a "Thank you, thank you so much!" as she ducks away. I raise an eyebrow at my date. "Pretty impressive pivot from shouting 'You asshole' in my face."

"I'm an actor. I know how to improvise."

Something strikes me. "How'd you get started acting anyways? It's always been part of my life, but I'm sure it hasn't been the same way for you."

"When I was little, this older girl down the street used to babysit me. She played classic movies. *Snow White*, *Roman Holiday*, *The Sound of Music*. I couldn't look away. I remember the first time I saw *Singin' in the Rain*. I realized there was this whole world I could be a part of. Acting has always been my dream."

"That's . . . impressive." Her eyes meet mine, brown as solid as desert stone. "That amount of passion? It must have been scary to commit yourself to chasing that dream."

She nods. "But I did. I've risked everything to get this far. My parents' approval, my chance to be out of the closet. And you'll never need to face those hard choices because you're Kate Ashton's kid."

*Being Kate's kid isn't easy either!* I almost say, but hold my tongue. I'm not mad at her. I'm mad at me. Because being anyone's kid is tough. But Kate can open any door for me she pleases.

"You could totally land another role," I say. "Don't give up. You're a good actor."

She shakes her head. "Wish I heard that from, like, anyone but the person who's literally pretending to care about me. Now she knows I'm getting fired, my mom wants me to come home and go to college. Quit acting and grow into a miniature version of her. I keep telling her I'm eighteen, that it's my choice—but she gets so upset. Says I'll break her heart if I leave her for Hollywood, never mind we're already living here half the year."

"She was really mean at the party."

"I know. She called you a hellion as we drove home." A shadow of a smile sneaks back on her face. "I nearly swallowed my tongue to stop from laughing at her."

"At least I did one thing right."

"Where, in that whole mess, did anyone do anything right?"

"I made you smile."

Color fills Greta's cheeks. *Crud.* I've said the wrong thing again. Quickly, I change the subject. "Does she know you're queer?" I say.

"Maybe."

"Maybe?"

"She clams up when I try talking about it. Says she's too tired or she's got work to do whenever I try to have that conversation. Honestly, I've sort of given up. She doesn't want to deal with it. Fine." She lowers her eyes. "She's still my mom. I'm not ready to say no to her. I just wanted a few more years on *Galaxy Spark*. Time to land my next role and save up some money. So, when I tell her this is my life to live, I'll be too strong for her to drag me down."

Her cool, steely determination sends a shiver down my spine. If she'd delivered that speech on film, she'd be a shoo-in for Oscar buzz. This plan of hers is impressively watertight. She knows what it'll take to stand up to her family. She knows one day she'll be strong enough. I'm not even sure what would make me comfortable enough to tell the world about my gender.

All I can do is save #Morganetta and help her buy the time she needs.

"You're going to be okay," I say, fumbling for words. "I mean. I believe in you. Seriously."

"You'd be the only one."

"Okay, then I'll believe in you twice as hard."

She looks down, brushing her hair back behind her ear. A diamond stud sparkles in her lobe. Tiny freckles lead up to her hairline, drawing my gaze like magnets.

Greta says something I don't catch. *Shit.*

"It's funny," I say, awkwardly changing the topic. "I didn't know you were jealous that I was Kate's kid. All this time, I thought you froze me out because I'm not worth your time. You got your role on merit. I got in on nepotism."

"Like I'm some great actor?" She laughs. "They probably just gave me the part because they liked my face."

"What are you talking about? You're literally perfect." *Perfect* comes out with a huff. Perfect Greta, who never forgets her lip gloss. Perfect Greta, who always knows the right thing to say in interviews. Perfect Greta, with her clutch that matches her butter-yellow skirt.

Who's perfect at being a girl. When I'm just a massive failure at everything, but especially at that.

Oops.

Worst of my faults, even more than not realizing I'm not a girl until age seventeen, is being a shitty friend. Not just to Greta. To everyone. Growing up at Kate's side gave me a totally skewed view of how the world works. Such a privileged vantage I can't even see all the times in my life I might have messed up and hurt someone by not *understanding*.

Which makes it that much more important I make it up to the world. That I do the job in front of me and save #Morganetta.

I mutter, "Check, please?" to the server and bury my head in my phone.

It looks like we've successfully murdered the internet. Pictures of me and Greta through the fishbowl window. The hashtag #Morganetta is trending. I scroll down, and so is #MorganettaIRL. *Yep, that's us. Just the characters we play.*

"Anyway," Greta mutters, shifting conversation back to safe ground. "Johann texted he's got three magazines asking for exclusive rights to our love story. I told him to run it by Kate. She can probably get us more money, and I might as well milk every dollar I can get from this town before Mom makes me leave it."

"You're not going to lose your job," I say. We're two weeks

from flying to Northern Ireland to film Season Six. Every day that ticks by makes it harder to change and fix the script. But now I know just how important this is to Greta. How much I need to do something more. "Peter sounded receptive to rewrites when I brought it up. If I can change his mind, he can change Wes's. Every moment the two of us trend online makes the case for why *Galaxy Spark* needs Alietta to survive. We're going to make this right."

"Why do you always pretend you can fix everything?"

*Because I want to.* Is that because I'm a guy? A maybe-guy? Guy-ish? I don't want to root my gender in outdated stereotypes, but stereotypes can carry a nugget of truth. My gender isn't something I'm brave enough to discuss outside of *Swordquest Online*. And that's not the right answer, anyway. I just refuse to believe this situation isn't fixable.

"Because it's not right," I say. "Someone has to do something about it. And I think I can. Don't you want to make a difference?"

"Of course. But I don't want to throw away everything I've fought for on a lost cause. I might lose out on future roles if I get a reputation for making trouble." She sighs. "Just promise me one thing. We're in this together. Please don't push this past a point I'm not comfortable going."

"Deal," I say.

We shake on it. But Greta's left-handed, so when I reach out with my right, we fumble a little before awkwardly lacing fingers.

From the outside, maybe it looks like holding hands.

I'm giving myself strange looks in the mirror these days. Either I structure my morning bathroom routine around avoiding it, or I spend an hour gazing at it after I shower. Staring at my body and seeking the places where it ends and Frey begins. That dark spot on my neck that makeup artists always paint over is like a shadow of his beard. My hands are bigger and broader than your average gi—and I can't even think that word anymore, can't apply it to myself. My brain skitters away from it like a spider from the light. I'm dreading Season Six shooting because it'll mean going through makeup and staring at myself for hours a day.

I'm more aware of myself now, too, in a strange and itchy way. How people call me "ma'am" and "miss" as they open doors for me. How it stings the back of my neck when Will says "Ladies first!" before flipping pancakes onto Kate and my plates. When one of Kate's older friends tells me once she cried after seeing Morgantha slay the Pitlord of Orbit Station X, because I was exactly the strong female hero she wanted to see as a little girl, and I'd rather hug a cactus than smile and say "Thank you."

"She did it!" the woman, now an Oscar-winning film editor, crows, squeezing my shoulder. "She wasn't anyone's backup or sidekick. She didn't need Bryken's help or anyone else. She's a hero. A hero! No men allowed."

A hero. I like the sound of that. Not for my ego. Hero feels like a title that doesn't come with gender attached. But people want to stamp it on me all the same. Squeeze me into the shape they want to see. A shape who's a little too curvy and small and covered in features I can't bring myself to look at.

The world finds that shape inspiring and meaningful. What sort of selfish person would take that away from others? What sort of selfish person would give up being Morgantha when it mattered so much?

While Episode Three airs, the one with the #Morganetta kiss scene, I'm playing *Swordquest Online*. I almost never watch *Galaxy Spark* while it's airing—I know what's going to happen, and it's strange watching my own face on-screen.

I have a name for that strangeness now. Dysphoria. An ache when I see how small and soft I look next to Chris. I can't even look at our costumes. No matter how much dirt Morgantha rolls in, none will ever muss her eyeliner and she'll never hide her face behind her helmet. Like the very world of *Galaxy Spark* is oriented around Morgantha being one hundred percent girl.

*Swordquest Online* rolled out a new play mode in the latest patch, player-versus-player team duels. I've never been big on PvP, but Aida convinced me to join in. There's a limited-edition mount drop, a big, fluffy flying white kitten, available for the first week only of the patch. Nothing like a made-up pile of pixels and the one person who really gets me as I am to distract me from what's on TV tonight.

Traditional MMORPG combat requires a delicate balance of roles: tanks to hold an enemy's attention and draw all blows into their meaty armor, healers to keep the players standing as their hit points fall, and damage dealers like me to actually kill the monsters.

But two-on-two, the trinity is broken. Partnering with a healer is risky. Aida can keep me standing for longer than I could survive alone. But I'm responsible for killing all our enemies, and I need to do that quickly before they find and slaughter us. It's a big responsibility, but at least it's one I'm happy to take on.

Besides, Aida and I have the advantage of taking this seriously. Hawk's partnered with Clay, who's high as balls and not particularly trying to hide that.

"Divine Blessing," I say, and my arrows flash gold as Aida casts. I shift-target Clay, who's ducked behind a shattered pillar—apparently forgetting he's still visible from the waist up—and roll out into the open. He throws up his hands, beginning the spell to turn me into a toad—but the blessed arrow strikes him speechless, and in the three seconds he's helpless, I fire two more shots and gut him with an ax. Hawk's still standing, but I've made a perfect, seamless kill.

It helps I've got limitless arrows and axes—game logic smooths out all kinds of everyday bumps and complications. My bag can carry unlimited gold bars. My horse materializes when I snap my fingers. My armor mends itself when I touch a magic hammer.

And I'm me. Looking exactly how I want to look. Seen exactly how I want to be seen.

"Back here!" Aida shouts. I don't turn away fast enough. My screen goes white—the dazzling light reflecting off Hawk's shield, damn it—and I'm stunned. Seconds tick past, each an hour-long agony without control, without knowing—and then the game snaps back on-screen.

Aida's health has dropped below thirty percent. Hawk's hammering her with combo strikes, and she can't cast her healing spells fast enough to keep up. I shoot a poison dart at him, paralyzing him for a nanosecond—and then Aida stumbles back into an arena fire jet, incinerating her in seconds.

Healer down, Hawk slices me to ribbons before I can leap away.

Damn it. Hawk is just that good. Even with Clay hopped up on whatever he found behind his local Walmart, I don't have the skills to knock him out.

After the third round of them mopping the arena floor with our corpses, Aida switches characters to her rogue. This character is called Aidina, a dwarven woman with a beard and a bunch of tattoos. She's still Aida in voice comms and in my head, though. Whatever character she plays is just another aspect of her. A few new tricks, but the same person inside.

Rogues and rangers make a good team, even if we don't have a priest keeping us alive. Aida sneaks around the battlefield, striking from the shadows to keep Clay and Hawk confused, while I leap atop a wall and fire arrows down when they emerge from cover. The game shifts in our favor, and fluffy white badges flood into our inventories. Every few minutes, the giant flying cloud kitten above the battlefield roars.

"It happened!" Aida gasps, high and excited. Static warps

her voice upward. "Sorry, guys. I'm watching *Galaxy Spark* in another window."

"Did they reveal Alban Moonblade is a clone?" Clay asks. "That's my theory. I haven't watched since Season Two."

"Don't be stupid." She steps from a puff of smoke behind his shoulder and stabs him in the back. His cloth caster robes can't protect him, and he bleeds down to zero. "They kissed! Morgantha and Alietta. I knew it was coming, but I can't believe they actually allowed that on TV!"

"Big deal," Clay says. "It's not like I watch shows for the kissing scenes."

"Just because you don't like them," I say, "doesn't mean they're not important." When he pops back up to life, I hit him with an exploding arrow and send him tumbling down again. "Some people have never seen someone like them fall in love in a major network TV show. Get used to things mattering to people who aren't you."

Then, with a pang, I realize what *someone like them* might have implied. *Sorry,* I DM Aida. *I didn't mean to sound like I was trying to out you.*

*What? No, you're good. I didn't think that.* A pause in her typing. *But I'm glad you were able to come out to the guild without trouble. It was really brave. Maybe that means I'll be able to, one day.*

*You're not less brave staying quiet,* I type. *We all have secrets we keep.* Like being the star of *Galaxy Spark. I'm happy your ship sailed.*

*You should really watch the show! I mean, it's a lot to catch up on. But it's got some incredible characters, and now it's officially gay as hell.*

I squirm. Talking too much about the show feels like a lie of omission. *Any other gay-as-hell shows you can recommend?*

*Sure. Here's my Pinterest. I made mood boards for all my favorite ships.* The link she sends leads to an account with only a smattering of followers, but walls full of screenshots, fanart, and comics. The profile picture is an artsy, out-of-focus shot of a girl's hand pressed to her jaw. Just seeing it makes Aida feel real. A girl who likes the same stuff I do. Brave, awkward, and earnest.

*Thanks,* I type. She sends me back a heart emoji. I blush. Even though she probably lives all the way across the city, I feel closer to her, warmth sparkling in my belly as we stand back-to-back facing down our foes. Something realer and more solid than concrete under my feet.

And I can't stop glancing at her Pinterest profile, at the little freckles just visible where her hand meets her chin.

I have a crush on a girl I've only met online. Who doesn't know who I really am.

Who knows me better than anyone.

By the time I collapse into bed, we've all got our giant fluffy kitten mounts and have flown them around the arena. My real-life social media notifications are blowing up—*that KISS! OMG did you see that KISS?* Someone's posted *WTF LESBIANS????* on my Quicshot, which almost makes me choke-laugh, because the poster sounds genuinely shocked that lesbians exist, like we're Bigfoot or something.

I guess I can't think of myself that way anymore. *God, what if I'm really a straight man? Oh god.* I get the worst online hate from those. But I'm not even sure I one hundred percent drop into the man category—I just know I'm not a girl, and there's so much space to explore between and up and down and around inside gender that I could land anywhere. Be anyone. Be anything.

I mean, I *could* explore. If my whole world didn't revolve around me being the girl hero single-handedly bringing feminism to the sci-fi genre, or whatever else people are writing about me online.

My phone chimes. A text from Greta. *Guess they like us.*

It's so open ended. Not even one GIF or emoji to signal how she feels. Professional Greta. Greta, who'd love to be dealing with my problems instead of her own, even if she doesn't know what they all are. I don't know how to respond but "Yeah." *Good job, Frey. Way to be smooth and flirtatious. No wonder you can't get a girl to like you in real life.*

I guess that's okay. My on-screen romance is what matters most.

But I can't stop thinking about Aida. About how maybe, just maybe, there's one person in the world who sees me as something else.

# Nine

Two days later, Callie calls when I'm in the bathroom, beneath my giant-tall mirror and glaring, pore-enlarging white light, engaging in the new worst hobby ever: staring at my weirdly round face as my stomach churns. I'd almost be grateful for the interruption, if she didn't sound mad as hell.

"I ran into Peter and his douchebag friends when I was out clubbing last night," she starts. "Of course, I bet you five hundred bucks he left his wife and baby at home, but that's another story. I said, 'Hey, how's the rewrites Lily asked for going?' and do you know what he said?"

"Um," I try to talk around my toothbrush. "That he's thought about it for a good long time, realized his mistake, and is planning to change the story?"

"He said, 'Oh, I think Lily's cool with the script. We talked it out.' Then he and his buddies did Jell-O shots."

I'm so shocked I almost jam my toothbrush down my throat. "Yeah. Um. I thought I made it clear I'm *not* cool. Not cool at all."

"Love you, kid, but I swear to god you were born with twice the THC in your lungs of a normal human. You didn't even lose your temper when we got trapped in the airport for eighteen hours thanks to that storm last year—"

"Hey, no one can control the weather—"

"But Peter and Wes can control the scripts. So if you're still up to take the lead on changing their minds, you need to get firm with them. Fast."

I wince. "There's a lot of cool stuff going on that'll help change their minds. Everyone loves me and Greta dating. When they see how popular we are, they'll have to keep her around. Then, while they're rewriting the script, we'll have an opening to get rid of all the hurtful stuff."

She sighs. "You can't change the world and have everyone like you. Don't be scared to make enemies. Trust me, it's fun."

"Gotcha," I say. "Yeah. I can do that. Get tough." Someone knocks on the bathroom door, and I lose my train of thought. "Thanks, Callie. See you soon."

"Excuse me?" Shyanne says as I hang up and let her in. "Sorry to bother you. I just needed to grab my shower bag before I hit the road." A purple bag, sized more for wilderness survival gear than holding makeup, hangs over the towel rack. "You look cute. I like that top."

The top is an old *Galaxy Spark* tee, a little tight now I've outgrown it, the black straps of my bra peeking through the worn collar. I feel absurdly visible. Separate from my own skin. Before Callie called, I was twisting my head back and forth to track which side of my face feels most like me. Which view convinces me I'm a person, and not a prop on a set.

"Are you okay?" she said. "You've been in here a while—looking for something? If you need any tampons, they're in my bag."

My cheeks flash scarlet. I already feel my skin crawling like it wants to run away from me. I don't need to think about how much my body hates me. "I'm fine. Um, how's work? Chris said you lined up a pilot." I'll say anything to change the subject.

"The production company is a mess," she says, and rolls her eyes. "But I shouldn't complain. A lot of actresses never get this far."

I think about what Greta told me, about why she came to Hollywood. "You must really love the work to put up with all that crap."

Her eyes light up. "I do! Ever since I was a kid, I acted out scenes from TV shows—*A Different World*, *That's So Raven*, *Living Single*—which *Friends* completely ripped off, don't get me started. My parents called me their little star. They worried a lot when I moved out here, but they always knew it was my dream."

Is that what all dreams look like? Either fighting your parents or making them worry? Wanting something bad enough it's worth upsetting your life and other people's lives to get there? That's how I feel about #Morganetta. But acting has never needed to be my dream. It was just handed to me.

I guess I should just be grateful and get back to work. Callie reminded me of the responsibility I took on. I'm not alone and I have to keep pulling. I'm getting fitted for my Season Six costumes today. With a week of #Morganetta blowing up the internet, maybe Peter will see the value of changing his mind. He admitted to rushing the Season Six scripts. If I can talk to him without Wes sliding in, maybe I can gain ground.

Unfortunately, Peter's not the only one attending the fitting. We're a week from flying to Belfast to shoot on location, and half the LA-based cast needs new pieces fitted. Greta's getting three dresses fitted, each in a different style to follow the planets we'll visit next year. I say, "Hi, cutie!" as I walk in, but she only yawns in reply, so I guess she's not up for pretending today.

Hot set lights beam down from the ceiling in round racks, painting lines of sweat down every face—the design team needs to make sure our costumes show up well under every possible light source, even if it means roasting us alive. The bulky warehouse doors of the studio's back are closed because we can't let anyone get photos of the fitting, and my heart longs for even the slightest stir of fresh air, even though summer blazes outside. Costume techs swarm around us both, though at least I only have to deal with three of them, measuring my cape. Twelve tailors work on Greta, sticking pins in her skirt and messing with her sleeves, as she yawns and tries to sip her Starbucks.

"Late night?" I ask her. "Do something fancy?" Then, so as not to look like an antisocial idiot, I add, "I didn't see you around, but the event I was at was pretty exclusive." The War-hawks raid team only runs twenty players, after all.

"Can't get more exclusive than me hanging out alone in my room." A hint of laughter plays around the edges of her words. A crack in the wall between us. "Reading episode reactions until three a.m."

"#Morganetta is still trending," I say. "The reviewer for Nerd Universe said us getting together is a bold and yet obvious development that opens exciting new story lines in a show once criticized for its lack of attention toward women's inner lives."

"I just swan-dived into queer femme social media and watched it light up like the Santa Monica Pier at sunset. Eighteen hundred fanfics went up overnight."

"Have you read the one where we—I mean Morgantha and Alietta—open an animal shelter? It's ungodly cute."

"God, no. I'm terrified I'll find something not safe for work."

"I can teach you how to use filters."

"Still. No." Her spine stiffens.

"Okay," I say. "It's not for everyone. Good to know your own comfort level."

She smiles, ducking her head as a man with a bulky headset slides a lace shawl around her shoulders. "Did you see the fans waiting outside? There's, like, fifty kids lined up outside with signs and rainbow banners. They screamed when I walked in."

"Damn," I say. "I must have taken the wrong entrance. That's awesome. Did you sign any autographs?"

She bites her lip. Her gaze skitters away from mine. "I mean. No? I'm scared they'd look at me, and . . . and I'd feel so guilty about raising their hopes that I'd completely spoil Season Six. What else can I say to them? 'Sorry, your big inspiring power couple is one hundred percent doomed?' I recommended the show to another queer person yesterday, and I've felt guilty ever since. Like I'm lying to the fans whenever I interact with them. That I'm just a massive fraud."

"That doesn't matter," I say. Because I'm a fraud, too. I'm not the girl everyone thinks I am, and with every passing day, squeezing myself into that mode gets harder and more painful. "No one cares what's really going on inside us. They're looking at us to be stars. You know. Shiny. Larger than life. Inspiring."

"It's hard to shine like a star up close," she says. "Especially with this stupid zit on my forehead."

"I don't see it," I say. "You're probably fine."

"The first time I signed autographs," she said, "was at New York Comic Con right after the Season Four finale. It was so crowded, and so dry. I spent an hour just trying to find a water bottle. Then I was so nervous, I didn't realize I'd signed 'Alietta,' on the first fifty headshots. Because that was who they came to see, right?"

I wince, sympathetic embarrassment twinging between my eyes. Perfect Greta making such a big mistake? But that's not right. Not even Greta can be always perfect. Maybe her stiff professionalism on set is because she's scared people won't like her, won't hire her again. I don't know if I can help her navigate that storm—especially because the rules are so different for her and me—but at least I can tell her she's not alone in dealing with it.

"The first time I signed autographs," I say, "I was three years old and played the toddler in a movie about a family road trip. Kate gave me a Sharpie to sign the poster at the premiere, and instead I jabbed it all over her ball gown. Ruined fifty thousand dollars' worth of satin." The tech pinning green silk to my shoulders gives me a hard look. I wiggle my empty fingers. "But eventually I scribbled something on the poster, and they auctioned it off for a lot of charity money. It made people happy. The little nice things add up."

"But they cost you something, too." Greta shrugs. Silk ripples pink and purple off her shoulder, sliding around the jutting line of her collarbone. "The fans ask so much of us. I need to remember there's pieces of me I should protect."

That stings. Because I, too, have something inside me I want to protect, something impossibly important and impossibly precious, the One Ring of my selfhood. *Frey.* A badass ranger and partner and friend. Someone who only lives inside a computer, but also somehow inside me.

I'm not the spoiled, stuck-up girl Greta sees when she looks at me. And the only reason she thinks that's me is because I'm committed to being Lily Ashton for the show's fans. For #Morganetta's fans.

So I'll keep Frey hidden. I'll save our ship. I'll help Callie, and

Chris, and everyone I care about who needs my help. That's the only way all this pain and confusion will be worth it.

I toss a coat over my costume—Morgantha's too-big leather boots, artificial gravity belt resting awkwardly on my hips—then march over to Peter and grab his elbow. "Let's go for a walk."

He seems bemused, but he lets me lead him around anyways, past the tape and out to the sun-washed parking lot. Security is keeping the teen fans clustered back from the building, but they still light up and scream when they see me. Their rainbow banners read *Morganetta for life!* and *Thank you, Lily and Greta!*

"Did you like the show the other night?" I ask, pitching my voice so they all can hear me. Performing. Pretending to be one of them. More cheers. Reaching hands. *It's not about me. It's about them.* I jab my thumb at Peter. "This guy here wrote the whole episode." Technically, making #Morganetta canon was my idea, but I don't need credit. "What do you have to say to him?"

Shouts rise. "Yes! Yes!" and "Thank you, thank you so much," and "I love it!" I whip some Sharpies out of one of my boots. Since age three, I've learned not to keep them near stainable fabric—but I always keep a couple on hand.

"Want us to sign your posters?" I say, and when they nod, I offer Peter a Sharpie. Voice lowered, I mutter, "Come on. They're excited to meet you."

Down the line we go. Girls squeeze my hands and pull me into selfies. I fix a grin on my face, bouncing off the energy of the crowd. Reflecting them back like a mirror as their voices echo in my ears, so happy and welcome that I almost forget I don't belong with them.

Peter is more cautious, hanging back. Unlike me, he's not used to being the center of attention. Still, after signing the first few posterboards, he loosens up. He's beaming by the time he reaches the last girl, nodding like a bobbing pigeon as they tell him how much the show means to them, how they love it, how it makes them feel like someone really cares.

"Thank you so much!" I say, waving to them. Then I break off, grab Peter's elbow, and drag him back into the stairwell, still waving. His face is flushed. I wonder how he can live out here so long and still not get used to that sun.

As we return, through the main studio doors, I put an arm on his wrist and stop him by the abandoned front desk. He stands stock-still. I look him in the eye.

"You can't kill Alietta in Season Six," I say, striving to be firm. Remembering what Callie told me. "Don't you realize that now? All those girls care so much about it. They've never seen anyone on-screen like them in a show like this. It's not just the same sad love story it'd be if Morgantha was a guy and his girlfriend died. This will really, really hurt all those very real people out there. I know Wes doesn't want to let random strangers on the internet do his job," I say, thinking about our conversation at the party. "I know he likes the story line and he wants Season Six to be good. We all want that. I just don't want to hurt real kids."

"None of us want that." Peter stares down at his shoes. "I . . .

Shit. This is really important to you?"

I nod. Hold my breath, cross my fingers. And hope.

"I'll talk to Wes. I can't promise anything, but I'll try. Hey, you and Greta weren't dating when we wrote that draft. If anything can change his mind, it's seeing how much people love you two together."

*Together.* There's the magic word. This is all happening—the girls are only here—because they think me and Greta are dating for real. Which is what we wanted. Which is part of the plan. If the whole world is talking about how great me and Greta are together, they're not talking about our motorcycle joyride or how the male fans don't like Alietta or anything else that can tear us down. We're in control of the narrative. How people see us.

And we're using it to lie. At least, I am. Not just about who I'm dating, but about who I am.

When I get home, I throw myself into the shower, crank up the water, and steam for a full hour. It wicks off the sweat from getting futuristic latex costumes sewn on for six hours, but nothing makes me feel less dirty. *Liar. Liar, liar, liar.* #Morganetta only matters because people care so much about seeing two girls dating on TV. Me and Greta matter as girls. Because we're girls.

Only I'm not. I thought I was, but now I know different, and it feels like I'm pretending for the followers and attention. I want to help. I want to be their hero, on-screen and in real life.

Maybe I am selfish. I'm not happy with just helping them

feel represented. I also wish what I was doing could make me feel more like me.

I don't realize how late it is until Chris knocks on the door the second time.

"We have four bathrooms in the house," I grouse as I storm past in a towel.

"Yeah, but your mirror has the best lighting." He pushes past me and inside.

Half an hour later, when I've finished my math worksheet and started turning on my gaming computer, he comes up to my room.

"Are you stealing my body wash?" Chris demands. "The bottle was almost empty. What's going on?"

I swallow. "Um. I didn't think you'd notice?" Something about the fruity, girly smell of mine leaves me physically unable to touch it. Smelling his pine-and-leather one on my skin calms me down.

"That was my birthday present. Shyanne ordered it from France. Two hundred eighty dollars a bottle."

"Sorry," I say. "I didn't know. I'll order you a replacement. Hey, why does your girlfriend want you to smell like a ski lodge anyway?"

"Why aren't you using the fancy stuff Kate got you for Christmas? It smells like powdered unicorn horns and costs just as much."

"Do not pull the fancy-soap card. Not when American soap isn't good enough for you."

"Hey, I've washed with my great-grandma's homemade soap. But she's gone, and so I'll use the stuff that's good enough for the best girl in Hollywood." He paused. "That means Shyanne. Not you."

"I figured."

"You're the second-best girl."

I wince.

"Shit." He bites his lip. His brown eyes are wide, concerned, soft. He genuinely cares. For all his joking around, he cares so much about other people that it leaps off his skin. But his care is poking deep into this strange new blister on me, and the soft edge doesn't stop it from hurting. "Forget I said that. I shouldn't rank girls. It's a dick move—"

"Please don't—"

"No, listen. Before my dad married Kate, it was just the two of us. My uncle, his wrestling friends—a real sausage fest. It wasn't until I met you and Kate that I had women in my everyday life. I saw what girls could achieve if men gave them the chance—"

I run from the room, hands over my mouth to hold in words. Hold in tears. God, I love my brother. But he doesn't know. He doesn't see me. No one sees me.

And I can't pretend it doesn't hurt like hell.

# Ten

Chris and I don't speak the whole flight to Belfast, even though he sits right ahead of me in first class. After the plane takes off, I sink back in my seat, roll the blinders up around my cubby, and bury my head in the first Ann Elise book, trying to see what Shyanne, Kate, and a million other women see in her. Trying to convince myself I can slip into her skin.

Ann Elise is a twenty-year-old virgin who loves books and is afraid of being kissed. She doesn't know anything about high fashion, but when she's offered a chance to break into publishing by interning at a fashion magazine, she decides to take it—only to discover she's accidentally been hired as the executive editor. Her billionaire boss, Michael Sterling, doubts her ability to do the job, but Ann Elise proves herself by designing a new marketing campaign involving her best friend's cupcake shop, and Michael falls for her. Turns out he's a really great guy, just cold and demanding because his estranged father asked too much of him . . .

Halfway through the book, I find I'm mentally listing reasons why I could totally play Michael Sterling, if I just started working out and magically grew a foot in height.

I can see why Ann Elise matters. I can see why people love her. It's the same reason people love *Galaxy Spark*. People need places for their imagination to escape into. Sometimes that's another planet. Sometimes it's falling for your rich boss. It's human, and there's something gorgeous in it, how we all have the power to send our minds and selves to other places. How we can imagine something entirely different and new.

I'll never be the sort of person who makes fun of the Ann Elise fans for loving this story. But I will never be Ann Elise.

That shouldn't matter. I'm not Morgantha either. I wasn't a poor orphan girl who wants a mommy for Christmas. I'm an actor. Pretending to be other people is my job.

It's just that pretending to be other people has sort of become my life.

"How do you like the book?" Greta asks, peering over the top of my cubby. She's got a pink silk sleep mask rolled up on her forehead and a box of Toblerone in her fist. Some ridiculous impulse in me wants to climb over into her seat and snuggle up—and I bite that down, because it's an awful idea. I can tell the difference between what's real and what can never be.

"It's fine," I say. "Um. Just fine. Smile."

I hold up my phone and snap a selfie of the two of us. She grins, a bright, obliging look that vanishes as soon as I lower my phone and start posting it. It unnerves me, how quickly she switches from pretend-girlfriend, light-up Greta to her normal private self. But the #Morganetta shippers will eat this up, and that's what matters. All that matters. We can both work together to save her job and the story we're trying to create between us.

"My mom and her friends really like those books," Greta says. "She's always trying to stuff them in my bag when I get home. 'See, Greta? Some people are just late bloomers! Sure you've never had a boyfriend, but once you have the free time, in college—look, Ann Elise doesn't meet her soul mate until she's twenty! These books will show you everything you're missing out on with men.'"

I wince. "That's some pretty, uh, conversion camp shit there." There are no gay people in the Ann Elise books, save for Cornelius, Ann Elise's gay hairdresser, who speaks with an exaggerated lisp. Kate's promised she'll get that turned down in the script, but still. We're certainly not welcome in the world of that story.

"It's just bullshit," Greta says, flipping through movies on the tablet in her cubby. "Like this selection. Only three gay movies, and they edit down the kissing for the airplanes. But they let this heterosexual propaganda slip through." She points to a wide swath of early '00s rom-coms. I guess whatever they could license for cheap. "I've never even watched these, and I can predict every single story line from the posters."

"No way," I say. "That's so judgmental."

She laughs. "But I'm right. Watch me." Greta picks one at

random, a movie called *All Wrong for You,* and offers me her other earbud. Her knee presses against mine as she balances the tablet between us.

An upbeat pop song plays as a woman in a blocky suit strides through midtown Manhattan. The film wastes no time in explaining her name is Chelsea, she's an interior designer, and she doesn't have a date for her little sister's wedding. Chelsea's agreed to a blind date with the nephew of her handsome, much-older boss. Unfortunately, he's a pimply college student whose mom drives him to the restaurant, and Chelsea runs off to commiserate with a hot businessman at the bar.

"She's going to go home with this rich guy," Greta says, "even though he's dropping all these creepy comments about her neckline." But a few lines later, unlike her prediction, the main character throws her drink in the asshole's face and walks out. "Okay, so . . ."

"Thank god," I say. "None of them are good enough for her. I feel bad for straight people."

A few scenes later, Chelsea attends a dance lesson to practice for her sister's wedding. The groomsmen are also present— whoops, turns out her handsome boss is the best man! They share a tango that ends in them intimately pressed, chest-to-chest, and something sparks in both their eyes.

"It's going to take the whole rest of the movie before they get together," Greta says, and the scene cuts to Chelsea and her boss waking up in bed the next day.

"Chelsea's a workaholic, but she's not dumb," I say. "Guess

you've been outsmarted by a rom-com."

Her cheeks turn pink. Greta looks down, embarrassed. *Seriously* embarrassed. *It's just a silly game*, I want to say, but I also know she's worried people think she doesn't really belong in this industry. Of course she wants to look smart.

"Hey," I say. "Sorry. That's what a good movie is supposed to do. Surprise you. But in a way that makes you think."

Chelsea's sister's wedding is ruined when a fire-juggling contest at the bachelorette party burns down the venue. The next day, Chelsea and her boss work together to find an alternate venue—the local Renaissance faire—and everyone dances in cheesy-looking costumes as both happy couples share a kiss.

"I haven't been to a Ren faire in ages," Greta muses, tossing back handfuls of popcorn. The flight attendants have kept us stocked. One slides down the back of my sweatshirt, and she reaches over and plucks it out. Her finger grazes my bra strap. I shiver. *Play it cool, Frey.*

"I've never been," I say. "Um. Is that fun?"

"You'd love it. Nerd paradise. It doesn't even matter what genre you're into. You can wear your *Galaxy Spark* costume and everyone will think you're doing a Morgantha cosplay."

"But that'd be so unprofessional," I tease. "Stealing costumes from set?"

She mock-hits me on top of my head. I dodge. Water leaps from the cup I hold and spills down my lap.

"Sorry!" She passes me napkins. "But I meant that. We should go to a Ren faire. It'd be fun."

"Like friends?"

"Like coworkers, forced into the terribly awkward position of dating to save their own bacon." She smiles. Just a flash of a thing. But I see it and smile, too. My heart thrums, and not just from the shock of ice cubes all over my sweatpants. "Fine, numskull. Like friends."

*Friends*, I think as the credits roll. Everything's changed between us, these past few weeks. It should cheer me up inside. Instead, my stomach flips. Cold creeps up my spine, sinking in deeper than the icy puddle on my pants.

Because here's one more reason I can't lose the fight to save #Morganetta. More than the ship, I can't stand by and do nothing while Greta's mom pushes her into a life she doesn't want. *Saving Alietta will save her in real life.*

One more responsibility on my shoulders. I shudder at how tall it feels; the scale of Greta's whole future looming tall before me. But I'm Kate Ashton's kid. My burden has always been pretty light.

I can carry one more thing. For Greta.

I close my eyes somewhere over the Atlantic. When I wake, the plane lights are up and the flight attendants are passing out customs forms. I scramble to fill mine out—averting my eyes when I have to check the *F* in the *sex* box—and drink a whole large coffee while waiting in the customs line. A driver holds a sign with our names just outside security and leads us into waiting cars. We wind through the neat green countryside and pull around the back of the hotel where we'll be staying the next few weeks, jet-lagged and groggy. Once the bellhops get my bags to my room, I jump in the shower and blast hot water for ages.

I don't usually game while shooting on location, but I knew I'd never get through filming Season Six without some sort of escape. I clear the minibar items off my room's desk, whip out my laptop and headset, and plug in my US–UK electric converter.

After the day I've had, I need to be seen. As the real me, scarred and scruffy and carrying two heavy axes.

*Fuck me*, I think as *Swordquest Online* loads. I'm so doomed. I'll never be able to paint Frey's image over the world's picture of Lily Ashton. It's hard enough to get people to take me seriously when they think I'm a girl. What would happen to me if they knew everything else?

What would happen if I told Kate? She donates money to support queer and marginalized teens in LA. She's fine with me dating girls. But me being a guy, or guy-ish, or even just not a girl—that wouldn't fit any of her carefully drafted business plans.

I don't know what I'd do if Kate didn't accept me. It feels like that would break my heart.

I slide on my headphones, lower my head, and force myself to concentrate on the screen. *Swordquest Online* is safe. Kate is a million miles away. I can be myself for these squirreled-away minutes, and that's all I can really ask for.

It's the middle of the workday back in the states, but Aida is online, PvPing in the Great Basin Arena. I group up with her and teleport to the overgrown, dinosaur-infested crater. We've got a small base to defend from enemy invaders—other players from all over the world—and while Aida rings our shelter in protection spells, I climb to the top of a crumbling wall and ready my bow to snipe down attackers.

"Warrior by the gate," Aida says. An enemy ogre berserker, twice my height and wielding two bloodred axes, grapples up to join me on the wall. I curse. A cocoon of light surrounds me, absorbing the strikes—but it won't last more than few seconds. I need to get off this wall, but it's too high to jump. "Step backward and wedge your foot in that boulder."

I do as Aida says. It's just a poorly rendered gray block, even with my high-end graphics card—a relic from an earlier expansion pack. But when I slide into that gap, I sink knee-deep into the ground. The ogre swings, but their axes don't hit me. Like I've slipped a half step outside their reality.

Aida grapples atop the wall, unleashing her plague cleric magic. Her face hollows into a skull. Her feet lift off the ground. An animated cloud of flies wraps around the ogre. But the enemy player is still focused on me, fixated and hopelessly swinging their ax—probably cursing at their screen some-where—until their hit points drop to zero.

I leap from the crack as the ogre dies. "The game totally breaks there! How'd you know about it?"

"I discovered it when the arena first came out. I was new to PvP and always getting killed. Came up on the wall and tripped into it when I was looking for a viewpoint. I've been using it to trap people for years." She laughs nervously. "You're the first person I've told. Don't pass it around, or I might get banned."

You're supposed to report bugs like this to the game moderators so they can fix them. I understand why. It sucks when you practice for weeks to kill a boss and another guild beats you to it by blowing it up with a bugged eight-bit squirrel. But this doesn't feel like cheating. It feels like a little piece of magic. Between the two of us, we've figured out a way around the world's rules.

"You can trust me," I say. "I don't share secrets. I mean, who would I trust enough to tell them to?" This next bit is fishing. I'm so curious to find this out. "I don't even, like, have a girlfriend."

By that, I sort of mean *Do you have one?* But I'm too chicken to ask outright. In case she guesses.

"Can I— Can I trust you with something else?" Her breath spikes oddly on that word, like my network is bad. "Promise you won't laugh at me? I just want to talk about this, and I don't have any friends I can trust like you."

"I'd sooner cut my own heart out than laugh at you," I say, and hope she knows I mean it, that my earnestness carries through my voice mods.

"I've never dated anyone. I'm scared no one wants to date ace people."

"Oh?" It's the first thing I can think of to say, and immediately I know I've fucked up. I didn't mean to sound like I didn't understand. "I mean, I'm glad you trust me with what you're going through. People really say they won't date you because you're ace?"

"Okay, I've never asked someone out. But I've seen movies.

A lot of movies. And even the gay movies make it seem like sex is the most important thing in the world. I want someone I can watch movies with. Get ice cream. Cuddle."

"That sounds pretty nice to me. Sex is . . . like, I guess I want it. But it's just one thing. Not everything." I pause. "I want a girlfriend I can game with. Or go to the beach with."

"Someone who'll fight against an entire enemy army to protect me."

"Someone who'll write me poetry so beautiful it changes the world."

She laughs. I can hear a smile hiding in her lips. "Do you like poetry?"

"Um," I say. "It feels important, I guess? I don't know much about it. I don't know much about dating either, but I'd like to learn."

"Me too," she says, and shoots a troll wizard as they try to batter down our gate. A phantom tiger rises from their corpse and lunges over the walls.

"Oh, god!" I yell. "It's the denmother!"

The swipe of a paw leaves us both lying on the floor, together and laughing. Like we have no bigger problems than this. Like we're normal.

Like we can flirt across the internet, across the world, and it can really, really matter.

# Eleven

Next morning, *Galaxy Spark* is shooting on the beach outside town. I wake at five to make it to the makeup trailer, ducking my face behind a big stack of coffee and walnut muffins. My brain and body all scream at me that I'm an idiot, that it's really bedtime, and why am I awake and working?

I focus on my lines, running them over and over in my head, wondering if it's even worth the effort when Peter could hand us his rewrite any minute. It's a distraction I need.

My newfound dysphoria is pushing on me hard today. Lurking in the mirror like the alien alligator who nearly killed Morgantha on that swamp planet. An itch, a spectral wrongness. Like if I rub my hands over my skin backward, it'll crack off like a snakeskin into something else. How my face and hands don't feel like mine.

"Chin up." Natalie, the head makeup artist, pushes my head up into the light. I squeeze shut my eyes, trying to avoid the strange, small face in the mirror. A girl's face. A face printed on T-shirts and merchandise all around the world. A face that could never belong to anyone other than Lily Ashton. It's like I've fallen into the second movie of a spy franchise, where the hero's cover is blown and his face broadcast to his enemies all over the world. The whole planet is a maze, and I can't escape anyone knowing I'm part of this stupid show.

"Lily. Lily?" Natalie pats my shoulder. "Relax a bit, sweetie. Do you have a headache?"

"I think she has a hangover," Callie says from the chair next to mine, Queen Aylah's massive dark wig glued atop her head. "Lily, there's some herbal pills in my bag that'll fix you right up. Don't ask me where I got them. Be sure to drink them with a lot of water."

"It's the water that fixes it," I say. "The herbs don't actually do anything. And I don't have a hangover."

Natalie shakes her head. "You know, Lily, my midwife tells me that herblore is the oldest form of women's magic. It embodied the power of sisterhood."

I wince. Do people care more about my well-being because they look at me and project *girl*? A technician walks by. I tap her arm. "Do you have any aspirin?"

"I'll get some," she says, and runs off.

Callie shrugs. "Your loss."

We're shooting a scene from the first episode today, where Aylah and Morgantha meet face-to-face to discuss potentially exchanging Bryken for information on the mysterious Galaxy Spark, the power source at the galaxy's core. As a child, Morgantha looked up to Aylah before discovering the evil queen sent her clone warriors to destroy her home village. It has the potential to be the most iconic confrontation on the show.

But we lack direction.

"More intensity, Lily," Wes says, yawning behind the camera. He stayed up late again last night, video-chatting with his family. I think his father's cancer is back, but he's not talking about it. Despite his limited time, he insisted on directing almost a third of the episodes himself. "This is your nemesis. The woman who killed your parents and kidnapped your foster brother. Get angry."

"What sort of angry?" I say. "Morgantha usually just threatens people with her stellar sword, but she can't do that when Aylah's holding Bryken hostage."

"Try this. Look at her—look at her like you're measuring up her and Alietta in your head. Like you know all her beauty is false since she uses nanobots to stay young—and you're judging her because she can never measure up to Alietta's natural beauty."

*Ew. Gross.* He does realize Alietta's played by a real person, right? Someone almost thirty years younger than him? "Is that really the right angle? We're at war. Why would I care how she looks?"

"It's symbolic. Because Alietta is good and pure, and Aylah is evil."

*Is this because Aylah killed a whole dynasty for power? Or because she uses her looks to manipulate men?* And I can't help but notice now Callie is one of the few East Asian actors on the show, and she's the one being framed as lesser than a girl played by a white actor.

I lower my voice and meet Callie's eyes. "Do you want me to say something?"

"I'm a grown-up. I can handle some cringe."

"Okay. And FYI, no one under thirty says *cringe* anymore." I fix on Morgantha's trademark sneer and meet Callie's eyes. It's impossible for me to see her as a villain when just three hours ago we were joking around in hair and makeup, but I imagine a real villain hanging in the air between us, someone I can target the vitriol at. Someone with Wes's face.

"I know how badly you want Bryken back," Callie says, slow and menacing. "But he may not be the same man you remember. Witnessing Alban's death changed him. Filled him with anger. Violence."

"Hold up," I say, breaking character. That line only makes sense if it foreshadows Bryken killing Alietta. And Peter promised he'd talk with Wes about changing it. "That line isn't right." I find Peter's eyes—he's curled around a steaming cup of coffee on the sidelines—and give him a little huh? gesture. He stands, cursing a little as the coffee splashes out on his vest.

"Cut that line about Bryken," he says. "Wes—you and I need to talk about that. Just the two of us. Later."

"Are you going to make me come back for reshoots?" Wes grunts.

"We'll talk about it later," Peter says firmly, and gives me a thumbs-up.

I relax and read on.

I wake up the next day to a notifications stream thick enough to choke on.

Like, my social media filters are pretty heavy-duty, especially when a new season of *Galaxy Spark* is on air. Thousands of fans tag me in their reactions. I need to block out most of that incoming traffic just to see stuff I'm interested in. Nevertheless, Episode Five has filled up my phone.

*What's going on?* I rub my eyes and sit up in bed. Video clips of Reggie Ainsley, dressed in Alban Moonblade's silver tunic, fill my Quicshot feed. #RIPAlban is trending. *Oh yeah. The episode where he died just aired back in the USA.* I've known that scene was coming for over a year now—longer, considering how Reggie's career has taken off and he's only doing blockbuster action films now. But it's fresh news for the rest of the world—and it's something everyone is talking about.

I watch the scene, in the background of a trending reaction video. Alban, bleeding from a dozen wounds, fights his way through Queen Aylah's prison ship to Bryken's cell. They share a teary embrace through the bars—my heart lurches— and then Aylah stabs Alban in the back, and he bleeds out in Bryken's arms. It's some of the best acting I've ever seen on the show, and reading through the early reviews confirms it. One line in the *World Dispatch* sums it up: *In his final episode,*

*Ainsley reminds us why we love this show: because the best science fiction captures the truth of our lives and our struggles, as wide as the vacuum of space.*

Pulling on a sweatsuit, I make my way to the set for rehearsal with our fight choreographer, Jeanine. We're preparing for a scene where Morgantha gets ambushed in a ruined temple, flips and spins as she tosses her enemies off a balcony. My stunt double will handle the gymnastics, but I want to do most of the fight scene myself—I love the rush of getting choreography right. Peter drops by to watch as I practice falling, butt-first, backward on a mat.

"Come on, Morgantha. Up and at 'em!" he cheers. "You should have killed at least three space bandits by now."

"Dude, you're the one who wrote this scene. They don't die until I throw the gravity grenade and send them screaming into the abyss!" I gesture at the abyss, otherwise known as the sheets of green paper lying beside the mat. "Have you seen the Episode Five reactions?"

"They've been coming all day." He pulls his ringing phone from his pocket. "Along with the calls from studio executives! Turns out I don't need a six-pack to be Hollywood's most wanted man." He lifts his phone to his ear. "Mike! Good to hear from you. Is this about the Captain Supernova reboot?"

"Happy for you!" I say as he ducks outside the soundstage.

"Focus!" Jeanine shouts, grabbing my attention. "We're shooting after lunch!"

The rest of my day dissolves into swordplay, backward

tumbles, and running through a maze of green screens. My stunt double is getting on a plane for Hong Kong in eighteen hours, so we have to get this done today. By the time the director lets us go, it's practically midnight. I don't even check my phone before I drop into bed.

Which is why I miss the shift in the discourse.

I wake up to another flurry of notifications.

#CancelGalaxySpark is trending.

My heart thuds in my throat as I do the social media forensics.

It looks like everything started when Black entertainment blogger Amanda Wells wrote a guest post on the *Galaxy Spark* fansite Geeks Run the Galaxy about her reaction to Alban Moonblade's death scene. I scan the text.

**The members of House Moonblade have all been played by Black actors—with the exception of Morgantha, adopted by Alban as a child. But over the show's run, most of House Moonblade has died gruesomely. Now Morgantha, played by Lily Ashton, and Bryken, played by Chris Arden, are the last living members of House Moonblade—and the show's already telling us who will fill Alban's shoes.**

The article goes on to detail Morgantha and Bryken's on-screen relationship—every time she beat him in a training exercise, every time she saved his life, every time she won Alban's praise. That scene in Season Three when Bryken tells

Morgantha, "You're the only one worthy of the Moonblade name." How the show foreshadows Morgantha, not Bryken, will inherit leadership of the family—and how we're supposed to want that to happen.

**Even in a far future where racism is supposedly long over, where a Black family rules a third of the galaxy, a white woman's story takes priority. If the rest of Galaxy Spark is the story of Morgantha's rise to power over her less-worthy brother, a show famed for its twists will have made the most predictable move of all: centering whiteness.**

All I can think is *Shit, I never noticed.* I always saw Morgantha's backstory as a Cinderella story, a talented outcast finding her place. But it's also a story that elevates a white person to heroism while characters played by BIPOC actors are villainous, conniving, or just simply sidelined. Amanda Wells is right, and that sits in my chest like a ton of bricks. I've been so focused on making a few tweaks to the story lines I never thought how deep changes needed to go. How the whole root mentality of the show slants in the wrong direction.

I look Amanda up online to follow her, see what else she has to say—but she's already locked down all her social media accounts, flooded by a torrent of harassment. Hundreds of the accounts are anonymous trolls, but some I recognize as #Morganetta fan accounts, accusing Amanda of homophobia for trying to get the show canceled. *But she didn't even say that! She just shared her opinions on the plot!* Someone's got #CancelGalaxy-Spark trending. People are tagging me in a million different arguments.

I open up Quicshot and film my reaction. "Leave Amanda Wells alone," I say. "Online harassment isn't cool." I hit send and then wish I'd said something better, something more *right*. I slide into the shower and fight the urge to reach out through the plastic and check my phone every two minutes as I wash. My stomach churns, and I'm not even sure why. All that online fury feels like an avalanche.

By the time I towel-dry, my mentions are flooded.

> You're dating @Greta.Alice and you won't
> even fight for #Morganetta? What a hypocrite.
> Butch girl dates bland femme. Yawn. Every
> WLW couple on TV is the same. #Morganetta is
> practically a homophobic stereotype. #Cancel-Morganetta
> LMAO everyone knows lily isn't gay she just
> fakes it for attention. kick her off the show.
> #CancelMorganetta

My guts flip over. I want to scream. Cry. Throw up. How could anyone say something that mean? *It's just a few people*, I tell myself. *A mean, vocal minority.* But it's like they're shouting in my ear. Bile rises in my throat. *How dare they say I'm not fighting for #Morganetta? I made it happen. I'm the one pushing Peter and Wes to keep it going.* But these strangers can't see how much work I've put in to getting this right. They just see I'm not giving them what they want—permission to harass a Black woman off the internet—and that's enough reason to tear me down for fun.

*Why am I working so hard for people like you?*

I turn off my phone. But I can't clear my head, and I'm glad to not be filming this morning.

Greta and I are doing an interview for the BBC. It's not much of a relief, being driven through a Belfast rainstorm, the sky dark and flowing water painting gray dockside warehouses grayer, but Greta's got a murder mystery drama downloaded on her phone and we can curl up and watch housewives solve crimes around lovely shots of the Pacific Coast.

"Okay, so Melissa definitely killed him," Greta says, her loose hair sliding down my cheek as I press in close to share the screen. Slippery and smelling of lemon shampoo. "Look how her eyes dart around in every scene. Like she's braced for them to accuse her, but she's too polite to show how uncomfortable she is."

"Anyone who'd willingly join the PTA is a serial killer," I say. "Helen should drop-kick those other moms off a cliff before they frame her."

Greta laughs. "You watch too many action movies. It's not that kind of story! I think it's supposed to explore how society expects women to be perfect."

She gives me a Meaningful Look. I wince. *All because I was assigned female at birth doesn't mean I like or understand girl stuff.* "I guess," I say. "It's just . . . not for me, you know."

She turns it off. "You don't have to sound guilty about not liking a show."

"Kate's worked her whole life to push movies and TV shows about women's lives into the mainstream. And like, what does it say about me that I'd rather watch dudes battle in space-ships?"

"Everyone has their favorites. There's no right or wrong way to like movies."

She says it like it's easy. "I always feel . . . I don't know. That it says something bad about me if I like shallow stuff for guys." Because I might be a guy. And I don't want to be a shallow one.

"It says you're overthinking things," Greta says.

I sigh. There's no way I can unravel everything I'm dealing with right now, not without telling her the truth. "Are you doing okay?" Something in the way her neck hangs says she's tired, and she's been tired for weeks. A sudden, irrational stab of anger sweeps through me that the universe has put more weight on her shoulders.

"It's been a tough week. I keep waiting for the other shoe to drop."

"I keep waiting to find out if the other shoe's Callie's sandal or Wes's work boot."

Greta laughs. "Can you believe that stupid motivation Wes gave when you were filming that scene between Morgantha and Aylah? That stuff about natural beauty or whatever? I swear, Wes ripped that from some reality show."

"At least the reality shows have better writing," I mutter.

She laughs, then reaches across the back seat to adjust the AC. Her hand brushes my knee on its way to the panel, and even though I'm wearing jeans, heat shoots up my leg. My cheeks redden. I turn to stare out the rain-streaked car window, hiding the blush instinctively.

Her reflection's smile widens when she thinks I can't see her. My heart swells against my lungs until I'm not sure how to breathe. *What's wrong with me?* It's like having a panic attack while eating whipped cream, scary and delicious all at once. I'm not supposed to feel this way about Greta. I'm not supposed to be anything to her but a coworker, a fellow actor in a complicated piece of performance art.

But nothing in my life is doing what it's supposed to do.

A crowd waits for us just outside the news studio, pressed back against the whitewash-and-brick walls. It's like the one I saw back in LA after Episode Three aired, but bigger and louder. Girls in raincoats, umbrellas flying back in the wind, hoisting rainbow-painted banners and chanting "Morganetta" so loud I can hear them inside the car.

They're here for us. Or at least the version of us they think we are. And I can't help but smile as I step outside to join them. Peter and Wes's bullshit weighs me down like an anchor, but I'm not putting up with it for myself. I'm doing it for my community. My art matters to them.

"Lily!" they shout as I slide out under a waiting umbrella. It's the wrong name, but the right welcome, and it cuts through the storm like a lighthouse beam.

"Come on," I tell Greta, pointing at the girls on the sidewalk.

"They came out in the rain to see us. Let's go say hello."

"What if I let them down?" she whispers. "What if I'm not the right kind of queer for them to like me? I haven't done . . . like, you know. That."

I pick up her meaning from her tone. "You mean, like, having sex with a girl? Neither have I! Or, like, anyone."

Her jaw drops. "You mean, you never? Like never?"

"It's hard to find someone to, like, even kiss you when your whole life is directors calling you up to set and your mom notices everything. That doesn't matter. Queer community shouldn't be about sex. It's about people. I'm the person inviting you in." I offer her my hand.

And when she slips her fingers into mine, it doesn't feel fake at all.

We rush over and into the crush of bodies. Girls reach for our hands and rain-slicked jackets. I whip out an emergency Sharpie for Greta and we're signing posters, jackets, arms. I try to make my writing neat, since I know some of them will rush off to get the signature tattooed in.

"This is sort of incredible," Greta says, grinning at me. Rain has flattened her hair against her freckled cheeks. Her mascara runs in thick lines. My heart swells against my ribs, all at once massive and aching and weird. For an instant, I let myself believe in this magic we're creating together.

"Miss Ashton!" A burly security guard squeezes my upper arm. It takes me a minute to realize they've been calling for me, that everyone looks at me and sees a "Miss." My heart sinks as I duck into the safety of the studio.

One distracted whirl through hair and makeup later, and Greta and I sit across from entertainment journalist Anjana Gupta, cameras glaring in our faces. She asks how we find the weather, and we make the usual jokes about being from a desert where it never rains—I mime drowning under an open sky. Then she asks if it's strange working on set as a couple. Thankfully, this doesn't feel like an awkward discussion to have with her—Anjana's openly bi and marches at the head of the Belfast Pride parade every year. It's only when we get to the meat of the interview that my stomach starts churning.

Because when something good happens in gay pop culture, everyone assumes it won't last.

"Recently," Anjana says, "the superhero show *Eagle Eye* came under fire for killing off its only gay character—Condor Man, who many fans hoped was being positioned as Eagle Eye's eventual love interest. Morgantha and Alietta's on-screen love story is an inspiration to many queer viewers around the world. But you're also starring on a show notorious for killing off main characters. Do you have anything to say to the viewers who worry one of the few pieces of on-screen representation they have will be snatched away?"

"I think," Greta says, weighing her words with a caution I doubt anyone who doesn't know her as well as I will notice, "that it's an honor to be part of this story line. It's been incredible to meet the fans it means so much to. It really has opened my eyes to so many things I've been missing."

It's a good answer. And it feels honest, one of the small honest things she can say. But I'm not sure it's enough for our fans. Nothing could ever feel good enough for them.

"Lily?" Anjana asks. "What do you say?"

*That Lily isn't someone I want to be anymore.* Those words seem to dry up on my tongue. Lily is who everyone here wants me to be. Morgantha is who everyone wants.

"I promise," I say, facing the camera. Studio lights blare in my eyes. I push words past the lump in my throat. I need to mean this. Those girls outside need to know I mean this. "Nothing like that will happen on *Galaxy Spark* as long as I've got any say in it."

"Well," Greta says, hurrying in to do damage control, "we trust the showrunners and their vision for the characters. We obviously don't have any control over the story. We're just actors."

Something defeated lingers in her words. I can't stand it. I need to do something, no matter how scary it seems. To give them what they want. To give us a way forward.

"I'm not just any actor," I say. "I'm Morgantha. And I'm brave enough to stand up for myself."

The studio goes quiet, save for the ever-present hot hum of the lights above.

"Well," Anjana says quietly, "it sounds like your fans aren't the only girls inspired by Morgantha's example."

I'm not sure if she means that as a question, or if my sudden declaration accidentally knocked her brain out of interview mode. But I nod, because yes is an easy answer to give.

Because if I could only be what she saw me as, I can't help but feel that alone would be enough to save our ship.

When I slide back in the car, my rush of courage has already worn thin. It doesn't help that Greta, sitting across from me, has twisted her lips into thin, angry lines as she stares out the window. The rain's stopped, but the gray sky promises it'll come and come again. I flick the window up and down aimlessly until she grunts and says, "Stop that."

"Sorry," I say, habitually apologizing, taking my hand off the switch. "I meant what I said in there, Greta. I'm not giving up on us." By *us*, I mean #Morganetta, but that should be obvious. Those girls outside the studio, the crowd at our fitting in LA—the most meaningful thing we've done together has been playing these parts.

"Which us?" That comes out sharp and briny, like the ocean at night. Like the slap of a cold wave. "The us we pretended to be back in there, or the us where you promised you wouldn't push your campaign to save #Morganetta past the point I was comfortable going? The fake us, or the real us?"

That's what she's so mad about? "Seriously? I meant, like, I wouldn't break into Peter's office. I just made a statement on TV. That's, like, the bare minimum."

"It doesn't matter. You didn't give me a heads-up. You didn't trust me to help plan what you were going to say and what the fallout would be. You're acting like you're the star of a one-man show, and nothing you do matters because Kate can rescue you from whatever mess you make. But you're not in this alone. And if you fuck up, it has consequences for me, too! How are you so selfish you care more about a fictional relationship than my real life?"

"You think I'm selfish?" I say. "Ever since you read that script, you've been focused on nothing but salvaging your career. So your mom won't make you go to college, which, by the way, is an opportunity millions of people would be grateful for. You're not the only super-privileged person in this fucking limousine! What about all those girls cheering for us, who want us to succeed? Who need something to show them that they can have a happy ending? At least I'm trying to do something with what I've got, instead of saving my own ass."

"I'm not going to apologize for caring about my career. What matters here is you act like my friend, but don't trust me—"

"What matters isn't us!" I shout. "Jesus Christ, Greta, we're just two people. What you want, what I want, isn't important when a whole community wants us to be this thing."

"Aren't we part of that community? Isn't that what you told me earlier when you led me out into the crowd?"

She is. But I'm not sure what identities I can claim right now. If I don't relate to my identity in the same way I once did, does that mean my place in the queer community has changed? I'm a mess of contradictions, an imposter pretending to be a queer girl because that's easy, a simple answer. Better to focus on the show and the story. Because a happy ending in real life feels like the most impossible thing of all.

"The thing you don't understand about me," I say, "the thing no one understands, is that being Lily Ashton means I can't be anything else, even if I want to be."

Back in the safety of my hotel room, dysphoria climbs back over me with a pulsating, ugly vengeance. I pull on the oversized UCLA sweatshirt I stole from Will's drawer and bury myself in its bulk. Curling up in the bed, I flip through old sitcoms on my phone—but just as the *Parks and Rec* theme song plays, I glimpse the corner of my face reflected in my phone and cringe inside. Round and small and awful. Everything is awful.

It's like I'm not myself. Or like myself isn't a person at all, just an empty hole.

I stick my phone under my pillow, curl up in my blankets and sweatshirt, and cry.

I don't know how long I lie there, shaking and trembling. Part of me thinks I should open up my computer and log in to *Swordquest Online*, flinging myself into the world where I get to be me. But I don't have the energy. All this trying I'm doing— trying to be normal, trying to pretend, trying to be the person everyone wants and needs me to be—has worn me down like an overused crayon.

Someone's knocking on the door. I dry my tears on a fancy towel and open it. Chris and Callie stand on the far side.

"Hey." Callie offers me a short, rueful smile. "I saw that

mess in your Quicshot mentions today. I'm sorry. People can be awful."

"You want to talk?" Chris says, offering me a carton of ice cream. "I heard you crying. Sounds like you need the help."

I throw my arms around him. "I have something important to tell you."

# Twelve

Coming out to Chris is easier than I thought. He's a good listener, which helps—just lets me go, and hugs me, and waits until I pause to ask questions like *Okay, so explain nonbinary again?*

Callie, however, is another matter. She quit social media after getting in a flame war with a Republican senator, and she doesn't quite have the vocabulary most people pick up on the internet. Maybe I should have waited until Chris and I were alone, but I couldn't—couldn't hold the words in once I'd given them permission to spill out.

"So, you're like that prisoner lady on *Breakaway?*" she attempts. "But, like, you want to go the other direction."

"Maybe?" I rub angry, frustrated tears off my cheeks, then wrap my arms tighter around the pillow I'm hugging.

"How can you not know? Isn't the whole point of being trans that you one hundred percent know you were born in the wrong body?"

I wince. To transition, to go through what so many trans people have done just to be themselves—it doesn't feel like something you can do halfway, wave off as *whatever*. How can you take that path if you're not one hundred percent sure?

Oh, fuck. What if I'm not really trans? What if I'm just a mess? A stupid girl who doesn't know who she is—but that *she* catches on the gears of my brain like a pebble in an engine block, and I can't escape how it jams up my brain like Silly Putty.

"Come on, Callie," Chris says, warmly but firmly putting up a line. "Let them be. They're having a tough night." I realize that, without asking, he's shifted to a neutral pronoun, and it feels so good and safe. Better than all the warm blankets around me.

"Thank you," I mutter.

"I'm sorry for not listening," he says.

"I'm sorry for stealing your body wash. And for raiding your closet. And Will's closet."

"At least you replaced the body wash," he says. "I think Kate's just glad all my dad's ratty college stuff is gone. Do you have another name you'd prefer?"

"Frey," I say before I can think twice. My cheeks are already burning, but heck—I guess they don't have to know it comes from a video game, right? And it's already the name I feel represents me best.

"Frey," Chris says. "I like it."

"Y'know," Callie says, sitting up on the bed beside me, "I

think I know something that might help, Frey. Give me five."

She ducks out of the room. While she's gone, I turn to Chris. I'm worried about him. "Did your socials also go nuts?"

He nods. "Kate let me know she hired a social media manager to watch my feeds so I don't have to deal with racist harassment. So that was a . . . weird way to wake up. I texted Reggie about it, and he said he hasn't looked at his own social media in three years."

"Lucky him."

"Yeah. Everyone expects a lot from us online. More than one person can give. So I guess I might as well have more than one person working on my brand. I wish Amanda Wells had that."

I nod. We both fall silent for a moment.

"Hey!" Callie slides back through the door, holding up an electric razor. "Let's see if I remember how to style with this thing."

"Go on," Chris says, eyebrow arching. "I'll watch. You two figure it out."

For the first time all night, a smile spreads across my face.

When Natalie sees me enter hair and makeup the next morning, her eyes practically leap from her skull.

"I see you've had your morning coffee," I say, dropping down in my usual chair. This time, I can meet the eyes of my own reflection and even grin at myself. I don't quite see Frey in the mirror, but I also don't see a lie. With half my hair gone, sides shaved flat and the top only a few inches long, floppy, I feel like I've let out a breath I didn't know I was holding.

Like I'm human. And welcome.

"How are we going to fit on your wig?" Natalie asks.

Oh. I didn't really think about this before giving Callie the go-ahead. A wave of shame threatens to knock me sideways— but my hair never felt like part of me until right now. I wish I'd given Natalie a heads-up, but I won't apologize for cutting it. I feel a million pounds lighter. The itch of wrongness isn't gone, but it's less painful now I know I can do something about it.

"Use extra glue?" I suggest, and Natalie scoffs and rushes off to get another tech.

A full pot of glue later, and I'm Morgantha, complete with black curls and thick eyeliner. Dysphoric prickles start sweeping back over me. I stare at myself in the mirror and tell myself this is the character I love. A girl with a blasting pistol and a stellar sword, a girl who single-handedly saved a whole planet once, a girl who cares nothing for the patriarchy or anything she can't slash apart.

But Morgantha is still a girl. Hearing Chris take that label off me last night made it clear how much I want it gone. And Callie's clueless questions made me despair that it would ever go away.

I'm twenty minutes late to the set, and my head is spinning from the smell of costume glue. But I make it, and join a bleary-eyed Chris, who's downing a cup of coffee the size of his head.

"Everyone's upset about your hair," Greta warns me as I run up, cape swishing behind me. "You've put everyone behind. It's not professional."

"I wasn't thinking," I say. "I'm sorry. I wanted to do something different with my look, and I went for it. An impulse, I guess. I'm sorry."

"Let us know in advance next time," Peter says, walking by my chair. "I'll shave mine to match."

I roll my eyes at the corny joke. "Did you read that article I sent you?"

"Huh?"

"The one about Alban's death in Season Five, and about how the show centers a white heroine—"

"Oh, that," he says quickly. Too quickly. "Okay, no. Sorry. I've been busy."

He doesn't sound busy. He sounds guilty. Because the article calls us out? I mean, I felt sort of ashamed reading it—but white guilt isn't productive. It just splashes your responsibilities onto people of color. We have a lot of work to do, both in this season we're shooting, and in future seasons. We need to roll up our sleeves and get to it.

"Busy with what?" I say. "Rewriting the script to keep Alietta alive? Because I think we need to change a lot more than one scene—"

"Lily, Greta, about the Alietta thing—" He sucks in a deep breath. "It stays in."

"Huh?" I shake my head. Like I've got wig glue plugging

my ears. Almost nothing in the Season Six scripts should stay. I don't know what he means.

Or maybe I just don't want to believe him.

"It stays in. I've been thinking for weeks about the best way to make Morgantha grow up. Just like Wes said: this is the only thing that can drive her to become the leader House Moonblade needs."

"Oh," Greta says, voice wooden. Quiet in a way that makes my teeth itch. Because she doesn't feel like she has the power to say anything else. "Okay."

"Not okay," I say. Too loud. The makeup techs give me a weird look. "I'm not sure we even need to push her in that direction. I mean, Bryken is the rightful heir to House Moonblade. And he's way more chill and grown-up than Morgantha. I know who I'd vote for."

"Space isn't a democracy." Peter gives an awkward laugh. "Morgantha is the hero. It's sort of expected she'll rule the galaxy in the end."

"Since when does the story have to have a single hero?" I shake my head. I don't want to get distracted. Beside me, Greta's gone stiff and pale as a Popsicle. Freezing up because she doesn't want to get a reputation as someone who argues with showrunners. I can take that risk. I need to take that risk. "Worrying about story stuff is Wes's thing. Come on. What's really going on? You owe me an honest answer."

"I don't owe you shit."

Anger flashes behind his words. Like his pleasant smile is

green-screened on. I've never heard anyone speak to me that way outside a scene.

Something's changed between us. And I don't like it at all.

"Is this about the phone calls yesterday?" I say. "The job offers you got?"

Peter nods. "I'm the twists-and-turns guy. My brand is in high demand right now, from people with even more power in this industry than Kate Ashton. No offense," he adds on. Like that's what's going to offend me. "Come on. Alietta's death will be great TV. Greta will give a great performance, and I'll get to show everyone I can keep the twists coming."

I meet Greta's eyes, arch my brow. A silent question. *Are you okay with me pushing harder?* She says nothing but twitches her lips in a half smile. *Go for it.*

"So you're killing her off anyway," I say. "Like you didn't see all those fans at the costume fitting. Like you don't care what this means to people?"

"Like you don't care what this means to me?" He frowns. "The next step in my career, more opportunities to provide for my family? I thought you'd be happy for me."

"Dude, I want you to succeed. But not like this. It's wrong."

He rolls his eyes. "Look, Lily, I don't mind helping you out, but this is television. A business. Not a moral crusade. And you can't honestly tell me your motives are totally pure." He shakes his head. "Admit it. You just want to keep your girlfriend on set."

My mouth drops open. Too stunned to respond.

"Be more like Greta," he says, already walking away. "She's professional. She doesn't make trouble."

Greta doesn't say another word before ducking away to the privacy of her trailer, brown eyes narrowed, massive blond wig swishing imperiously behind her. I watch her go. If we were really dating, I'd go after her, but she clearly wants a little peace and quiet while waiting to be called up to film. Especially when the alternative is hanging out with the person she had a massive argument with last night. But I feel a little lonelier without her all the same.

*Tight schedule.* Alietta's death scene films in just a few days. Greta's losing her job. The fans are losing their hope.

And the little voice in my head screams it's all my fault. For trusting the wrong people. For thinking Peter's friendliness to me meant he cared about all queer people, instead of just one rich white kid whose mom knows half of Hollywood.

I stumble through the rest of my scenes that day in a haze, head spinning through lines I barely track. At last, I can rush back to my hotel room. My laptop hums to life beneath my fingers. I can't stay away long from a body that fits me wrong and a world that wants me crumbled. But once my headset is on tight and the *Swordquest Online* music ripples in my ears, I can pretend this is just a normal day.

"PvP?" Aida asks when she logs on, just minutes behind me. Somehow, she knows exactly the right thing to cheer me up after an awful day.

"Let's go kick some ass," I say, and three minutes later, we're defending a cliffside fortress from an army of trolls with the aid of giant, deadly rainbow glitter cannons.

"I love this level," Aida says. "It reminds me of the time me and my friends snuck out to the Pride parade in NYC."

"That sounds awesome!" I say, and throw a Carp Grenade on the advancing enemy players. It's a joke item that does nothing but turn them into flopping carp for three seconds— but just imagining the looks on their faces, scattered all around the globe, is priceless. "I'd love to go to Pride. My mom says I've got to wait until I'm eighteen. She's, like, scared I'll try to jump onto a float or a firetruck."

"I can see that," she says. "God, Frey. You're such a teenage boy."

I grin. Warmth seeps from my heart to the pit of my stomach and down, tingling, through my legs. It's more than just being seen as a guy—it's being seen by her. Being welcomed in with open arms. Being part of something.

"Not that I mind," Aida says quickly. "All my brothers were teen boys once, and they turned out okay. Not that you're like a brother to me, it's just— Fuck, I don't even know what to say. I just want to say the right thing to make you feel affirmed."

I throw a Carp Grenade at her. Her avatar morphs into a flopping fish on the parapet. "Count me affirmed."

My phone buzzes beside my laptop. My heart jumps. Kate has texted me: *I heard there was drama on set today. Everything okay?*

The twisty knot of my guts goes slacker. I pick up the phone, about to let her know every shitty thing that happened, when she adds, *Did you really cut your hair? I wanted you to go blond for Ann Elise.*

I roll my eyes. Of course that's her priority. For a moment, I consider asking for her advice on how to deal with Peter and his obstinacy—but what if she tells me to stop pushing back? Worse, what if she pulls another move like with the Motorcycle Incident, constructs another scheme to protect my image? Kate keeps her eye on the bottom line. She may have activist friends and causes she funds, but she didn't become who she is by taking risks to help people. And that certainly isn't in her plans for me.

*It'll grow back soon,* I text instead.

The screen flashes. Enemy players charge against the fort. I curse, shooting traps and arrows as they approach the narrow entranceway—but we're outnumbered. A druid in the form of a giant ox tramples me, and I'm down for the count. Aida crumples to the ground beside me. Thankfully, in close-quarters combat, we only stay dead for ten seconds before we pop back up again, alive. Ten seconds feels like agony when you're watching your teammates fall and your enemies snatch your flag, but it's nothing at all in the great span of life.

Ten seconds is less time than it takes for Morgantha to kiss Alietta in Episode Three. Less than it took for me to ruin my newfound friendship with Greta in that interview. I wonder how long it would take to tell Kate I'm not a girl. I wonder if it would feel this agonizing.

"You're the first one who knew I was trans," I confess as we pop back to life and speed away from the fort, seeking cover. A moment of peace so my heart doesn't skitter outside my chest. "It doesn't feel real anywhere but here. I don't feel real. And I know that's stupid because it's just my gender people don't know about me; it's just this one thing—but if no one knows who you are, are you really a person? Or just an empty place for people to put their own ideas about who they think you should be?"

"That sounds really tough," Aida says. "I wish I knew the right thing to say. I'm sure a lot of trans people feel that exact same thing."

We turn around the curve of a mountain peak. The virtual sunset hits at full blast, sparkling up the snow and painting the misty sky diffuse orange. It's only an image, but it still takes my breath away.

"Having you around is right enough," I say. I hope the meaning carries through my voice mods. I wish my character had an animation option to take her character's hand.

She laughs nervously. Like she's sitting atop words too big to easily fit through her mouth. "I'm really glad I know you, Frey. I'm glad we have this place where we can hang out. Just the two of us. It's really special to me."

*Frey.* She's speaking to me, the real me, in a way that touches me down in my gut. Like the clouds have parted and a real ray of sunshine has swept in.

"When you're in LA next," I say before I can outthink

myself, "we should meet up and hang out. Go to the beach, grab dinner, see a movie—I mean, if you like movies—" I'm babbling now. I want to work the word *date* in there, but I'm suddenly a huge coward.

"I like movies," Aida says. "It's a da— I mean, let's make a day of it."

Did she mean *date*? I think she meant to say *date*. But she stopped herself. Because she doesn't like me? Because she's scared?

Her character goes still. Her comms cut out suddenly. I give her a few minutes, but she doesn't come back online. Maybe she's having internet problems? I teleport to the underground market and start selling off the ore I gathered this week. Aida will send me a message once her Wi-Fi is fixed.

And she said yes. I almost giggle, thinking it over. She said *yes*.

I can figure out if it's a date once I meet her in person.

Five new messages from Kate wait on my phone. Asking about my hair, my schedule, my fake dates with Greta. Not one question about me. I always tease Greta for her strict devotion to professionalism, but Kate acts like we're working even when she's trying to yell at me.

I love my mom. I really do. I know she works her hardest to protect my career so I can advance, so I can have the life she wants for me. I know none of this is personal and she's not doing this to spite me.

I just. You know. Want a mom whose first priority is how

I feel. A boss can fire you. Abandon you. But a mom has to listen, even when you're saying something she doesn't want to hear. Like I need help. Like I feel lost.

Like I'm not actually a girl after all.

A soft knock comes on my hotel room door.

"What's that about?" Greta asks when I open it, eyes flicking like X-ray scanners down the *Swordquest Online* T-shirt I'm wearing. Part of me almost wishes she could see right through me, like Superman. Make existing easier. Let me be open. "Do you game?"

"It's just something I got at a con," I say, changing the subject. I don't want any of my cooler cast mates learning about my nerdy hobby. "What's going on?"

"Kate texted me." Of course. She went to Greta when I didn't reply. "She heard there was some drama on the set about your hair and wants us to go out and be photographed so the fans have something else to talk about. She said she doesn't want Lara Brown thinking you're hard to work with."

"Why can't she just ground me if she's mad?" I roll my eyes. "I mean, I shouldn't complain. Your mom is trying to drag you back to Pennsylvania the first chance she gets."

"She just wants what's best for me."

"Nuh-uh. You want what's best for you. And you're you, so you know what that is best of anyone. Don't let her get under your skin."

Greta smiles. "God, just when I think you're an obnoxious, clueless little twerp, you say something charming like that."

"I'm an incredibly charming person." I wink at her and then remember what I need to say. "Greta, I'm so sorry for arguing with you on our way back from the BBC interview. I said the first thing that popped into my head, because I felt responsible for the ship and the fandom. But I'm also responsible for you—I mean us. As a team. Like we decided to be." *Way to go, Mr. Charming.*

"That interviewer put us all on the spot," Greta says. "Like, we're not the writers. Neither of us had good answers to give."

"I just . . . I don't know. We're sort of stuck together, and I want you to feel comfortable hanging out with me, even if you think I'm obnoxious."

"Dude, I'm my own person. If I didn't feel comfortable doing this, I'd walk away." She shakes her head. "And I'm sorry I got so mad about the hair stuff this morning. It's your body; you can do what you want with it. Now that I can see it up close, it looks cool."

Greta thinks my hair is cool. Greta thinks my hair is cool. My heart skips a beat—and then it slides away. I want to hear someone tell me my hair's cool. But I want to hear it from someone who genuinely likes me. And Greta never will, not in a million years, even if we hadn't fought after the interview— because she can't like the real me. No one can. Only a handful of people even know I'm there.

"Here's the list of sanctioned dates," Greta says, handing over her phone. "Pick a place we can spend at least two hours. I don't like this either, but we've got no choice. At least we can get a decent dinner out of it."

I look over the list of Kate-approved date venues. Nice restaurants near the center of town, *NO DRINKING* typed in all caps. There's even a list of approved outfits—for me, not Greta. I guess she trusts Greta.

"Can I touch your hair?" Greta asks. "Um. Sorry. I know that sounds weird. It just looks really fluffy and soft—"

I shrug and sort of lean into her hand. She pets the top of my head, and a shiver runs down from my temples to my tiptoes. I've never had anyone touch me this long when it wasn't a scene, and it's electric, and strange. I never want her to stop, and I don't know why. Because it's literally just my head, and Greta and I almost chewed each other open last time we were at arm's reach.

*Keep it together, Frey. Focus. You have a job to do. Kate's orders.*

Only, suddenly, I don't need to follow them to the letter. Kate is a whole world away. I want to feel like a real person, and that means doing something real. Even if it gets me in trouble. *I should ditch Greta. Go back to* Swordquest. But this fake date will help #Morganetta. And if Aida's still offline . . . I want to give Greta a chance to touch my hair again. I want to see what happens after that.

"Hey," I say. Take a deep breath and try to deepen my voice a little. "Fuck the list. Let's go have an adventure."

# Thirteen

Greta's eyes flicker wide, but she does say, "Yeah. Sure." I pull on Will's borrowed/stolen sweatshirt and a loose pair of jeans, covering up the outline of my body. Greta throws on a heavy sweater and a pair of dark sunglasses. I google *gay bars Belfast* and pick the least-assuming pub. Greta calls hotel security and says we'll leave for our date in an hour. Instead, we sneak out early and text our driver to meet us in the empty lot across the street.

I feel like James Bond.

The bar, an out-of-the way spot named Rowdy Rory's, sits wedged between a closed tailor's shop and a convenience store downtown. Our driver gives us a strange look as he pulls up and parks, but doesn't correct us or tell us we're not supposed to be here. That's nice. It isn't any of his business.

The bar is dark on the inside, weathered wood and musty air, but lit by neon rainbow lights that streak by overhead. The dark room is filled with older men and a few older women, gray streaks in their hair. Greta and I shoot each other nervous glances like tiny lightning bolts zigzagging between us. Do we belong here? But then I straighten my spine and pull all of Morgantha's confidence over me like a blanket, and swagger up to the bar.

"Two pints of Doom Bars," I say, sliding into a stool. The bartender gives me a look. The drinking age here is only eighteen, but I guess I'm on the edge, because he looks at me and huffs, "Try mother's milk."

Greta shoulders up to the bar a few people down from me and repeats the order, with much more success. She brings me the beer, and we sneak off into a side corner. Seventies disco hits play softly from a speaker. Two men who must have been our age when those songs came out sway quietly in each other's arms, heads low and foreheads pressing together, but no one else is dancing.

Oh, god. I've brought Greta somewhere lame. She's going to hate me forever for this.

"This is . . . different," she says, taking a big gulp of her beer. "I sort of like it, though. It reminds me of the bar my big brother snuck me into once back home."

"Is your brother gay?"

She almost spits out her beer. "God, I wish. I didn't mean, like, gay bars. Just, this place is a total dive. And I like that." She scuffs her foot on the ground. "There's even beer stains on the floor."

"Did your parents catch your brother and you?"

"Nope. But I almost wish they had. God. Mom and Dad want me to be their picture-perfect heterosexual grandkid-making, money-earning daughter, and I can't—they want so much, and it's not me, and fuck that shit. Sometimes I want to scream in their faces, but I don't. I never do." She punctuates her point with a deep swig. "You know what the real difference between you and me is, Lily? It's not that I'm more professional or anything. I just make choices about when and where I tell people what I really think about them. A skill you apparently have no interest in learning."

I wince. "You're right. I'm not an expert in how other people feel. I'd probably have a real girlfriend if I was, instead of a fake date with expert knowledge of all my fuckups."

"I didn't mean it like that," Greta says. "Er. I'm going to the bathroom. Be right back."

She stands and heads to the rear of the bar. I watch her go, awed by her fearlessness. How she seems to have figured out everything I struggle with, and more besides. She's effortlessly cool and effortlessly real, and all I want is to be effortlessly cool beside her.

Before, I might have defined that feeling as jealousy, but it isn't, not really.

"Aren't you a bit young to be drinking, lad?" An older man, blond hair gone to salt, claps me on the shoulder. "You're what? Twelve? Thirteen? Does your mum know you're out?"

*He thinks I'm a boy.* A thrilling shiver runs up my spine. A light flashing on from all corners of the stage in my head. Like

I'm being seen. Like a great, heavenly spotlight is finally sliding my way. "She doesn't," I say, careful to keep my voice low. "I just wanted to be in a place that was meant for me."

He cocks his head. "American? You're a long way from home. Are you a student? Oh." He rubs his eyes. "You're the girl from that show with the evil space queen."

"No!" My voice squeaks. I tug down my hood. "I mean, yes, but no. I'm not a girl. That's why I'm here."

"Oh." He pauses. "You're one of those new folk. The nonbinary type."

"Maybe?" I squeak. I don't know about being new. Nonbinary people have always existed. Besides, after the week I've had, I feel approximately five thousand years old.

"It's good to see new types of people here," he says. "We've had a lot of dark days. Good to see there'll be another generation to take up the fights we left them."

I don't feel like a fighter. I just play one on TV. I always thought fighting would be as simple and easy as Morgantha makes it look. Stellar swords flashing, cool explosions at my back, poetry in motion. I feel less like a poem than a spattered mess on the concrete. I tried to stand up to Peter, but now I'm here, with nothing to show for it but burning cheeks and a career I might have blown up if my mom wasn't protecting me.

"Um. I hope we can do it justice?" I say. Morgantha would say something like that. Only she'd be more confident. Frey would be a little uncertain, though. I can channel Frey.

After all, there's a pretty decent chance I am him.

"So, how did you know you're nonbinary?" the older guy asks. "Just curious. I never met one."

I shiver. Not because I'm scared—it was an honestly meant question—but it feels more personal than I think he knows it is. And because I don't have an answer. Because I'm not sure. How can I put myself into words when my whole life will topple if I do?

"Aren't you a handsome lady?" says an unfamiliar voice. An arm snakes over my shoulder. I turn to see a butch woman with a tattoo sleeve, a few years my senior, breath reeking of alcohol. I've never seen her in my life.

"Nope." I try to peel the arm off my shoulder. "Nuh-uh. Pretty sure you mistook me for someone else."

"Please?" She drops her voice. "My ex is here with her new girlfriend. She'll think I'm such a fool if I came here alone."

*Oh, god.* I want to help. Like, I want to help everyone all the time. But I really don't want to get involved in strangers' personal lives. *Boundaries. I need boundaries*—but now an older woman clomps over in heavy boots, a hand on her hip.

"So that's how it is, Tally? This girl's not even in uni yet!" She turns to me, eyes narrowed in suspicion. "What are you playing at?"

"Absolutely nothing," I respond, and try to slide off my stool, back away. *Whoa.* My head spins. I didn't expect the beer to be that strong. And I definitely didn't expect to get sucked into strangers' drama.

"At least she doesn't snore like an asthmatic hippopotamus, *Hannah*," Tally says, making her ex's name sound like a curse word. "At least she doesn't forget my birthday and call me a bitch when I get pissed at her—"

*She. Her. She. Her.* God, it needles. Maybe there's something I can do to help, though. "It sounds like you two have an unhealthy codependent dynamic." I scramble to think of advice I didn't hear on a comedy podcast. "Have you tried therapy?"

"You think I'm crazy?" Hannah rolls up her sleeves. "That's it. You and me, little girl. One-on-one."

"Nope." I hold up my hands and shake my head. "You're drunk—"

"And you're a coward." She leans in. Grabs for the front of my shirt—

"Duck." Greta says from behind me, ice cold. I don't hesitate—I lower my head, and what's left of her beer sloshes out over me, hitting Tally and Hannah in the face. The feuding exes back up, stunned and cursing. "Fuck off, both of you!" Greta shouts. "We were minding our own business before you barged in!"

I slide between them—hesitate for a second, because how do I do this?—then gently grab Greta's shoulder. "Come on," I say. "We're getting out of here. Now."

She looks back and glares at me. I swallow. Oh, god. I decide there and then I never want to get on her bad side for real.

"All of you." The leather-clad bouncer smacks a heavy wooden baton against his palm. The sound it makes does all the talking for him. "Out."

# Fourteen

Greta and I make for the exit. Behind us, Hannah and Tally argue with the bouncer, words growing more heated every second. My cheeks burn as I turn and follow Greta up the street. She ducks into a shop and pops out two minutes later with a shopping bag on her arm, then keeps walking.

At the edge of town, an old railway bridge goes over a small creek. Water burbles below, and the reflection of the full moon ripples. It makes me think of our hike in Griffith Park, even though here the air is cool and moist with evening. Maybe that's for the best. That kiss wrecked my heart.

"Fuck!" Greta shouts, dramatically sprawling back on the gravel of the bridge. With one hand, she pulls a beer from the shopping bag on her arm. I bet the clerk didn't even card her.

"Yeah, fuck," I agree, dropping down beside her and grabbing another beer. The wind cuts through my sweatshirt, and part of me wants to slide an arm around her waist, but I'm scared she might evaporate into sea foam if I dare. "I didn't know you were that, uh, badass."

"People need to learn to mind their own business. I see enough weirdos with boundary issues on my social media profiles. You have to be firm sometimes. Even if it means everyone thinks you're a selfish bitch."

I run my hand over the back of my head, just so I can have something to do with my hands, shivering at the prickly, stubbly feel. Despite everything I've done to figure her out, I'm always seeing new sides of her. Realizing she's one of the most interesting people I know. "You're not selfish at all. It's okay to know who you are and want what you want. Honestly, that's what I like best about you."

"Seriously?"

"Seriously."

"Thanks." She tucks her knees under her chin, balled up at the bridge's edge. Even though she's six inches taller than me, she looks small, folded in like this. "I'm just so . . . not used to trusting people. Did I ever tell you how I knew I was queer?"

I shake my head.

"So, the summer of seventh grade, my best friend, Amy, comes to me and asks me to keep a secret. She had a crush on a girl from her soccer team. And like, before then, I didn't even know that was an option? *Gay* was a thing adults were on TV. The secret my grandparents used to whisper about my uncle Ted, who ran off to San Francisco with his boyfriend. I didn't know it was something I was allowed to be. But I knew I didn't get crushes on guys like the rest of my class all did. By the time school started, everyone in my group of friends realized they were also queer."

"That sounds great," I say. "Like something from a fanfic."

"And it was." Emphasis on the *was*. "Then I got cast as Alietta and went out to LA. I was thrilled, so thrilled, but I also missed my friends like crazy. They were the only people who knew who I was. We tried all sorts of things to keep in touch—chat groups, phone calls, gaming together—but everything just drew us further and further apart. I couldn't talk to them about school stuff; they couldn't talk to me about the show. The last time I visited home, three months ago, they wouldn't even go to Panera with me. They didn't answer any of my messages, and they didn't care when I finally removed myself from the group chat."

"Wow," I say. My fists tighten. "I'm sorry, Greta. You don't deserve that."

"You were right about me," she whispers. "I chose acting over them. I was selfish. I left them behind. It was my fault, and I shouldn't feel like you betrayed me—like, when have I ever been a person other people could stick around?"

"You're a great person. You're cute and funny and you're fun to watch movies with." I wrap an arm around her shoulder and pull her close. "You shouldn't give up your dreams for anyone, especially not people who'd treat you that badly. They sound like total jerks. I was a jerk, acting like your career doesn't matter. It does." I suck in my cheeks. "Can I trust you with a secret? I don't . . . I don't think I really care about acting. Not like you do. Maybe not at all."

Her head whips around. "You don't care about acting?"

I shrug. "I mean, it's always been part of my life. I practically grew up on a set. When they needed a kid in a shot, I was there. Like that plastic potted plant that's been in, like, every major sitcom since the eighties. And I was good enough that directors started writing me speaking roles, and . . . yeah. Acting is just there." Nothing like the rush of joy racing Peter's motorcycle down the highway. Nothing like the piercing light of the desert sun. "If anyone leaves the show, it should be me."

"I'd miss you," she says grudgingly. But she says it, and my cheeks catch on fire.

I fold my arms and kick my legs where they dangle over the bridge's side. "You deserve all the good things. Everything I was born with. Everything I'm not sure I want. Instead, you're just stuck hanging around a screwup like me."

"You're not the worst screwup in Hollywood," she mutters. "I mean, have you seen my manager? Johann can't even wipe his ass without complaining for twelve hours."

A laugh bubbles out of me, surprising and rich, splitting the night and echoing off the stars. Being with Greta feels so right, so natural. Things have always been so confusing between us. I've spent so much time thinking about where our characters could develop that I never thought about what lay between us. But what lies between us is solid and strong.

Whatever Season Six shooting brings us, we're going through it together. And that matters. It shocks me how very badly the connection between us matters. A connection as tangible as my arm around her shoulders, bright and shiny as the flutter of her red eyelashes in moonlight, the way my heart lurches when I make her laugh.

A connection that matters as much as that awkward kiss between us in Griffith Park. Feelings she made clear she doesn't share. For a girl who doesn't exist.

*Aida*, I tell myself. *I'm going to meet Aida soon.* She'll understand why I never told her about my job. She understands me in a way Greta never will. So what if I'm attracted to the girl sitting beside me? I want more than just that from a relationship. I want something real.

We don't say anything more for a long time, just drinking and waving our legs off the side of the bridge. Greta drinks more than me. I hold her hair as she throws up in a trash bin, and help her walk back through the snaking city streets, staggering along the harborside where only gulls linger. We sneak up the hotel back stairs before anyone sees. I stand in her hotel doorway, her weight leaning on my shoulders, my eyes darting everywhere but her face. I can't let her see me looking at her. I think I might explode if we keep standing this close together.

"That was fun," she says. Her breath washes over my cheeks. It smells like stale beer and a little bit of throw-up. Not her usual fruity perfume, but I don't mind. I'm sort of messy, too.

"I'm sorry." I wince. "Shit, this night was a clusterfuck. I'm not even a good fake boyfriend—I mean girlfriend."

Her eyes narrow at that, but she doesn't comment. "Well. Anyway. I had fun."

She slides into her hotel room and closes the door. I stand staring at it for far too long. Like I expect it to come to life and grant me three wishes.

Like I want something so big and meaningful it weighs down my whole heart.

It's okay. No one has to know. I'll sit on top of these feelings and push them down, like holding in my pee on a long drive. I won't let how I feel about her affect how I behave or make shooting together uncomfortable in any way. That's the absolute last thing we need.

I keep my head down and avoid Greta all through the next week of shooting. Most of the time, whenever I'm not filming, I hunker down in my trailer or hotel room. On set, I do whatever the directors say, because that's easier than getting into arguments. I hold her hand and smile at her whenever we're on camera, and she smiles back, and my heart skips every time.

*It means nothing. She won't ever love you because you're not real. Aida. Think about her. The one girl who knows you.*

I act my heart out and leave it all on the set. And when we call for the day and I walk back to my hotel, I'm playing the part of the girl who couldn't care less.

*Still need to go on your weekly Greta date!* Kate texts on Tuesday. None of the pictures from our bar trip have made the papers, which I guess I should be glad for, though part of me aches at the feeling that night never happened. Every part of my public life is arranged to fit a very specific image. I wish someone had snapped photos of us. I wish there was just one piece of real out there to balance out the lies.

*Did she show you the list of approved restaurants? I've gone to one of* them. *They have the best sea bass—you'll really love it!* Kate types. She knows I like seafood. She's trying so obviously hard that I hug my phone to my chest because it's the closest I can get to her.

*Greta's having a hard time this week,* I text back. No mention of how rough this feels for me, or how much I'd rather be playing *Swordquest Online* than dining in a five-star restaurant. *We're filming her death scene tomorrow. We'll go out after she's put that behind her.*

*Of course,* Kate answers. *Sorry, forgot about that. That's very thoughtful of you. Are you sure you don't want to make her your real girlfriend?* There's a wink emoji and a laughing emoji that follow, but I'm not sure what those imply. Is she encouraging me to ask Greta out? Does she find the idea of us dating for real hilarious? I love my mom, but she has no clue how to text.

It strikes me *I love my mom, but* is something I find myself thinking multiple times a day.

*It's not real,* I type. *None of this is real.* I'm not even real. I'm a lie in the shape of a girl, with no room to become a full person.

*Right. Well. You only need to keep doing this until we start filming the first Ann Elise movie. It'll be a good long time away from your motorcycle stunt, and then we can stage you two breaking apart.*

*Can't wait,* I start to text, but those words just feel mean inside me. Because I feel like I'm lying. I'm not playing a role at this point; I'm just lying, about who I am and what I want, even to myself.

It doesn't matter. What matters is the task ahead of me. Get through Alietta's death scene. Get through the rest of the shoot. Go home and meet Aida. Go home and start preproduction on the Ann Elise movies. Dozens of people have worked hard for years to situate me in this position. Thousands of people want to see me on-screen. This heavy, cramping weight on my chest, the pressure of no one really seeing me—it only matters to me.

And I want to matter. Not in the way Morgantha matters so much to people—because I can never hope to reach that—but matter in the same way Frey matters to the Warhawks. As part of a team, a unit working toward some common goal. I want to be a person, connected with other people, and I don't have that with anyone but my guild, and maybe with Chris when he switched pronouns for me the other night. Now I've tasted how it feels to really be alive. I want to hold on to that.

It shouldn't be this complicated just to be who I am.

# Fifteen

They make me do hair and makeup super early the next morning, that black check mark on my schedule calling me in at 5:00 a.m. Did Peter schedule me in that slot as payback for getting mad about him not changing the scripts?

And I don't know what I'll be shooting that day until an intern passes me an updated schedule. Grief stills. They want to film me weeping over Alietta's body, and they don't want to go through the trouble of making up Greta as a corpse more than once.

"It's smart," Natalie says. "That gaping wound on her chest—boy, that's tough to duplicate over multiple days. Peter will have our heads if the blood is flowing one way in today's shots and another direction in next week's."

How could these little details mean more to him than the main message the show sends? I think about all the plot holes and inconsistencies I noticed rewatching the show, how they convoluted characterization and theme for the sake of a twist.

Peter thinks people want stories that mess with their minds and hearts, but he doesn't realize that those stories have to go somewhere. Say something. Have meaning beyond just messing around.

The work behind the costumes and the sets and the makeup isn't reflected in the story. Even the work I'm putting in as an actor feels wasted. It's hard to feel like we're making art, and hard to feel proud of it. If the point is just to shock people, I could be starring in YouTube jump-scare videos and I wouldn't have to wear this heavy wig.

I was so excited, last year, to finally be shooting a role that was queer, like me. But I'm not the same person I was then, and never have I felt less like I'm doing something valuable as when I sit on the benches near the side of the soundstage, fighting the urge to run off to my trailer and hide from this mess of feelings and people.

A tech points a battery-powered fan at my face. I try not to sweat through my costume as I watch Wes explain, over and over, the expression Greta should make as she dies.

"I want your lips to make an O," he says, contorting his face. Like he's practicing making out on a basketball.

"Like this?" Greta says, and opens her mouth. Her lips have been glossed perfectly pink, and even though part of me wonders where Alietta got lipstick while fleeing for her life, part of me can't help staring and remembering how they felt on mine. The flutter. The soft breath. The way the world seems to swell up and then dim with every fake kiss.

"Like a perfect circle. Like you're shocked. Neither of you can believe what's just happened. Chris, get in there and practice the thrust."

Chris peels himself off the bleachers and walks over to the pile of rocks, dirt, and broken boards, surrounded by green screens, where another planet will be pasted in. Bright morning light streams into the soundstage. He winces as it reaches his tired eyes.

Last night, I heard him tossing and turning behind our shared wall in the hotel. At two a.m., I went to check on him. "You're not actually killing her," I said. "Peter and Wes made up their minds to kill Alietta. No one will get hurt. Greta's not going to hate you."

"Everyone's going to hate my character," Chris says. "Everyone's going to bitch about it online, and I'm going to have to answer for it, even though it wasn't my choice."

"Maybe we can talk to SAG-AFTRA?" I suggested. "If you have a union, might as well use it."

"If there were unsafe working conditions on set, maybe, or if we were being underpaid. But I don't think they've ever intervened because actors didn't want to do a scene as written. It's not a big deal."

"You deserve better."

"Oh, I know." He sighed, and *I* knew he'd felt the weight of the show's problems for a while now, from the writing to the awful wigs picked out by the mostly white hair and makeup team. I knew I hadn't been there for him, and I knew

194

I shouldn't say that, shouldn't put him in a place where he felt obligated to reassure me. I just needed to keep my eyes open and be there for him more.

I really wish I could make the world perfect, safe, and happy for everyone I love. But I can't. Not in every way that matters. I'm not even sure I can do it in the fictional world of *Galaxy Spark.*

"I'll hate myself if I let this be my story."

"It's not your whole story," I say. "It's just one show. There'll be other roles."

But will we ever be part of something as big and popular as *Galaxy Spark* again? Both of us know this matters, for the platform the show gives us. Both of us see something good and important slipping away through our fingers.

Now Chris walks over, joins Jeanine and the choreography team, and practices driving his blunted stellar sword through the air between Greta's chest and armpit. She reacts as he does, stiffening in shock and surprise, a basic acting exercise we've all done a hundred times. Act and react. Action and response.

They're really good, but I can't watch. It's like seeing all my hopes getting stabbed before me. They rehearse, and I get to hear Greta beg for her life, and I— Fuck, I should have brought my headphones. I just left them in my room to look professional. In front of a girl who I can't save or do anything to help.

"Let's do this for real!" Peter shouts enthusiastically. He's the only enthusiastic one on the stage.

"Action!" Wes calls, and the set goes quiet as fate. I wonder if he knows none of us want to be here, doing this. I wonder if he cares.

"Please," Greta says, fast and frantic and yet still crystal clear. "This isn't my uniform. I just found it. I didn't kill those villagers; I'm not—"

"That damned Vorlian accent," Chris hisses. "I hear it in my dreams. Laughing as they pull my mother away from me. Do you know what they did?"

"I'm not like them!" Greta gasps. "I lost my family in the war, too! We're the same—"

"Do you know what they did?" Chris's voice grows into a shout. "I'll give you a hint. It'll make what I do to you look like a mercy."

"Please!" Greta shouts again, and I turn my face as Chris raises his sword, because I can't keep watching. Not as two people I love suffer so Peter can add one more shocking death scene to his résumé.

Plastic clatters to the ground. I turn around and look up.

"I can't do this," Chris says, standing over his dropped stellar sword. "Nope. This is not okay."

I exhale, relieved. Thank god. We can't let this continue—

But of course it will. The show must go on, and we've got a multi-million-dollar machine breathing down our backs to make it so.

"Come on," Peter says. "I know you can do it. You were awesome in Alban's death scene in Season Five. Show us those acting chops—this is for your awards reel!"

"Bryken is a soldier, but he's not a violent man. He wouldn't do this."

"Bryken is a fictional character we made up," Peter says. A hint of anger simmers low in his voice, then bubbles up to the surface. "He does what we write him doing."

"I don't want to do this," Chris says. "You know how long a GIF lasts on the internet? This shot will follow me around my whole life."

"Everyone loves an antihero," Peter says. "Like, this might even make Bryken more popular. We're on a tight schedule. Get back to your mark and shoot the scene."

"We always leave four weeks in the filming budget in case we need to do reshoots," Chris points out. "There's room to make changes if we want to. We did that last year."

"Come on, guys," Greta says to the writers, looking up from the floor to meet their eyes. "Neither of us is comfortable shooting this. We haven't even rehearsed much, and it's really violent and messing with our heads. Maybe if we had more time to get our heads around the scene and what it means for our characters, we could get it right."

"Let's move, kids," Wes says. "The scene's on today's schedule, so we shoot it today. You're supposed to be professionals. Belly up and just do your jobs."

*Just do your jobs.* It feels like a slap across my ears—but then the echo ends, and I think, *Really, Wes and Peter?* Is that supposed to scare us? Because sure, he can fire us all and recast our roles, but the negative publicity for that move will follow the show around forever. It's our faces that sell the T-shirts, after all. Who will keep watching once we're gone? We have power here, all of us, if we're willing to use it.

I have the power. It's like I told Anjana in my interview. *I'm Morgantha. And I'm brave enough to stand up for myself.* They need me. Without Morgantha, the pop-culture phenomenon they've created ceases to exist. I can push this. If I have to. If I'm willing to face the consequences.

But is this really the fight worth fighting? Is this the thing worth risking the fallout for?

I think so. It's not just a job. These characters have become part of us. We've been playing them almost as long as we remember—they're wrapped around our lives like broken-in favorite jackets. Our characters are part of the story we tell the world about who we are. Peter and Wes may be the writers, but we've made the characters our own. It hurts like hell how they want to rip it out from us. How they don't even care.

I care. And I won't let them put my brother through something he's not okay with. I won't let Greta risk all her dreams alone. I won't let them make Greta or Chris feel uncomfortable or unsafe.

Chris is still arguing with the showrunners—well, *arguing* is the wrong word for how quiet and measured his voice is. He has every reason in the world to be pissed off, and instead he's simply explaining. He doesn't want them to see him as the angry Black man they wrote in their script. They're straight-backed, arms folded, brows furrowed. They're the ones with all the power, and they're the ones projecting they want him to shut up.

I meet Greta's eyes, wishing this was a game so I could draw her into a private voice channel and talk this through. But she gives me a small nod, and I know she gets me. In this, at least, unlike everything else in our lives and this fake connection we've manufactured between us, we sync up.

"Start filming," I mutter to one of the cameramen.

"But—"

"Trust me. Just film."

He hesitates, then presses his finger down on the red button. I unsheathe my stellar sword in a dramatic arc—a move Jeanine spent hours drilling into me—and leap off the bleachers.

"It's one of Aylah's soldiers!" I shout. "Bryken, watch out!" I barrel across the set and leap at Greta, moving my sword high like I mean to cut off her head.

But Greta knows my actions like her own. And when I cut down, she rolls out of the way.

"It's me!" she gasps, rolling up onto her feet.

"Alietta?" I stare at her, shocked, and then at the stellar sword in my hand. Like I can't believe I'm holding it. The moment hovers, drawn out, tense—and then I drop the weapon. "I can't believe—it's you. I—I . . ."

I bite my tongue. There's nothing more Morgantha can say here, but Greta knows that. She picks up the thread I'm offering her.

"Your anger has blinded you, Morgantha!" she shouts. "I

didn't know you were this wrathful. I don't want to be with you like this!"

"Are you ending things with me?"

"I'm ending things with the person I thought you were. But you were never really her! I never realized who you were until just now!"

Her anger lands like a slap across the face, vivid and captivating and raw. And a little too close for me to feel I'm just acting.

"Cut!" Wes shouts, throat as grumpy if he'd just chomped a cigarette. "I said cut!" His anger isn't pointed at us, but the bank of screens he's following the shoot on.

Because we've just given the performance of a lifetime and he only had one camera rolling to catch it.

He's still panting, red-faced, angry. We defied him. But we gave him something, too. A flash of the twisty drama *Galaxy Spark* is famous for. An idea he can ride all the way to headlines and awards.

"Don't you think it makes more sense this way?" I whisk my tongue around my mouth. Try to drum up more saliva, more sound, in a throat half-dead from nerves. "Morgantha has anger-management issues, right? That's why she's so popular. It's okay for both girls and guys to like her because she deals with her problems like a guy." A toxic, stereotypical guy. "If she takes a dark turn and messes up her relationship with Alietta, it'll be the sort of plot twist that gets the whole internet talking about her." Because everyone online talks about Morgantha, loves Morgantha. She's written to be the most popular one on the show.

"Seriously, Lily?" Peter says, but Wes holds up a hand to stop him.

"Let her speak," he says. I'm so focused that, for once, even the sting of wrong pronouns doesn't slow me down.

"You said it yourself, Wes. Morgantha needs a challenge to grow up. Why can't her challenge be learning to fix her relationship with Alietta and deal with her temper? Everyone expects her story to be about slaughtering her way across the cosmos to avenge her father and overthrow the evil queen. Instead, it can be about learning and growing while Bryken takes on that role. No one expects it. What could be a bigger twist?"

Wes lowers his head. Stares at the script in his hands, the screens showing off different camera angles. The set falls quiet as we wait for his call.

"Look," Wes finally says. "I always knew I got into this business because of my dad's connections. And I told myself I'd learn to write as good as anyone else to earn my spot here. But that article you forwarded me, Lily . . . there's shit I'm not seeing, that I need to see to do my job well. So let's have a conversation about the script issues, and we'll fix it. Cut the bad scenes, write some better ones. Easier than everyone getting all upset."

Easy. For Wes, learning about his privilege and his place in the world will take thought, education, reflection. And taking action to right systemic inequality in Hollywood will mean standing up and saying uncomfortable things to the men who gave him a career. I'm not sure that's easy. It'll sure take more than one conversation to fix.

Wes stands and nods to the camera team. "Take an early lunch. I need to talk with my team." Peter shoots me a death glare as Wes pulls him in. The two showrunners draw together in a tight knot, talking about shooting schedules, plot lines, character arcs. Everything we wanted them talking about in the first place. I wait for the rush of victory, for the thrill that makes our win real. But Greta can't take her eyes off them, nervously chewing her lip, and Chris only squeezes my shoulder and mutters, "Thanks for backing me up."

"Thanks for starting it," I say.

Because we all know this doesn't make anything okay.

We've changed the story.

But we have way more work to genuinely make it better.

# Sixteen

Wes's makeshift office is in his and Peter's trailer, a cramped, orange-carpeted camper from the 80s that smells of tuna salad and coffee. We gather on the folding chairs spread around his desk. Three open laptop screens separate him from us as we all do our best to distill the whole unfair history of American film and television into an action plan.

". . . and you know I've always taken the representation of racial minorities seriously," Wes says. "With my father so sick, and Peter dealing with his new baby, we've both been stretched thin."

Chris nods along, in a way I can tell he's done before. He's heard this stuff, if not from Wes then from other white directors and writers he's worked with. "Hey, there's no shame in needing help with your work. You and Peter are only two people." He taps his phone screen. Wes's computers beep. "I just emailed you the résumés and contact info for six Black staff writers. They're all available for work in the next few months.

And I know you're busy, man, so I'll just go ahead and coordinate the interview dates with your assistants."

"Good, good," Wes says, sounding relieved. "Interviews. That'd help. And what about you?" He turns to Greta. "I know you've been quieter about all this—"

"Because I haven't known how much I could say," she answers. "But it hurt, learning you wanted Alietta gone. It felt like you'd sided with the men who trash my character and harass me online. You created this character and you hired me to play her—I deserve better than for you to throw me away."

"I hope you all know none of this was purposeful or intentional." Wes leans into that point. I'm not sure how much his intentions matter. "We didn't mean to . . . to hurt feelings. We're on top of this now, and we're going to do better."

His phone buzzes. "Hold up," says Wes, and fumbles in his pocket.

I squeeze my fists in my lap and will myself not to say anything sarcastic. It's like we've been teleported to a TikTok star's apology video for using a slur. *Next he'll say, "I was barely forty-six when I wrote the pilot episode! So young and naive!"*

"*God.*" Wes makes a strangled sound. His phone drops from his hand. The upside-down text message is brief:

*Mom: He passed in his sleep.*


As Wes sinks down behind his desk, we three mutter polite excuses and duck outside. The brightness of day and the crisp grass seems oddly out of place with the weight of the moment.

Even the bustle of the crew feels slower right now.

"You were really brave in there—" I start saying to Chris.

"Nuh-uh." He shakes his head. I hold my words, nod, and step aside as he walks off toward the soundstage. He'll probably go call his dad, or Shyanne—we're family, but I don't think talking to a white person will help him feel better.

Greta flags down the shuttle bus to the hotel. I stumble on board behind her. We slide past some lighting techs and an apprentice carrying a whole box of model spaceships, and collapse in a seat together. My head flops down on her shoulder. I should move, but I don't. *We're in public*, I tell myself. So it's okay to pretend.

"Thanks," Greta says. "I . . . I didn't realize how much I needed to get that off my chest. Let loose at Wes a little."

"It was very impressive," I say. "He looked like he'd swallowed bees."

"Do you think Chris is okay?"

"No," I say. "I mean not as okay as I wish he could be. Not in a way that means he can feel as comfortable on set as we do. But he has a good support network, with Will and Kate in his corner." The bus pulls up outside the hotel. "Do you want . . . ?" I start, and pause, because I don't know what comes next.

"I really need to rest," she says, and stands. My head slides off her shoulder.

"Me too," I say, and we're split up as the apprentice with the model spaceships sets the prop box down between us to answer his ringing phone. Awkward. Separate. Like the people we really are, underneath it all.

My phone buzzes as I ride the elevator to my room. An email from Peter. Wes is flying home to be with his family. Peter is going to rewrite the Season Six scripts. More writers will be hired for next year—god, I hope they actually reach out to Chris's contacts. I email Peter and volunteer to help consult on the script as he writes.

*It's my story,* he writes back. *I'll fix it. Wes wants it done fast.*

*How fast? This work needs care and thought.*

*As fast as it goddamn needs to be. This isn't your job, kid. Stop bothering me so I can do my job.*

I roll my eyes and shove my phone back in my pocket. He's acting like he's the hero in a war movie, taking a bullet in a grand act of sacrifice. I get he's stressed out, but he's making this all about himself. All I've ever tried to do is show him why it matters to other people.

I'm tired. Not just from getting up early, but from worrying. From carrying this weight on my back, the physical burden of other people's stories. Back in my room, I order a meal delivered and curl up in front of my computer. I need to slip away from all this mess for a while. To spend some time being the self I can't be around my cast members. I need to be with my guild. With Aida.

"You ever wonder if you could be as badass in real life as you are in a game?" I ask my party as we explore the newly opened Wind Temple dungeon together. Apparently, the air elementals of *Swordquest Online* don't have enough brains in their windy heads to stay dead after we've beaten them once.

Hawk laughs. "I drove a tank through a mudslide in basic training. I don't need to wonder."

"Considering my role in this guild is to get shot full of arrows and crumble before I can get off my fifth fireball," Clay says, "I'm exactly the same level of badass here as I am in reality. Why are you asking, Frey?"

I sigh. "I'm just dealing with an asshole boss. Calling him out on his bullshit is exhausting. Like, if I can't even defeat him, I sincerely doubt I have any real life badassery in me."

"I feel that," Aida says. "My boss is a jerk, too. But when me and my coworkers get together, we can push him to do the right thing. Sometimes it just takes teamwork."

"I guess," I say. Wishing I could bottle up her faith and hold it secure inside me. "I don't know. You can push against people, but they can swing right around and push back at you. When it's your boss and they call all the shots—"

"I guess it depends on what you do," she says, "but there's all sorts of power out there, especially if you're brave enough to use it. And I know you're brave, and smart. Maybe you have a way to get leverage on them."

*Leverage.* That makes me think of Kate, weirdly. Spending twelve years abroad learning the ins and outs of the film business. Building a name for herself brick by brick. Everyone treats her like some unstoppable force, but she didn't start out unstoppable. She built her life on what she had. I know she had to deal with more than a few jerks along the way.

And Aida thinks I've got some of the best parts of her inside me.

"I tried to negotiate with my boss once," Clay says. "He fired me. Course, that was Dairy Queen and no one really gives a shit who maintains the milkshake machine. I guess I was replaceable."

"What do you do now?" I say, sniping down an air monster that's about to wipe him off the map with a devastating frontal attack.

"I work at GameStop now. It's a block farther away, but the air-conditioning works all the time and I get an employee discount."

It sounds so nice and normal. Like having a job isn't a matter of life and death and a million expectant viewers. *Galaxy Spark* is such a big part of everything I do. But work comes and goes. Life comes and goes, and some days you wake up and realize you're totally different than who you thought you were, and you're in a different place than you ever thought you'd be.

And in the end, maybe you wind up as successful as Kate or Will. Or maybe you crash and burn. Or maybe you don't even go anywhere. You keep on trying to figure out your way through the world.

But I know where I am, right now. I'm here, in *Swordquest Online*, and in Belfast, and I have a job to do. Not for Peter, but for the show. For the fans and the people I said I'd stand up for and help.

I'm on the verge of triumph. Does it also matter I'm on the verge of breaking down?

Filming is canceled the next day—officially because of weather conditions, unofficially because Peter is rewriting the whole second half of the season in a day. I stay up late playing *Swordquest Online*. When I make it down to the hotel restaurant for breakfast, I'm bleary and buried under the hood of Will's big sweatshirt. Habit leads me to my normal seat, a big booth with plush blue leather seats, beside Chris. The server brings me the full English breakfast: sausage and beans steaming on my plate, toast and poached eggs and a half tomato. I try to puzzle out what the tomato is for and look over at Chris's plate, only to see it untouched—and his fingers blurring across his phone screen.

"What's up?" I say. "Is something wrong? Is it Shyanne?" They better not have broken up. Shyanne throws the best karaoke parties, and I'd like to still be invited.

He sighs. "Remember how she had that big role lined up? Starring in that sitcom pilot about the guy who has a giant pet snake living in his apartment?"

I nod. I'd helped her do some reading for the pilot—lots of "Oh, Corey, it's a snake!" and "I like snakes!" C-plus dialogue, but she somehow made it funny. Filled it with life and just enough self-aware sarcasm to make you buy it. I couldn't imagine that project going forward without her.

"Apparently, one of the producers is a total mess. She wanted them to fly to Vancouver to shoot this park scene—even though there's a million parks in LA they could use. So, Shyanne gets on a plane and flies to Canada, only to have them say the location won't be ready for another week, and they won't pay for her hotel. The producer says she'll pay for her plane ticket home, like it's a big favor, even though *she* fucked up. Then Shyanne gets the email saying the park is clear, shooting is back on—but she'll have to pay for her own plane ticket, since they don't have the budget to fly her back to Vancouver again."

"She should drop out of the project," I say. "If that pilot gets picked up, she'll have to work with that asshole for years. No one would think less of her for walking away."

Chris sighs. "Frey. That's, like, one of the whitest things you've ever said, and you say a lot of those. People decide Black actresses are too difficult to work with if they breathe too loud. Shy just wants to act, and she doesn't want to let anything get in her way. If she wasn't having an anxiety attack, she probably wouldn't have called."

I hadn't even thought of that. I nod, once again reminding myself not everyone has things as easy as me. "Is she okay?" I ask.

"She can't sleep." He stares down at his phone like it's her, tossing and turning half a world away. Like he wants to reach through the metal and hold her hand, and every mile between them tugs on him like a string.

"How are you holding up with all this?" I ask. "After yesterday, I mean?"

"I don't know," he says. "I wish I was more like my dad. He's great with people. Spend five minutes in a room with him, and he'll charm you into anything. But me, I'm just stubborn. I worry a lot that if something goes wrong at work, I won't be able to take care of the people I love. Like Shy, like you and our family."

"You know I'd do anything for you, right?"

"Yeah, I do." He gives me a crooked smile. "Will you let me be the man who takes care of his family?"

Man *doesn't only mean* provider, I might have said. Still, Chris makes space for me to define my gender on my terms, and I owe him the same. We can't easily alter the systems of identity we live in. But we can build up ourselves and support each other as we go.

"I absolutely will not let you take care of everyone alone." I shake my head. "We can both do that. Together. Do you think there's anything we can do to cheer her up?"

"Let's order her some breakfast delivery when she wakes up. There's that brunch place near her apartment she loves."

I grab my phone and punch in the order. At least I can help Shyanne smile while she's figuring this out. But I can't help wondering what I'd do in her shoes if I hit that sort of wall and didn't have Kate and her money to bulldoze my way through. People put up with all sorts of terrible, annoying obstacles to do the thing they love, because acting is worth it, and producers know this, and know they can do whatever they like because actors will stick around.

At what point does loving something stop being enough to keep going on?

# Seventeen

All I can do today is make peace with this moment and cheer up the cast. I slide over to Callie's table, where she sits like a queen in a gauzy pink minidress, diamond-flecked sunglasses flashing, and get her on board with my plan. Both of us start making calls.

"I've secured the equipment," I tell her, trying to sound as conspiratorial as a superspy.

"I've rented a van," she says, in the same voice I'd expect someone that glamorous to say *The yacht awaits us.* "It'll be here in twenty minutes. Do you want to invite Peter?"

I hesitate. We usually invite Wes and Peter on cast outings, even though they're not actors. But he's busy rewriting the script, and I just—I just don't want to deal with him right now. "I think he can't make it," I say, then stand and raise my voice. "Hey, everyone! We're going on a cast bonding trip. Our treat!"

After breakfast concludes, we file out to the van—sneaking

through the garage so no photographers can get shots of us leaving. Greta pats the seat next to her as we climb in, but even the thought of being near her sends my stomach churning, like a whale crashing back into the sea. I climb in back next to Ruby, and then we're off. Rolling through the smooth and soft-edge green of the countryside.

"Anyone have any clue what Peter is up to?" Callie asks as we turn down a windy, sheep-lined lane.

"I asked if he could give my character more development in the new scenes," Ruby says, sighing. "Remember when I had that arc in Season Three where I saved that space pirate after his ship blew up and we fell in love?"

"Oh, yeah," I say. Wow, that subplot was random. Like, they got a good fight scene out of it in the season finale, but Captain Thorta hasn't spoken about her love interest in years. "Did your character ever actually do anything about that?"

"Shoved the pirate into a cryopod and never spoke of him again."

"I'll send my space navy to find him," Callie says. "He'll be pretty scrawny after months in deep freeze, though."

"I like them scrawny," Ruby says. "And, uh, ladies. I like them to be ladies."

A somewhat-awkward pause falls over the van for a bit. Did we know Ruby was gay? Did I know? I mean, I assumed she was queer just from her hair and bodybuilding habits alone. But I don't know if she's ever said it out loud. That's the weird part about being a queer actor—you can tattoo a rainbow on your ass and people will still ask you what it means and get shocked if you tell them you're gay. You can be as butch as you want, but spelling it out crosses lines for people. Makes a distant thing real.

Maybe sensing the awkward still, Ruby holds out her fist to me. I bump it.

"Solidarity," she says. "If it wasn't for #Morganetta, I don't think I'd ever have the guts to talk about it."

A wave of guilt rushes over me. Really? There isn't solidarity between us, at least not in the sense we have the same mission. Ruby's a woman; I'm pretty sure I'm not. #Morganetta is for queer girls—for all queer people, I guess, but mostly for girls.

How can I make that known without breaking the new warmth in her eyes when she smiles at me? How can I be myself while still being everything they need me to be?

*#Morganetta.* That reminds me. I haven't checked the fanfics I'm following in ages. Looking away from the cast, I pull out my phone and sneak a peek. No updates—but a new #Morganetta fic is trending. I click on it.

### Deliverance (Galaxy Spark): Morgantha/ Alietta, Canon Divergence, Kidnapping, Hurt/ Comfort, No Death.

Looks good enough—I open it and dive into the story about Morgantha rescuing Alietta after she's carried away by a masked stranger on a hoverboard. Lots of cuddling, wound bandaging, whispered reassurance, and then Morgantha rips off the kidnapper's mask—

A face like her own peers up: messy brown hair, round nose, confident smear. Yet the stars-damned abductor has no honor in her eyes. She growls: "I am Lilian of House Ashton, and I will smother you in the void of my undefeatable tackiness!"

Author's Note: Yeah, I wrote a fic of Morgantha kicking Lily Ashton's ass. God I hate her. She's so fake.

My stomach lurches sideways. I flip off my phone and shove it back into my pocket. Are people still mad about the motorcycle-stealing thing? Or that I said show fans shouldn't harass anyone online? Do they even realize I'm a person, who can see this cruel stuff? Or do they think Lily Ashton is just as fictional as Morgantha? I try to tell myself it doesn't matter, that I'm not even the person they think I am. But that's how the world sees me. As a girl. And that means, when I do something they don't like, I'm a target for rage.

I've always been more engaged with the show fandom than Greta. I thought she just didn't get it. But we've had completely different experiences. Her character has always attracted negativity. And, after catching even a taste of that backlash, I want to bury my head in a hole.

The van pulls up in a small lot overlooking the bay.

"This is it," Callie says, and we climb out.

"What's going on?" Greta says. I wave her forward. Lead her to the edge of the rocky cliffside, and point down to where new, state-of-the-art Jet Skis bob in the natural harbor where the two cliffs close in. No work to do. No photographers to bother us. Just the deep blue-green water and the untouched grassy sand.

"Like it?" I say.

"How'd you set this up?" she asks. "It's so private."

"I sent the press on a wild-goose chase by posting on my Quicshot the cast would spend our day off at a luxury spa." I wink at her. "Then I booked the Jet Skis under Lara Brown's name."

The cliff is narrow, twisted, and turn-backed, and Callie almost trips twice climbing down in her stilettos. We split up at the small changing hut on the beach to put on our bathing suits. It's become so much a matter of habit that I follow Greta in when I need to get changed, but seeing the little placard outside the women's restroom hits me like a needle in the side.

I duck into a stall and pull out the bathing suit Callie brought for me, since I didn't bring my own along to the shoot. She's got incredible taste, and I know all her gifts are super expensive, but this black bikini held together by gold rings is just—

It's for a girl. For a femme, at least. And that's not me. And it hurts in a stomach-twisting sort of way that Callie has missed seeing such an obvious truth, especially since I came out to her. She knows, and she's still treating me like a girl.

I pull a T-shirt over my bikini top, and try not to look in the mirror as I slather on sunblock. Some painful, awful part of me whispers that it doesn't change anything—that everyone can see my chest underneath it, that everyone knows what I've got there and I can't ever change how they look at me. How I don't even know who I am.

I bite my lip. The dysphoria is getting stronger with time, with every second I spend in *Swordquest Online* being Frey, whenever Chris uses my pronouns in private. How good it feels to be myself. How my lungs close up when I can't.

*Just enjoy yourself*, I think as I come out of the changing hut and join the rest of the cast on the sand. I'm the last one out, even after Callie, who's been applying her waterproof makeup.

"Want to share a Jet Ski?" Greta asks me.

I shake my head. I want to be alone. When I'm with other people, I have to pretend I'm not floating outside myself. Never sure how to make my own feelings right.

"You've got a smear of sunblock." Callie runs a thumb down my nose, rubbing it in. I wince. My head spins, asking, *What other details does she notice on my body?* I pull away and walk toward the water.

"You know what you're doing?" Chris asks as I hop on a solo Jet Ski. "I did it in Miami last year. I can show you."

Normally, I'd be happy to take lessons from Chris. But I can't piece together what he's hiding in his voice. If he's offering because I'm younger, because he thinks I can't do this, or because he sees me as a girl and some part of his subconscious says that means he doesn't trust me to do this alone, for myself.

"I've got this," I say, biting my tongue and trying not to snap. Because I can't know how he meant it. I only know it made me feel confused and unseen.

When I turn on the Jet Ski and feel the engine growl to life, my heart sinks down in my chest. Like a horse that could buck and throw me to the sharks. I know it's not any more challenging than piloting Peter's motorcycle, but I guess I feel smaller than I did when I gave Greta that ride. Or maybe I'm just aware of how small I am in the grand scheme of the world.

I've learned something, I guess. But I don't like how crappy and worthless the lesson makes me feel.

*Push, Frey,* I tell myself. *You don't want to feel crappy? Don't. Be brave.*

It's so easy to be brave when you're pretending to fight CGI villains. It's so hard to be brave when you're not even sure what bravery looks like.

I twist the throttle.

The Jet Ski growls. I shoot forward like I've been launched from a rail gun. Wind and water slap against me so fast my lips ache and my racing heart feels left behind. Twisting the handlebars, I slide through a smooth figure eight, picture perfect as I cut through the glassy stills. The sea breeze tingles strangely against the shaved side of my head. All my fears and worries feel like they've been swept out of me by the rush of acceleration and pounding adrenaline.

Out here on the open water, there's no one but me to decide who I am.

"Race you to that cliff!" Chris shouts, coming up next to me. Callie sits behind him, holding on tight, while Ruby unpacks the beer cooler on the sand. I grin at my brother and open up the throttle, shooting ahead of him and twisting sideways to cut him off—with a long spray of foam that slices through the air and hits him and Callie in the face.

"Move it, slowpoke!" I taunt over my shoulder, giving the engine all I've got. The ancient gray cliff rises up before me, moss-draped and storm-weathered, so close I can see the waves slapping its base. I'm about to win.

Greta laughs wickedly as she cuts a long, spraying arc across the bay entry, white water spewing up from the Jet Ski engines, glittering in the sun. Sliding in just before me and grinning like she's won the World Cup, light glinting off her red hair like it's full of fireworks. I pull to a stop, smiling so hard my face hurts as Chris pulls up behind me.

The truth is, I can't imagine not being happy to be near her, in whatever way she wants. The way she laughs and smiles, the way she simply *is*. I feel like I'm only just beginning to get to know her and like I've known her for a million years.

That whole day, we race and swim and eat packed sandwiches like we're normal people with nothing better to do. I lie out in the sun and crisp dry, stealing some basketball shorts from Chris's duffel bag to half cover the bikini. Greta and Callie convince me to join them in building a sandcastle, though we don't have buckets or shovels and basically wind up building a giant wet lump of sand. Chris frowns when he discovers the red peppers on his packed sandwich are roasted, not fresh, and we all share a laugh over how in the UK they call arugula "rocket." The sun hangs high in the sky, even as the hour grows late, thanks to the northern latitudes. I bury my feet in the stand and stare at the prickling of hair down my legs I haven't bothered to shave and wonder if Kate will kill me for that.

"This is nice," Greta says, sliding down beside me and burying her own feet. I can feel her toes twitching through the sand. "You think anyone would mind if I got a little hut on the beach and sold driftwood for a living?"

"I'd mind," I say. "Um. I mean, Kate would mind, since I'm pretty sure me being so awful that everyone who dates me runs off to be a hermit isn't good PR." Her face falls. I scramble. "And, uh, I'd miss you."

That just hangs in the air. It feels dangerous. I don't pull it back.

I guess I've kept a little bit of Morgantha's courage after all.

"You could visit," she said. "I don't want to be a total hermit. Just, you know. No weirdos allowed."

"I'm not weird?" I don't know how I feel about that. "I mean, I'm an actor. I think I'm supposed to be a little weird."

"Yeah, but, like, you're a good type of weird. I don't know. Your weirdness and my weirdness sort of vibrate together. If that makes sense."

"It makes absolutely no sense," I say, though I'm joking and she smiles as I say it. "But thanks. I'm glad to be your kind of weirdo."

"What sort of fresh hell do you think Peter will come up with in the rewrite? I'm half expecting him to give me a scene where I wear a gold bikini and dance for Jabba the Hutt."

"He'd probably put both of us in gold bikinis." A stab of dysphoria shoots through me at the thought, a pain like feedback from a dying microphone. "You know. Lesbians. Two for one."

Greta buries her face in her hands. "Ugh. Fuck. At least I still have my job." She looks up and smiles at me. It's tired, vividly real, and absolutely stunning. My heart flips over again. I press my fingernails into the ball of my hand before they can reach out and reveal something I can't take back with a joke.

*Stupid body. Cut it out.* Greta's just grateful I saved her job. And all because I think she's cute doesn't mean I want to take this any further. She made her feelings clear after our kiss. And Aida will be waiting for me back in LA.

"I didn't just do it for you," I say awkwardly. She's not really being close and friendly. She's following Kate's PR plan. She has to be, even though there's no photographers or fans watching, even though we already saved her job, and that might mean—"I did it for Chris. And for the queer kids who watch the show."

It's not honest. I love Chris, and I love the fans—and I also love how Greta's eyelashes glint red in a sunset and how she's always full of surprises. *I did it for you.* But that feels too important, too romantic, for how she's made clear our relationship stands. And that's not entirely true either.

Because honestly? I did it for myself, too. Because I was sick of feeling like a brand, not a person. I wanted to make a stand

and say something real for once in my life.

"I did it maybe thirty percent for you," I allow. I don't want her to feel like she doesn't matter. It'd just be awkward if I made it sound like she mattered too much.

"Maybe fifty percent?"

"Forty percent. For sure."

"Deal." She wraps an arm around my shoulders and pulls me close against her. Sand and freckled skin, the sweat on her neck, the pulse beating in her chest. She's close, real, and welcome as my favorite hoodie. I freeze—or rather, I tell myself not to freeze, not to react in a way that makes her think I'm mad.

But I'm a little mad. Because she isn't even hugging the real me.

"When this is over," Greta says, "we should go see a movie or something. Together. And do dinner after."

"Sure," I say, pulling my towel tighter about my legs. Trying to hide the shape of my thighs.

"Sure?" Her voice peaks. Excited. Oops. "So, it's a date? Like a date date?"

"Like a *date* date date?" I'm just echoing her now. But I don't understand. "You don't need to keep up the ruse when we get home." We can't. Not if I want a chance with Aida.

"I want to stop the fake shit. I want . . . I want a chance to date you for real."

My eyebrows arch. "You sure? Because you kissed me in Griffith Park, and again at the premiere, and then basically acted like it meant nothing to you. Like I'm your own personal romantic kryptonite."

"Okay, I shouldn't have done that and left you hanging. But you're not the reason those kisses went flat. I just wanted to see how it would feel, if something would spark, and maybe it did, but not in the way most people would expect. I don't know. All I know is you're the one person I can actually trust in this industry. You came through for me when no one else did and, Lily—" She swallows. I flinch as that name cuts me like a diamond blade. Pain I can't even express out loud without outing myself. "I think you're cute, and brave, and— Please say something. Please. I feel so stupid."

"I think you're really great," I say quickly. Too quickly. Like my veins are Mentos and Dict Coke. Like I'm shook up, toppling over, and bursting apart on the ground. "But I don't think we line up. Not that way. Not when we both want such different things from our lives. Also, there's this person I met online, and she's really great—"

The sound cuts out from my ears. All I can think is *I'm doing this wrong* and *I'm a total disaster.* How could I never have imagined the scenario where Greta would develop feelings for me?

Because I was only thinking about myself and what I wanted. Again.

Callie groans, breaking through my brain freeze. Her many-ringed hand points up toward the road.

A lone figure, out of place in jeans and a wrinkled button-down shirt, is scrambling down the trail to the beach.

"Shit," I gasp, recognizing him and rushing back to the group of cast members to stand at attention—even though it's my day off, it's my day off—

"You're all out here?" Peter asks. He doesn't really need to make it a question when he can see us, plain as day. "I didn't get the invitation."

I freeze. *Crap. He is mad.* This is my responsibility. I'm the one who shut him out. I should take care of it.

"Sorry, man." I improvise with what I hope is a chill half shrug. "We thought you were busy writing the new scenes. Didn't know you'd want to come along."

"I can always make time for fun," he snaps, sounding like a little kid. I fight the urge not to roll my eyes. If he wanted to come to cast events, he could have treated us better. "Enjoy the rest of your evening, team. Lily, I want you in my office first thing tomorrow."

Needless to say, *I* don't enjoy the rest of the evening at all.

# Eighteen

"If he's made it worse," Chris says at breakfast the next morning, "we leak it online."

"I'm down to cover the NDA penalty," I say, mouth full of roasted tomato I can't taste. I'm not even sure it's supposed to have a taste. "But Kate will kill me."

"There's got to be a way," he says. "Sir Charles Kittswillow could leak it when he comes over to film his cameo as the Master Terraformer. He's, like, eighty. He'll click any link if we tell him it sends messages to his grandkids. No one'll retaliate against the old white grandpa who played Poppet the Penguin."

"People sue everyone." Ugh. I know he's just trying to cheer me up, but I can't keep thinking about how awkward things went with Greta yesterday, how much I want to be online chatting with Aida, how three more trending #Morganetta fanfics popped up last night tagged *fuck lily ashton*, how much I dread what's coming.

"I'm serious," Chris says. "I won't let you deal with Peter's bullshit alone."

"And I'm grateful," I say, fighting the urge to grit my teeth. His concern is earnest, but it *lands* wrong. Like he's not offering it to me, but my shadow on the wall. "But you can't control what Peter does, and you can't make my choices and messes for me. I'm going to deal with him one-on-one."

"Like hell you are." He sighs. "This is ridiculous. Don't go to that meeting. Tell him if he's got something to say to you, he can say it in front of me—"

"I'm not a kid anymore," I interrupt. "Just because you look at me and see a girl doesn't mean you get to be in charge."

"I don't—"

"But that's how you make me feel! If you saw me as your brother, you'd treat me differently." The low, slow ache in my chest pulses right next to the place where my heart sits. The part that wants to not have to crawl through a maze of thorny words and genders to be seen as a brother and a son. "I don't know. Maybe I'm crazy." If I was really trans, wouldn't it shine out of me like a beacon? Wouldn't people *know*?

Wouldn't telling them the truth be enough to make them realize who I am?

"You're not crazy," he says. "I—I'm trying, Frey." Even hearing that name from him doesn't help. "It's hard to adjust your whole view of someone overnight."

"But I've always been me!" That comes out loud. Everyone turns to look at me. I flinch. My phone beeps, reminding me that I'm meeting Peter in five minutes. My stomach does back-flips around my breakfast. I don't want to be here. I want to throw up. Disappear. Transform into a curtain.

Anything to save me from the legendary scolding I volunteered myself for when I stood up and said no.

"Wish me luck," I say, sliding out of the booth past Chris. He says nothing. He doesn't know what to say to make this better, and neither do I.

I'm not brave, I'm not strong, I'm not a Warhawk. I'm not the girl Greta's convinced herself she's got a crush on. I'm a collection of missing pieces, a massive, fucking phony, and it feels like the tiniest crack will split me apart.

Peter's set up a makeshift writers' room in a business-center office on the hotel's bottom floor. "Come in!" he shouts impatiently from behind the door as I arrive. I square it up, plastic with a squeaky hinge and a paper sign reading *DO NOT DISTURB—CONFIDENTIAL* taped on. Try to convince myself it's just a portal into a dungeon for a boss battle. That Peter can't actually hurt me in real life.

I wish I had Aida and Hawk with me. I'm never scared around them.

I square up my shoulders and march in.

"You're sunburned," Peter says first, which is the last thing I expect. He waves me toward a seat before his makeshift desk, which is covered in empty compostable coffee cups and notes scrawled on a forest's worth of Post-its. I sit down. "Forgot the lotion on your shoulders and the back of your neck. Good thing you're not shooting much more."

"I'm not?" I ask. I mean, it's not like I want to stick around much longer after how things have gone down. But if I'm not filming more, does that mean I'm not in the rest of the season? Does it mean—

No. They couldn't. Not after everything I told them about how you should treat queer characters. They wouldn't.

I mean, of course they *could*. But they need Morgantha. She's the most popular character on the show. That's what I knew when I stood up to them, why I did this. They can't push me too far.

"Read it," Peter says smugly, and tosses a script across the desk. He's even bothered printing it out and binding it. Just so he can clearly see the reaction on my face.

Tense like I've got a live wire pumping volts into my side, I open the script.

And as I read, all the fighting energy seeps out of me.

INT: MORGANTHA's ship.


Lights flash wildly across the dash panel. Her fingers fly over the controls. Stars whirl outside as the damaged craft spirals toward a crash landing.


                    **MORGANTHA**
           The AI's gone dead! It can't

pilot us out of the spin!

                    ALIETTA
          So fix it!

                    MORGANTHA
          Some things can't be fixed.
          Didn't you tell me that?

MORGANTHA bites her lip. Despite everything, she can't let ALIETTA die.

                    MORGANTHA
          I'm using the experimental
          neural link. Hold on.

                    ALIETTA
          But that hasn't been tested!

MORGANTHA draws electrodes off the panel
and sticks them to her temples. An image
of a human brain appears on the screens.
Lightning flashes. She slumps over on the
control panel.

EXT: We see the ship level out and
successfully land in a field.

INT: MORGANTHA's ship.

ALIETTA weeps over MORGANTHA's comatose
body. A message plays on the screens,
where ALIETTA isn't looking. "I'm in here.
I'm in here."

I know this scene. Or at least, I thought I did. He's rewritten a scene from Episode One, which we've already shot, where Morgantha and Alietta argue before crashing their ship. Only he's moved it forward a few episodes. And completely changed what happens in the end.

"So, this is it?" My fingers shake, though whether it's with shock or anger I'm still not sure. "Morgantha tries to fix her broken spaceship and get electrocuted until her consciousness is sucked into the computer AI? Alietta holds her comatose body while her imprisoned essence looks on and weeps? Because the two of them broke up and never got a chance to say goodbye?"

"It's brilliant," Peter says as if it's not his own work he's complimenting. "We can capture all that emotion and suffering, but the show's most popular character isn't actually dead. The way I see it, there's two ways this could go leading into Season Seven. I haven't picked which."

"Oh?"

"Morgantha has to come back. She's the most popular

character in the show. You were right when you said I couldn't afford to lose her. But she doesn't have to come back in the same body." Peter grins. "It's science fiction, after all. I can make a genetically modified clone or whatever. So, it'll be up to you how it goes. Who plays your role next year. Be nice, and there won't be trouble. Keep talking about how *problematic* the script is—"

Holy shit. He's threatening to write me off the show. Because I stood up to him.

Morgantha goes on. They need her. But I might no longer be the one bringing her to life. Peter's found a writing device that lets him have his cake and eat it, too. I can't tell if he's an evil genius or an uncreative hack. If he spent just fifty percent of the energy he devotes to trolling his employees to creating something new, we'd actually win Emmys.

"That's a dick move and you know it," I say. "What'll you do if I walk out?"

"We've already filmed plenty of footage we can repurpose. I can use a body double for your remaining scenes. But come on, Lily, you don't need to make this a problem—"

"I'm not the one making this a problem. You need me. I don't need you. I have the Ann Elise franchise waiting; I can step into that at any time and make twice what I'm getting here."

"But you won't." His grin grows wider. I suddenly hate even looking at his face. "I know you don't want to do this stupid chick-flick franchise your mom's lined up. It's a pandering cash grab designed to empty the purses of women who don't even care what real art looks like."

"That's not true," I say. I don't like the books, but they're not written for me. That doesn't mean they're stupid or worthless. If art has value to someone, then that art matters. Even if the art only has value to girls. Maybe even especially then.

"You want to stay on *Galaxy Spark*. What we're doing here is real art. We're making something that matters to people. I know it *matters* to you that it matters to people."

*Art?* I want to say. *That's such bullshit.* His show has sex and violence and curse words, but it's not better art than the Ann Elise books because it speaks to him personally.

But before I can fling that in his face, a wave of shame surges up and swamps me. Because *Galaxy Spark* also speaks to me. For all its flaws, I like it ten times more than the Ann Elise books. I'm attached. This is something Peter and I have in common, even if pissed-off me wants to deny we share anything at all.

And Morgantha and Alietta's relationship doesn't become less important, less vital to the people who need it, all because I'm mad at my boss. What if they cast an actor who doesn't care about the story? What if they cast an actor who isn't queer? People need me. The people following me on social media need me. The girls at the airport cheering for me and Greta need me. Okay, they need Lily Ashton. Who I'm not, or not quite. But I can be close enough.

After all the people who've helped me get this far and all the people who want this and everyone who's fought for me, how can I walk away from this fight?

"Think about it." Peter gives me a nasty grin. "But don't think too long. We're going to need to put out a casting call for Season Seven soon."

I bite my lip and flee.

# Nineteen

I'm numb all over, shivering even though it's a nice, sunny day outside for once. Staggering through the hotel lobby, people staring and whispering at me as I pass, eyes flicking my way in the elevator. "She looks sick," a woman mutters to her husband, and when I realize that *she* means *me*, my stomach clenches and flips over.

That was a threat. Peter threatened me. He might tell himself he's just being a tough boss, but that doesn't make it right. What sort of boss leaves everyone who works for him wishing they could run screaming a million miles away? What sort of leader leaves everyone who follows him wanting to hide under the bed rather than meet one-on-one with him ever again?

Worse, I can feel it working. I can feel his hooks slipping further and further under my skin. Erasing me. Controlling me. As long as they can still put my face on a T-shirt, it doesn't matter to the showrunners if I feel dead inside.

In fact, I think they might prefer me broken.

I lock myself in my hotel room and pull out my laptop. Thank god I have a place to escape and be myself.

Because I don't think reality is big enough to hold me and every one of my problems.

"You're not asleep?" I ask Aida, opening up my voice channel. She's gathering herbs in some underground caverns. I teleport down to join her. You'd think a cave would be dark, unfriendly, but this one is lit by glowing crystals up and down the walls, carpeted in glittering soft moss. It's a psychedelic wonderland of light, so strange and comforting I wish I could just dive into it and disappear into a safe, familiar world.

Except I guess I sort of can. Because I'm here, aren't I? With her. And she can be like the world to me.

"I can't sleep," Aida says. "I'm too embarrassed. I asked this girl I knew out on a date and it turns out she's already got a girlfriend."

"Oh no! I'm so sorry!" A tug of sympathy threatens to suck me through the monitor, across the world to her side. Even though I want her to still be single when we meet in real life, I can't help aching for her. It's so hard to be honest about who you are and what you want, especially when being queer means there's already an extra layer of vulnerability there.

"Yeah. It's pretty awkward, especially since we work together." She laughs. Static bursts with her voice. "I'll recover. And I'm glad I did it. I don't think I'd have had the nerve to open up about how I felt if you hadn't been such a great friend to talk about queer stuff with."

"I'm always happy to talk to you," I say. "And that girl obviously doesn't know who she's missing out on." For some reason, I think of Greta. The girl whose best parts I missed out on, until I screwed up my courage, admitted I could be wrong about her, and looked deeper. Greta let me in. She told me about her friends abandoning her, about her issues with her mom, shared her love of movies old and new. But she did that all for the girl she thought I was. I don't know if she'll like me when she knows the truth.

She doesn't know me like Aida does. And this girl who said no obviously doesn't know Aida like I do, because how could anyone talk to Aida for five minutes and not fall in love with her?

I bite my lip. *Fuck.* These feelings I have for her feel bigger than the whole ocean between us. Like if I dive in, I'll either float off into the sunset or get eaten by a shark.

We scrape moss and fungus off the walls, killing the occasional animated mushroom when it pops to life and attacks us. Clay will take them later and turn them into potions we can use in the new dungeon—healing magic, fire spells, shielding potions—because, in video-game logic, drinking weird mushroom juice is a good idea. Not everything in *Swordquest Online* makes sense.

Still. It makes more sense than reality.

"I'll be coming back to LA next month," Aida says. "I'll be in town until the holidays. Want to . . . I don't know, start by grabbing some coffee? I'm warning you, I'm super weird in person."

"Me too," I say, grinning into my mic. Hoping she's smiling at me, too, through her screen. Warmth bubbles up inside me. Gooey and sweet as chocolate melted on a marshmallow. "We can be weird together."

She goes quiet. For one awful second, I'm scared she's mad at me. Then she mutters something, and her voice crackles with static.

"What?" I say. "Your mic's bad."

"Maybe I need to reinstall the driver?" She sighs, speaking louder now. "One second. Let me restart my voice comms."

Static. A strange clipping. Her voice peaks and trails off. Something about it strikes me as familiar. How did Aida recognize so easily that I was using vocal mods? They're pretty good these days. I wouldn't recognize one, unless—

That clipping. Aida's using a voice mod, too.

But why? Is she also trans? Using mods to move her voice in the opposite direction of mine?

"Frey?" a voice says. A *new* voice. But one I know all too well. "Can you hear me?"

There's a click, and Aida's high pitch returns. "Can you hear me now?"

I yelp and slam my computer shut. Because it all makes sense. Everything crashes into place. *That was Greta Thurmway's voice.*

My heart pounds like I accidentally stepped on an EpiPen. I push back the chair and swivel aimlessly, like I can keep pace with my spinning head. *Greta and Aida are the same person.* And I feel like a popped balloon, all my hopes and wishes draining away in a hissing trickle of air. How did I never notice? The game groups players up by location—she must have just started once she moved to LA; of course there'd be a chance we'd wind up on the same server. The guild full of old friends who kicked her out, the way we're online at the same times even crossing continents—I should have seen, suspected.

"Fuck!" I roll out of the chair, onto my bed. Kick the chair halfheartedly so it spins back across the rug. *Weak. Pathetic.* As pathetic as me, for not noticing, for not wanting to see. Hoping one small part of my life could be untainted by the giant mess of everything else.

The girl I like is just two hotel rooms down, and I turned her down for a date yesterday. Because I was so busy daydreaming about a new start; a girl who knows me as only ever Frey, and not Lily. There's no easy answer, no fantasy made real. No escape. If I want to make this work, I'd have to tell her everything.

Once Greta knows I'm Frey, she'll know I'm not as brave in real life as I am in the game. How I let Peter scare me with the threat of losing my job. How I still haven't found the words to tell my mom or the world I'm trans. How the one thing I've done that actually makes the world a better place, #Morganetta, is slipping through my fingers, and part of me would be okay with walking away from the show and that story line if it meant never having to deal with Peter again.

I'm so tired. So confused. And every step I take, every choice I make, tangles me up further. I'm more than tired of fighting—I don't know what to fight for, or even if I should fight at all.

So I do the only thing that makes sense. I pull out my phone and call Kate.

"Sorry if I'm rushed, baby. Lara's people are pressuring me to set a filming date or they won't renew the option. I told them no one could match what I'd put in place and they said Geraldo and Henry Montez had already reached out with an offer—"

"Hi, Mom." My voice sounds small. Like it only matters when I'm saying someone else's words. "Peter wants to write me off the show."

For the first time I can remember, she goes quiet.

"I told him his script was a problem, and . . ." It all pours out of me, word by word. All the pushing back. The persuasion. The interviews. The arguments. "I'm doing everything I can to keep fighting. Someone needs to push for queer girls to be represented on TV. But I can't—I can't keep walking onto that set and seeing Peter and Wes. I know I sound like a total coward, that I should be brave. But I don't want to keep doing the show. Not after this season. Not after this."

That comes out as a whisper. Very quietly, so no one can hear me. It feels like I've said something dirty, but I can't take it back, and I don't want to. The thought of being done with this mess makes me feel a thousand times lighter. I want to cling to the only light I can find.

"That's no problem at all," Kate says, smooth and satisfied as a cat with a bowl of cream. "Screw Peter and Wes. Come home. Just tell them you're going to my birthday party next weekend. You don't need *Galaxy Spark*—I'll get my contracts team to find a way to get you out of it. You're going to star in the Ann Elise movies. We'll tell Lara Brown we've got a date to start shooting. With your obligations to the show cleared, you'll be able to start working right away."

*Come home.* I want to grab that invitation. That shimmering golden ticket to home, to dreams. But I'm not even sure that's what she wants to offer me. It feels like she's solving her problems. Not mine. Making me happy is only a bonus.

But I can't save #Morganetta. I can't make my relationship with my dream girl anything more than a fantasy. Going forward means leaving something behind, and I'm too scared to pick what I'm losing after I've already lost my hope in Aida. Better to let Kate handle things. Better to let this and everything else drift away behind me until the whole world vanishes into formless gray.

I bury my head in my pillow and cry until I finally fall asleep.

# Twenty

From my first-class window seat, the shadows of clouds on the southwestern deserts paint baked orange in swathes of mauve and dark violet, the hues of the lesbian Pride flag I draped across my shoulders two years ago when I came out on Quicshot. I'd felt so certain then. Like I understood every part of myself and every inch of where I fit in the world.

How can I even begin to understand other people, enough to think I could have a girlfriend and a good relationship with my boss, when I don't even understand who I am?

LA unrolls from the desert, clapboard and terra-cotta and the concrete slabs of soundstages. Hyper-saturated flashes of blue pools dot the landscape. Punch through the clouds and across Mar Vista and the knot of interchanges, where my city flashes up a bright rainbow of color. Nothing like the rolling green and boring brick of Northern Ireland, a location we pick because it could look like anywhere. LA is distinctly LA. Belfast can stand in for anywhere people are mostly white—more "real world," a location scout once told me, with no trace of irony.

I guess I'm the sort of person who'd come from a fake world. Shallow and empty inside. I'm not even drawn to the flash and glamour of my home city. I didn't come here to make my dreams come true. I just arrived on top of the heap people fight their whole lives to climb.

The plane touches down. Outside my window, palm trees wave in welcome. A comfortable sight, but it still makes my throat tighten and threaten to close. It feels like I'm trying to squeeze back into a shirt I wore in middle school. Like I've been gone a million years instead of six weeks, and everything and not enough has changed.

The first time I went to shoot on location, it felt like going on an adventure. Like traveling to another planet full of incredible sights and thrills. Now I've got Peter's threat—he'd never call it a threat, but I know one when I see one—dangling over me. If I was really Frey, I'd shoot him full of arrows. Since I don't have that option in real life, I don't know what to do. I only know I'm tired down to my bones and everything that feels familiar also feels like it belongs to someone else. To the girl I was supposed to be.

Worse, it feels like part of my heart is back in Northern Ireland with Greta. That I left things ugly and unfinished and full of so much wanting and mistakes. You could crush on a cool girl who stood up for queer rights even when it cost her something in return. You could plan a date with a fun, dorky boy you met in a video game. But once you realized they were both the same clueless mess of a person, that everything you'd expected and projected onto them was nothing like their reality, all those feelings would evaporate like water spilled on hot sand.

Greta won't like me anymore, not when she figures out who I really am. And that will hurt every last piece of my heart I accidentally, stupidly, let get tangled up in hers.

Kate sends a driver to pick me up from the tarmac. It's a nice gesture. Part of me wishes she'd come herself, like the movies where normal families reunite at the airport. But I guess she's busy planning her big birthday party, and besides, what does normal matter when your family is about to launch the Ann Elise franchise to new heights? I wish Chris had come back with me, but he's determined to stick it out, and I respect that choice. I just wish I wasn't so alone.

I pull out my phone and start looking for more #Morganetta fanfics. Even after the recent negativity in that hashtag, some part of me can't stop reaching for the thing that used to help calm me down. But real life bleeds into the ship tag on every platform. Someone photographed me at the airport this morning and noted I'd left the set earlier than expected. Some speculate that means Morgantha will die in Season Six. Some people think it means me and Greta are fighting. A few are even speculating that we only pretended to date for PR—and that's true, but seeing it discussed by strangers makes my ears burn.

My identity is about me. My dating life is none of their business. Navigating my public and personal life is hard enough without the internet blurring all the lines in between. These people aren't even friends of mine online, not like how the Warhawks are. They're just spectators. And it makes me feel like an animal in a zoo.

By the time I get home, I feel absolutely crushed.

"I had a meeting all afternoon," Kate says when I finally see her—at eight o'clock—as Will and I are playing darts in the game room. We're both evenly terrible players. Despite that shot in his last movie where he throws a bullet into a bad guy's eye from five hundred feet away, and the scene where Morgantha sniped an enemy shooter with her blasting pistol while balanced atop a hoverboard, neither of us actually has good aim. "Lara's people were so happy to have a filming date, they invited me to a barbecue at her ranch. I don't have the time to fly to Oregon, so I invited them to my birthday party instead—"

"I'm back from Northern Ireland," I break in. She hasn't even acknowledged me, though it's been six weeks. "Hi, Mom."

"Hi, Lily." She kisses the top of my head, then runs to the game room fridge and pulls out a bottle of white wine. "Lara's hothead agent said I don't respect her time if I'm not going to fly cross-country—"

"Is that all?" I mutter. I can't believe I've said it out loud until both she and Will are staring at me.

"What?" Kate looks up mid-pour. "What do you mean?"

"You didn't even ask how my trip was."

"I follow you on Quicshot and get alerts every time you

post. I saw you and Greta had a nice date on the beach the other day. I left a comment. I'm busy, sweetheart."

"No *shit*."

The words, deep and sarcastic and razor-blade angry, are out before I can stop them. The room goes quiet. I bite my lip. I should take it back. But I don't want to. I want Kate to know how much I'm hurting, even if it means hurting her, too.

"Hon," Kate says, and the flare of her Texas accent means I've stepped on my own neck somehow. "I was working for you. To get you out of the show where you don't want to be and into the role that'll set you up for life."

"How do you even know that's something I want? To be 'set up' in something? Hasn't my whole life just been you setting me up in stuff I didn't ask for?"

"Oh," Kate says, and now she's sarcastic, mirroring me but cutting ten times deeper. "I'm sorry. I'm sorry I worked my ass off for ten years to make you famous. To give you everything other girls dream of—"

*Girls.* A string snaps in my chest. "Just stop it!" I scream. "Everyone in the world has their own idea in their head about who I am, everyone expects a million different things of me, everyone expects me to be something I'm not and I hate it! I hate it! No one ever asks me what I want!"

"Lily." Will's voice is low and smooth. Soothing. Like he sees a hysterical girl he needs to talk off the ledge. "Your mom's asking you to get along so that you can cash a multi-million-dollar paycheck. That's a pretty ungrateful thing to be mad about."

"This isn't about the money." There's a fortune to be made squeezing myself into stupid Ann Elise, to selling the next ten years of my life to her, and if I do it, I'll wither so deeply inside there's nothing left of me. Can't he see that? Doesn't he know how much it hurts? No. Because he and Kate and everyone else knows as much about my real life as what I post on Quicshot, which is nothing at all. How can he get a say in this argument when neither he nor Kate knows what it's really about? "This is about me. It's my choice. Not that you'd care about that since you're not my real dad."

Then I slam my darts into the table, hard enough that the tip breaks on one, and run upstairs to my room. I slam the door behind me for good measure, since that's what teens do in movies when they fight with their parents, but it doesn't make me feel better at all.

I bury my head under my pillow like there's someone underneath it who understands me. Oh. God. I've become one of those movie teens who fights with their parents. I got passed over for one of those roles in a screen test because the director thought I didn't test angry enough.

Fuck.

My phone rings. It's Chris. "Fuck," I whisper, because it feels good. I consider flinging the phone across the room, but then remember what a pain it is to text with a broken screen, and answer.

"I don't need a third parent yelling at me," I say, cutting him off.

"What you need is to get your head together."

I wince. "Kate didn't even ask how the shoot went. She doesn't even care. And Will—like, he just—I mean, it's not fair, I know it's not, but they keep treating me like a girl and it hurts. It hurts like hell." I don't even know why I'm talking to him about this, after our argument back in Belfast, but I can't help it. He's one of the very few who know. "I'm sorry for snapping at you. I was taking out my own frustrations, and that was really rude."

"Glad you know it," he says. "What you're going through hurts, more than I can guess. But you can't just randomly yell at them, Frey. I don't know what it's like being in your shoes, but you know our parents are on your side—" He cuts off. "Don't worry about it, Greta; it's a private thing. I'm just talking to my sis—my sibling here."

Greta's there. My heart twists. I wish she was here, with me, facing this. I don't know how she does it, considering how many people around her just want to feed off her light, but she's got a gift for carrying sarcasm-wrapped joy into even the darkest spaces. I sort of love her for that. I know I'll never be able to look away from her.

"I don't know," I mutter nervously to Chris. "I just . . . what if they don't want to hear it? What if they don't accept me?"

"They better," he says. "If my dad gives you trouble—look, he's buff but old. I could take him one-on-one. Got all that stage combat training. Kate—all I'd have to do is hide her cell phone and she'll do whatever it takes to get it back."

Despite myself, I giggle.

"But that's not what we're dealing with now," Chris continues. "The ball's in your court, Frey. You've got to figure out who you are and how to be them. I've got to figure out how to be a brother to *you*, not to the person I thought you were. So, you do whatever you have to do, and then you'll find out where our parents land. Not before."

What am I supposed to do? How does coming out even work when I don't know what I'm coming out as? I don't have a label for this thing inside me, not yet. I just have a name and a general direction. I'm not a girl. I'm a ball being tossed in the general direction of masculinity, I think. I'm not sure how I'd explain that to my parents. It sounds absurd, like I've picked up a new fad diet. Maybe I've lost my mind. Maybe I'm just sick of being a girl in a world full of hostile men. Maybe I'm—

But it feels real. And there's a million other people out there who feel the same way I do.

I feel so awful about losing my cool. I'm not sure if I'm a dude one hundred percent—maybe eighty percent, maybe seventy-five—but I don't want to be the sort of angry, controlling mess of a guy Peter is. So much of our friendship feels tainted now, so much I wonder if I maybe only liked him to begin with because he made me feel like I was "one of the guys." But that's not a good enough reason to keep him in my life.

There are kinder ways to express my gender, my masculinity. I want to be more like Will and Chris. They genuinely care about the people around them and don't tear others down because they have something to prove. And maybe that's the best part about being trans. Being free to invent whoever you'd like yourself to be.

Maybe that's the best part of being alive.

Of finally, finally being real.

# Twenty-One

"Hey," I tell Will, slinking back down to the kitchen. He's kneading a slab of fresh bread dough. Kate's head is bent near his. They're probably talking about me and what a mess I am. "I'm sorry. To both of you, but especially Will. You're a really great dad." My eyes swell up, thick with tears. I didn't expect that to happen, but I can't stop thinking of Greta and how her mom doesn't even bother considering her dreams while making plans for her future.

I trust Will and Kate. It's the strangest thing of all, but I do. I can't think of a time when they haven't had my best interests at heart. When I spoke up and said what I wanted and needed.

I just haven't had a firm enough voice to make that known until now.

Okay, I decide, I'm doing this. One at a time. Make it easier.

"Mom," I say, surprising myself. Because I've finally started this conversation. Because it's *Mom* that slips out, not *Kate*, and that brings home how much I need a mom right now.

"Can we talk alone, please?"

We curl up on the back deck together, out by the pool. The sun's setting over the hills, turning everything red and violet, painting the nooks and crags of the bracken chaparral slopes with pockmarks of shadow. Peaceful and smog-touched and perfect. It looks like home.

Kate's the first one to break the silence.

"I did some bad things back when I was your age. And I had some bad things done to me. I've always wanted to protect you, from the guilt and the shame. From getting an amateur shiv stuck in three inches above your kidney."

"Is that why you don't ever wear bikinis?"

"That's because what my tummy looks like is my and Will's business." She sighs. "And there I go again. Joking about my sex life in front of my teenager. Pretty sure normal parents don't do that. I . . . I had you because I wanted you, real bad. Once I started making big bucks, I had this idea in my head that I could give a kid everything they wanted. I could make you a real-life Disney princess, like I always saw on TV but could never be in real life. And you—don't get me wrong, you're the best kid in the universe. It's me. I'm the one who messed up. I'm so focused on giving you the life I always wanted myself to have that I'm not asking what you want for you."

"What if I told you . . . ?" I swallow. Swish spit around to keep my tongue damp. "What if I told you that I could never be a princess? That I'm pretty sure I'm not even . . . a girl."

Kate's quiet for a minute. Then she leans over and kisses my forehead. "I said I wanted to be a mom to the best kid on earth.

That's you, sweetie. It'll always be you."

Tears well up in the back of my throat, spilling out of my eyes. I throw my arms around her shoulders and bury my face in her neck.

"I hate feeling like I'll lose by quitting *Galaxy Spark*," I say as Kate strokes what's left of my hair. "I fought so much to save the queer rep on that show. People want it so badly, but I can't deliver. I can't even be the girl they want me to be." The weight of #Morganetta twists inside me, like I've swallowed a bunch of USB cables.

"What do *you* need? What do you want?"

"I want to never confront Wes and Peter again, but—"

"No buts. You want out. That's okay."

"Yeah." I lick my lips quietly. "I guess it is."

I thought I'd feel sad, saying it out loud. Committing to quitting the show. But I'm not. I'm relieved. Let them try to splice together the rest of my scenes from preshot footage, like Peter threatened. It feels like a massive weight has been lifted off my shoulders, like I'm not scared to see what tomorrow will bring. I feel like the world is a little brighter and more open than I felt a minute ago.

I guess she's right. I do want to go. Even if that means letting people down.

I can't keep carrying this weight for other people. Not when it's grinding me down. Not when it now feels as distant from me as the moon.

"Sweetheart," Kate says. "You did your best. Some people can't be reasoned with, and I never thought Peter and Wes were all that smart or worthwhile to begin with. There's so much out there in the world. So many chances to do good and help other people. The world is bigger than *Galaxy Spark*. Put that aside and move forward. You're going to be the star of the Ann Elise franchise. I can get us more creative control of the project. The screenwriter I'm hiring is an old friend. She'll work with us to make sure everything is perfect and that nothing in the script makes you uncomfortable. You'll see when you talk to Lara at my party. Everything will be different on this project. Everything will be better."

*Different. Better.* I could really use that. Kate always has my best interests in mind. She's thinking one step ahead, to my next career move. I'll need a new project if I'm not doing *Galaxy Spark*, and I know working with Kate's team will give me much more control than anything else I've ever done.

But I don't know if safer will be good enough. Or if safer means it'll be the right fit for me. Still. Kate wants me to do this, and I trust her. She's led me the right way so far.

"Okay," I say. "Yeah. This'll be fun."

She wraps an arm around my shoulder and hugs me. "Will you need a dress for the party? I mean, do you still want to wear dresses?"

"I've never ever wanted to wear dresses," I point out. "Like, ever." Wow. I'll have to wear a lot of dresses as Ann Elise. At least it'll be only a costume. I bet with Kate's backing I could get the production team to use he or they pronouns for me.

"How about a tux?" When I nod, she adds "Classic black? Colored? Sequins?"

The twisted lump of nerves in my chest relaxes. She does see me. Or close enough, and she'll get better in time. Maybe I'll get closer to seeing me, too. I tell her my pronouns, and my new name, and she promises she'll try her best to get it right. She asks how much I want to be out to the wider world yet, and I say I don't know. I tell her I'm thinking about coming out and using my name and pronouns professionally, but I'm not there yet.

"I'm sorry," I say after that. "I didn't want to put this—this burden on you. It's a lot to ask. I don't want to take away the daughter you've always known, but—"

"Don't even worry about it," Kate says, smiling. "You could have told me sooner. I'm a good ally. I give thousands to the LGBTQ youth center. I don't care what your gender is."

Of course she doesn't. The swell of relief is fading back into the reality of Kate, of what's always been between us. "No. I couldn't. Because how was I to know you wouldn't tell me coming out would hurt my career? That you wouldn't say I'm not allowed to be nonbinary."

"What?" She's still smiling. But her face is frozen now. Only animated where tears run down her lip.

"I never know what I'll get with you," I say, and the words feel brittle and plastic on my lips. Like sucking on dice. "I never know if you're my manager or my mom. I can't trust that you really see me as I am when I feel like part of you sees me as a product instead of your kid."

Kate stands and turns her back on me. Staring at the wall. Shuddering. Finally, she asks, "Would you like me to tell Will?"

"Yeah," I whisper. Cheeks burning. That'll make it easier. I don't know what else to say.

Because I've heard Kate rage at executives screwing her over and howl in triumph as she wins a hand of poker.

But I've never heard her sound hurt. I've never done the hurting. And I can't take it back, because I know it was right, what I said. True to how I feel and the tangled mess between us. I need my mom to support me now, and as long as there's a dollar sign attached to our relationship, the support doesn't feel real.

Not as real as I need it to be.

With Kate gone, I hide in my room, fire up my rig, and check out *Swordquest Online*. Aida—Greta—isn't playing right now, and though a small part of me is glad I don't have to talk to her, a bigger part of me misses her. It's like a hole's been ripped into me where she isn't. I try to tell myself that doesn't matter, that I only miss the person I thought she was, because how could I miss the real Greta when I hadn't recognized her after weeks of gaming together?

But that's not true. Aida is a part of her, even if it's different from the way Frey is part of me. I miss the fantasy I constructed in my head of meeting the perfect girl, but I also miss the real her. I miss her more than I ever expected I could miss someone.

"Dude," Clay says, throwing a handful of animated leaves in the air. "I'm so high I painted my nails. You should come over, bud. There's plenty to share."

"I'm not running any dungeons with you until your reaction time is back up. Are you even anywhere near LA?"

"Spokane! America's best little city." He blows a kiss at an orc lady berserker. A trumpet of music announces she's challenged him to a duel. I step back and watch as she wipes the floor with him. Wishing Greta was here to watch with me.

I can't talk to her again and lie about who I am and how we're connected—because it would be a lie, to hide everything from her that I now know. *You're using vocal mods because people might recognize your voice from TV. So am I.* But that conversation leads straight to me letting her down and breaking her heart. Selfishly, I hope Peter and Wes are keeping her busy with nonsense filler scenes. So busy she's forgotten entirely about me.

She's still on the show. And they'll still have a Morgantha, even if she isn't me. There'll still be queer rep on *Galaxy Spark*. It's just I won't be able to do anything to protect it.

I know I need to quit. To escape the showrunners. To move forward. If anything, I won't be able to bear working with Greta much longer. I just wish I could do more than cross my fingers and hope it works out okay.

Clay and I blow up some giant slimes, empowering our Rings of Titanic Might. Then he gets the bright idea to create new level-one characters, strip them to their underwear, and make them race defenseless across the continent.

"He with the fewest deaths wins," Clay says, and I laugh and take him up on it. We're halfway across the world when Will comes into my room, puts a plate of fresh-baked bread down for me, and slides an arm around my shoulders in a hug.

"Your mom told me," he says when I mute my mic. "I'm sorry you didn't feel like you could tell us."

"I'm sorry I yelled," I say, speaking around the bread I've shoved in my cheeks. "I've been carrying this so long, but it wasn't fair to lash out like that. Especially at you. You've never been anything but a great dad to me."

"Don't worry about it. My dad would have kicked my ass if I'd said that stuff to him. Always told myself I'd be nicer to my own kids."

"Seriously. I was out of line. Ever since you married Kate, you've been there for us when we needed you. Your respect means so much to me. I won't do it again."

He rolls his eyes. "C'mon, kid. Hitting me with the emotional stuff? That's cold."

I laugh. I hope we're good. I think so, anyways. And I hope one day I can provide more emotional support to my family, even if I've got a lot of growing up to do first.

Will stares at my screen. "That a fun game? I haven't really gotten into anything in years."

"If you like fantasy games," I say. Will's thing has always been first-person shooters because he likes the competition and he's got fast reaction times. I'm more into exploring the game world than beating other players. "You'd probably have to use a voice mod if you wanted to play with other people and not just your friends." I can't imagine any human on the planet not knowing Will's voice. His catchphrase as Duke Beaumont, Tennessee mechanic turned superspy—*Someone's looking for a good old beatdown*—has been memed across the planet and back.

"I do. Maybe I'll give it a shot. Do you use a voice mod?"

I nod.

"Do you think you'll ever tell your friends in the game who you really are?" he asks. "You always talk about them like you're pretty tight. I bet they'd understand."

I shake my head. "They already know who I really am. I mean, they know everything that matters."

It's not like hanging out in the #Morgantha fanfic spaces. That part of the internet just makes me feel like a commodity people want to consume. With the Warhawks, I'm part of a team. We all give equally.

I think it's maybe time to let the #Morganetta fandom be its own thing. People can find their own ways to enjoy the ship and be happy. I can't help anyone if I let all my resources drain away. And I deserve to be able to help myself.

*Frey?* Clay's chat message floats across the screen. *Is your mic down?*

He's stopped to wait for me at the crossroads ahead. Hoping I'll catch up.

Will squeezes my shoulder. "I'll let you get back to your friends, kid. Are we cool?"

"We're cool," I say, flashing him a grin and sliding the headphones back on.

I hope I'm doing the right thing. I hope I can be cool with this.

Even though the tightness still grinds across my chest. Telling me I'm not as free as I need to be to breathe.

# Twenty-Two

Kate's birthday party is a no-holds-barred affair, with gold-foil-rimmed invitations proclaiming it a "fantasy black tie" gala. My tuxedo jacket, when it arrives, is made of the same silver fabric as Morgantha's tunic, and Kate has turned up a perfect replica of Glinda's gown from *The Wizard of Oz*. (I hope it's a replica, anyway. She probably knows someone who could get her the original, but it's a priceless antique.)

Under the epic touch of her decorators, the house is transformed overnight. Dark curtains woven with fiber-optic threads turn the halls into shimmering palaces of light. An ice statue of a mermaid leaps out of the pool. Laser projectors blast dragons and wizards over the walls.

It should make me feel like anything is possible. It can't still the itch in the back of my brain insisting this is all fake.

"Do you want me to do your makeup?" Shyanne says. She's come as Brandy's Cinderella, in a floaty blue-white ballgown, a delicate tiara atop her spiral curls.

"This eyeliner is all I'm wearing," I say. Hesitate, because I don't know how much I want to say. I want her to know who I am, since she and Chris are so close she's practically family and we're all convinced they're getting married one day. But I'm not sure I have time for such a lengthy explanation, and the more people I tell, the more it slips through my hands to the world; makes it more likely the press will out me—

"Do mine if she doesn't want any!" Jeanette, Shyanne's best friend, drops down on the makeup bench beside me, dressed like Okoye from Black Panther. I think her armor is actually from the film, it's so pro—and then I flinch, because I realize that *she* was directed at me, and there's no way Jeanette could have known, there's no way anyone can know—and that's the part that stings. Because of course no one knows.

I slide out of the room and sit by the fountain. The smooth flow of the water helps me calm down a little, but I'm still aching at the thought of going back in there. With my hair chopped short, wearing a binder and a tux, I'm as masc-coded as I can ever hope to be—and yet anyone who looks at me will just see a girl who's being a little daring about fashion.

Maybe I'm just nebulous and weird. Maybe I made all this dysphoria stuff up for attention. It can't actually be real—I mean, it's totally real for other people, but not me. I'm just a stapled-together collection of wadded-up script pages for all the roles I've played in my life. Fakes on top of fakes. Other people can be really, truly, genuinely, trans, but I'm such a mess that I'm sure I don't deserve it.

"Party's starting, kiddo," Kate says, stepping up behind me. "Come on. Lara will want to say hi."

*Kiddo.* She shifted to something gender-neutral on purpose; I can hear it in her voice. The knot beneath my tuxedo loosens. Maybe I can do this. If Kate can embrace the unique mess of me, maybe the rest of the world will follow.

I just hope she's using those words because she really sees me. Not because she's humoring her future star.

I follow Kate across the room to where Lara sits on a gold-backed love seat, wearing a flimsy witch costume that must have come from Party City even though she's worth twice as much as Kate.

"Lily!" she gasps, flinging her arms around me and giving me a sticky red-lipstick kiss on the cheek. I flinch. The sound of my name—that name—hits like the crack of a whip, a wrong and sour note in a piece of music. Kate gives me a concerned eyebrow lift over her shoulder and mouths, *Want me to correct her?*

I give my head a little shake. What if Lara doesn't understand? What if she doesn't like the real me at all?

"Lara!" Kate swoops in with a mouthful of sugar, kissing the woman on both cheeks. "How are you, sweetheart? How was your daughter's wedding?"

Lara's whole face lights up. "It was gorgeous! Absolutely dreamy! Let me show you both the photos!" She grabs me by the arm and levers me down beside her. The phone she whips out is a battery-busting nightmare with a giant screen. When she opens the photo album, a caption flashes: *1 out of 990.*

"Oh my god," I whisper.

Lara jabs a finger at the picture of a tall girl gripping a weedy man's arm and wearing a dress with more fluff and petticoats than Kate's Glinda gown. "There's my Marryanne. Isn't she lovely? That'll be you one day, Lily."

"Well," Kate says. "There'll certainly be a girl involved. And a fancy dress I pay for."

Lara flips through the photos—her daughter with her bridesmaids, all made up in matching orange dresses. Girls with matching tall hair getting their makeup done. I feel the same distance I did when Shyanne and Jeanette offered to do my makeup earlier. *I don't belong here.* The thought pounds in my ears like the beating of a second heart. *I don't belong here and I never ever have.* Something separates me and Kate and Lara, me and all girls, something fundamental and bone-deep. Like a wide gaping trench carved between us, or the ocean where you can't see another shore.

I want to be something else, something other, something firmly and clearly set apart—no. I've always been something different. I've always been looking for a way to pack my bags and move to a different place.

And that'll never happen if I take this role and become Ann Elise. Because that's what that story is about, I suddenly realize. It matters to so many girls and women because it celebrates that closeness, that sisterhood, that inherent femme-ness of which I am not a part. I can pretend to fall in love with a billionaire, I can pretend to run my own international fashion magazine, but I can't embody who she is and what she means.

I can't take on that part.

But what other option do I have?

"Kiddo?" Kate puts a hand on my shoulder. "You're looking a little green. You okay?"

"I'm fine," I whisper. My throat feels tight and twisted, but that's nothing new. I can't breathe right when I'm not me. I know Kate's trying to make me feel affirmed, but I'm still not sure *why*. I want her to be my mom, only my mom. I want to be me, only me, not Morgantha or Ann Elise. I want to be a person, not a girl or a face on a T-shirt.

I *want*. And I want to find a way to work all that out.

Out by the front door, an engine growls. Ruby's red convertible, top down and lights flashing. Wasn't she still filming in Belfast?

"Frey!" shouts a familiar voice, winding through the crowd. Like someone throwing me a lifeline in purgatory. It can't be.

Dressed for travel in jeans and Will's old UCLA sweatshirt—which she must have stolen from my hotel room—Greta Thurmway jumps out of Ruby's car, dodges the valet, and charges into the house.

She flew back from Belfast. She borrowed Ruby's car. Greta Thurmway has crashed the party where I'm supposed to seal the most important deal of my acting career. She's panting, out of breath, her hair a red-gold tangle from driving with the convertible top down—in fact, there's a smear like a wind-squashed bug at the top of her hairline—and she's so thoroughly beautiful and real that she takes my breath away.

That's what I want. Where she's going is where I want to be. And just knowing I can want things this deeply, with my heart and soul and every inch of me, puts all the rest of this mess into perspective.

I grab Kate's elbow. "This isn't me. I can't do this. I'm not the right person for the part and it's not right for me. And if you're disappointed, too bad. I'm firing you as my manager."

Kate freezes. So do I. I've crossed a red line, tossed a bomb, and I'm not taking it back. My fists ball in concentration. I breathe deep from the bottom of my lungs. Seventeen years of work lie in shambles, and I'm so, so glad.

Kate laughs. Thoroughly and loudly, so much that she squeezes an ache at the bottom of her corset. "I'm so proud of you."

"What?" Everything's on fire, and I'm holding the fuse in the smoke. Greta calls my name again, I think, but I can't hear anything over the hammering of my own heart.

"I'm proud of you, and everything you fought for on *Galaxy Spark*. You saw something that needed to be done and you went to do it, because other people needed it from you. But you don't owe it to the world to crack yourself open to help them."

"But someone has to help, Mom." I swallow. "Someone has to do the hard work. Like . . . you have queer and Black family members, you love and support us at home, you donate to charities supporting marginalized people in LA, but you don't take risks within the industry. You make safe choices, when you have the power to make moves that could help so many people."

Kate's eyes widen. I think it's been a long time since anyone spoke to her like that. Told her that, even though she's struggled to find her place in filmmaking, other people are struggling worse—and giving back isn't just optional, but a responsibility.

Finally, she nods. "When I came into this business, I was fighting with all I had just to carve out a space for me. But a space for me, a cis white lady, isn't good enough. So, you do whatever the hell you want, Frey. Take the role or not, go to college or not, dye your hair purple and sail around the world if that's what you want. You're just a kid. I'm your mom, and it's my job to go out and make the world a better place for you. I know I'm not a TV mom. But I'll promise to do this for you. Are you sure?"

Am I sure? There's nothing incredulous or pointed there. Just a simple question. Am I sure I want to say no to the plan to make me a star? The multi-million-dollar car she's set out for me to ride to the very top?

I think so. Because it's not driving me anywhere I want to go. When I think about my life and everything I have in it, I want nothing more than to hold my breath and dive into the whole wonderful world I know is waiting beyond.

I'm never going to run out of things I can do for other people. But I also need to take care of myself. And that means going after what I want. Not what anyone else wants for me.

And the first thing I want is to figure out just *what* I want to do.

"Frey!" Greta shouts from across the room, so loud two

executives with champagne glasses shoot her dirty looks. She storms past them. "Where are you?"

"What's going on?" Lara Brown asks in a big, hiccupy voice that says she's on the edge of tears. "Why did Lily fire you? What about my movie?"

"Mrs. Brown?" Shyanne steps over to the couch, voice high and excited. She takes a deep breath, steadying herself, and waves to the author. "I'm so sorry to bother you, but I wanted you to know how much your books mean to me and my friends!"

"Thank you, dear!" Lara presses a hand to the giant brooch on her chest. "Good to hear *some* people appreciate my work." She pats the open seat I've vacated. "Call me Lara. What's your favorite book in the series?"

With the grin of a fangirl ascended, Shyanne sits down. I lower my voice and tell Kate, "She really loves the books. And she's available to start filming right now."

"Shyanne?" Kate's lips purse thoughtfully as she turns to the women on the couch. "Let's talk business."

Shyanne looks up, white-frosted eyes wide and glittering with confused hope. Wanting, something she's held so long it's hard to understand when it's coming true. The sort of want that means she's the right fit for this world. A want I want to find inside myself.

I kiss Kate's cheek and run down the stairs to Greta.

"We need to talk," she says. Not in a bad way. Her cheeks are flushed a rainbow of reds.

"And we need to get out of here." I point out the door, where the valet is stammering excuses at the drivers waiting to leave their cars.

She plucks the keys out of her pocket and jerks her thumb back out the window, where the night air is wild and crisp. "Let's go."

We run through the patio, crashing through the scrub bushes, to where she's left Ruby's convertible. I slip the poor valet two twenty-dollar bills, mutter "Sorry," and slide into the passenger seat.

"Ready to fly?" Greta asks, and I nod, draping myself over the side of the car. I've been waiting for this my whole life.

"Let's go," I say.

The engine growls. Greta pulls us smoothly out of line and whips us down the long hill to the road. Wind rolls smoothly back over my skull, the night air humming and potent with smog and potential. Suddenly, I feel shy.

"I overheard you and Chris talking on the phone," she says. "He called you . . . by a name I know from this game."

I nod. "Hi, Aida."

She swallows. Her throat dips in a big, nervous, diving gulp, highway lights painting yellow streaks over each ridge and hollow. "Nice to finally meet you."

This is ten times weirder than I ever thought it would be. But it also, somehow, fits. How we pulled ourselves together, two Hollywood misfits who found a safe space in our messed-up lives by seeking anonymity, exploring a whole world without the pressure of being noticed, connecting to others without the massive weight of living up to expectations.

It was always a fantasy that meeting Aida would make everything in my life better. I'm still me. Dating anyone won't change that, for better or worse. But this can make both of us happy. I think. If we take it slow and figure it out as we go, just like we figured out being friends and allies in the doomed cause of saving #Morganetta.

And I think I'm excited for that.

"You're a really good driver," I say as she pulls us onto the highway. It brims with life, a vein of the city, but she smoothly slides us between cars and trucks and guns the engine. I hate myself for saying it—because it feels like such a weird thing to say—but she smiles and says "Thanks" and I hold on to that.

We rocket up the fast lane, a million miles an hour, my heart jerking up into my teeth. Other drivers honk and stare as Greta cuts a lightning-fast path through traffic, but I can't bring myself to look at her. My eyes are glued awkwardly to the dashboard.

Finally, I speak up.

"Did you really buy a plane ticket halfway around the world because you thought I was someone you'd met in a video game?"

"I know, it's weird. But I kept thinking about you. I just needed to know if I was right, and I couldn't imagine having this conversation over the phone. There's no way I can concentrate on the show with all this hanging over my head."

"No, I mean—did you do it because it was me? Because if

I thought Frey was"—*someone worth falling in love with*—"cool, and I learned he was *me*, I'd be totally disappointed. Who'd be excited to meet *me*, knowing I'm not Frey or Morgantha or any of that? I'm just an idiot who doesn't even know what gender they are."

She falls quiet. Then, she adds, "What are your pronouns?"

"Um. He and they, for now, I guess. I'm still not sure."

"Okay," she says. "You don't need to be sure. And if you change them, just let me know." She pauses. "Want to get milkshakes?"

"Yeah. That sounds great."

Greta pulls in at an all-night diner straight out of a 50s movie—literally, I know I've seen it on TV; it's the perfect set piece. Like everything in this town, it's built with an eye to the story it fits in. I'm pretty sure it wasn't built for a story like mine, but I'm claiming it tonight anyway.

"I'm going to grab us some food." Greta hops out of the car. "Be right back."

While she's gone, I also climb out of my seat and perch atop the hood. The sky is clear, for once, and stars and helicopter lights beam down from the back. The world feels infinite beyond this parking lot.

And suddenly, I realize I don't care what Peter and Wes do, or what sort of story they want to tell. If they can't imagine this sort of happiness for someone like me, then they don't deserve to have me around. They don't even know Morgantha, or the story they're writing, or why it matters. And the *why* of why it matters isn't their writing. It's what everyone's brought to the story—every actor, every crew member, every fan—that's given it life.

They're missing out on the most important part of the world they created. And I don't even feel sorry for them.

In fact, I don't think I want anything to do with them ever again.

But what Peter said the last time we met still grinds away at me, like an anchor tied around my feet. How he thinks he can use my love for the show to control me. How refusing to play his game is the best way to keep me safe, how it's okay for me to back away—and how maybe I can win after all.

Because, for these last few precious moments, I'm still Morgantha. In all the ways that matter most.

"Hey," I tell Greta when she comes out, joins me atop the car hood, and passes me a strawberry shake. "I think I'm going to come out. To, like, everyone."

"Okay," she says. "When?"

"In, like, fifteen minutes?" I pull out my phone. "I just need to think of what to say. Something epic." Kate could have one of her people draft a statement for me—I mean, we've got a whole team of lawyers dedicated just to that—but I need this to be my words. Not perfect, but real.

"That's really brave of you," she says, slinging an arm around my shoulders. I fit perfectly into the haven of her hug, resting my head on her shoulder, back leaning against the windshield. "I mean, I don't know if I could. If I posted about being ace, trolls would come and say awful things about my sex life. Like, things in my life keep slipping away, and I'm holding on by my fingertips and—ugh. I just want to feel safe for a while. I don't want to deal with explaining my identity to the world."

"You don't have to," I say. "In some ways it's easier to say 'I'm gay' because people sort of know what that is and what to expect from you. It's harder to say 'I'm nonbinary' or 'I'm asexual' without getting into a big debate defending that your identity exists. Like, when I had my first crush on a girl, I thought *gay* was the word for me—but that was because I didn't have better words yet to fit all my feelings in. I didn't realize yet I could be a guy. Or, you know. Guy-ish."

Greta nods. "Mine, too. So, if you're guy-ish, does that make our relationship actually straight?"

"It's physically impossible for anyone as cute as we are to be straight. But let's give it a try and see how it goes." Those words tumble out of me rapid-fire fast. My cheeks feel sweaty and plastic. It's the bravest thing I've ever said.

"Are you asking me to be your girlfriend?" She bites her lip. "I mean, like, in real life? And you're okay if we don't have sex; if I don't always like kissing?"

"I want to date you," I say. "And you're ace. That's part of you."

"Okay," she says. "Seriously. In the future, if you want to, we can talk about ways to make it comfortable for both of us."

"Definitely. We can work that out later." She's what matters. She's everything that matters. "Do you want to date me?" And

I hold my breath because I don't know what happens next. But I'm ready. Ready for everything. If she is.

"Okay." She nods, blushing red. "Yes. That's great. You're great—" and she buries her face in my neck. Her long, beautiful eyelashes flutter with happy tears, and we're suddenly holding each other, laughing, happy and stronger together than we ever were apart. And I'm with her, every piece of her. The lonely parts, the funny parts, the nerdy parts, every part in love with the art she makes and the world at our fingertips. "I just— Fuck. I forgot how good it felt not to be alone."

"I'm here for you," I whisper. Skin tingling. Heart singing. I snap a quick video of us, arms entwined, me in a tux and her in a sweatshirt, the open night sky wheeling above us. It's so peaceful and quiet out here, like the rest of the world doesn't exist. Like we're just two people who found each other and like what we found. I know real life is more complicated than all that. But, then again, maybe it isn't. Maybe this is just how it feels to be really alive.

I upload it to my Quicshot and caption it *Update for everyone: they/he.* And I go into my settings and change my display name and pronouns.

"Are you actually changing your name to your *Swordquest Online* character?" Greta asks. She sounds impressed.

I wink at her. "I'm not changing anything. I'm just making it true."

And then, before I post, I add one more line. "Yes, I'm trans—and so is Morgantha."

There. If Peter and Wes write around that—which I know they might—the internet will blow up in their faces. I suppose it'll blow up either way. I've tossed them a live grenade, and it might mean I never act professionally again. That thought fills me with bubbling glee, because for the first time in forever, I'm doing only what I want to do.

I think I'll do this more often.

# Epilogue

We stay out in the parking lot until well past midnight, holding hands and talking. Mostly about *Swordquest Online*, which is good, because I had no clue what being part of a couple would mean before tonight and now I know I really like it. Greta's yawning by the time we get back to the house, and Kate offers her a spare room. She climbs in with me instead, and I wake up the little spoon in an overheated tangle of quilts.

*Your big announcement was incredible PR for the show!* Wes texts me in the morning. *Good news. We're casting a man as Morgantha next season. It's going to get so much coverage!*

*Are you casting a trans man?* I text back. The response takes a while to come, three little bubbles bobbing too long on-screen—but it comes back *Yes, of course.* I screenshot and save it. Between Kate and my Quicshot followers, I can hold him to that promise. I've done something, even in leaving, and hopefully that will radiate out and do more good.

Hopefully. Hope can be a skinny thing, but in the end, it's

all I get to hold on to.

Especially now that I'm moving on.

I slide out from Greta's arms and get dressed in something that isn't the crumpled remains of my tux, then limp downstairs to where the staff and the rest of the overnight guests are picking through the party rubble.

"I'm sorry," I tell Shyanne. "I completely panicked and ran off and left you alone with Lara Brown. I hope it wasn't too awkward."

"What? No! She was amazing. We talked about the books for hours! I was scared she'd run off because I was such a total dork about it, but no! She was really cool! Anyway, she went to your mom and said, 'Who's her manager?' And Kate, because Kate's fucking incredible, said, 'I am,' and Lara asked if I could play Ann Elise and—" She sucks in a deep breath. "Li—Frey, I know this part has been part of your career plan for years. Say the word, and I'll step down."

"I don't want a career plan anymore," I say. "I want a me plan."

And with that, everything clicks into place.

It's weird, seeing my name on a business card. My real name, ink-printed and real: *Frey Ashton, Development Associate, Ashton Productions.* Having that just beneath the logo of Kate's company is a clear reminder I'm here because of who my mom is—but I'm here, and I need to do the best I can with that.

"Do you have the latest version of the pitch drafted?" says a voice from across the writers' room. I share my current open file with Amanda Wells and nod at her. She gives me a thumbs-up, the pink custom band of her Apple Watch sparkling in the sunlight. Kate's signature ultra-white modern decor style extends to her office space, and the whole open-plan floor shines. I still think it's a bit dramatic, but I'm getting used to it.

Kate, Chris, Will, and I worked together on a plan to overhaul the production company, offering priority on contracts to companies that hired and retained diverse staff at all levels. Will donated to fund twenty full-ride scholarships for low-income students interested in studying some aspect of film production; Kate opened job postings for eight writers from marginalized backgrounds to develop new shows and movies, reserving six of the slots for BIPOC writers, and provided full salary and benefits, including relocation costs. The goal is to build a new cohort of people in the business of telling stories, equipped to portray a wider variety of lives—and, at all stages, make sure all people are paid for the work they do.

I reached out to Amanda after she unlocked her social media and asked if she was interested in the job. Turned out, she had a great rom-com screenplay drafted. We're having dinner with an A-list actor tonight, one whose name I'm trying not to even think about in case I jinx it. If things go well, we'll have our star.

I was shocked when Kate invited me to attend the dinner. "You do realize I'm just stapling papers together around the office, right?"

"You're funny, earnest, passionate, and you're great at telling stories," she'd said. "People feel comfortable around you. You can smooth things out and make people want to come on board."

"I didn't realize that was a work skill."

"It's a *you* skill." She nodded. "Of course, not everything you're good at should be part of your job. It's healthy to keep some boundaries there. You have real talents, kiddo, and how you use them is up to you."

"I'll do it," I said. "I want to help."


I head home from the dinner, yawning, worn out but proud of myself. The star loved the pitch for Amanda's screenplay. There's still a million scheduling details to work through, but I'm optimistic. And relieved. No matter what happens next, I know I'm doing this work as part of a team.

And I know I have other things in my life—for one, college applications. I still have to finish my online high school classes—deal with Will's expectation I'll choose UCLA, persuade Kate I really don't need her to pull strings with her Ivy League contacts—but it's starting to feel like something I can really accomplish. There's a whole world out there, beyond *Galaxy Spark*, beyond Hollywood, and it's time I went to see it. I'll still be working with Kate part-time, but I'm excited to think I can learn anything. Be anything. Whatever I want and choose to make part of me next.

"I'm proud of you," Hawk says when I tell him. We're in the

new raid, the Fortress of Lightning, three bosses in. Finally making some decent progress. "College. That's a big step."

"I just hope he stays local," Greta says. She's set up her rig using my laptop and the desk beside mine, her voice echoing weirdly doubled. Every so often, her foot brushes mine, reminding me she's here and close, and everything that makes me smile.

"College *and* a new girlfriend? Wow. Sounds like a perfect Hollywood ending," he says, chuckling.

"Nope," I say, and a grin breaks across my face. Only Greta can see it, but I hope he hears it in my voice. Hope it carries all around the world. "Sounds just like my real life."

## THE END

# Acknowledgments

Writing my second YA contemporary novel was a completely different experience from my first, and I owe so many people for their help along the way. Kaitlyn Johnson, my incredible agent, has always been there with a tissue and a plan. Stephanie Guerdan, my editor, cheered for Frey and Greta from day one. So many people shared their knowledge of film and television with me: Alexandra Overy, Kianna Shore, Molly Knox Ostertag, and more—and I'm especially grateful to Alexandra for letting me crash on her couch while I did research in LA! And, of course, special thanks to my World of Warcraft guild, HKC, for always tossing me a resurrection spell when I'm on the floor.

Working with HarperTeen has been an incredible experience. Production, marketing and publicity, sales, and editorial all came together to help launch Frey and Greta into the world, and I'm grateful for every ARC sent and comma corrected. Thanks to the many booksellers who put queer books in the hands of queer readers, especially Sol Garza and Ally Scott, and the librarians and teachers who fight against all odds to get stories to the kids who need them.

Finally, my wonderful readers. Thank you, thank you so much.